MURDER AS
A FINE ART

MURDER AS A FINE ART

Carol Carnac

with an introduction by
MARTIN EDWARDS

This edition published 2025 by
The British Library
96 Euston Road
London NW1 2DB

Murder as a Fine Art was first published in Britain in
1953 by Collins, London for The Crime Club.

Cataloguing in Publication Data
A catalogue record for this book is available from the British Library

ISBN 978 0 7123 5517 9
eISBN 978 0 7123 6853 7

Original front cover image: *Tate Gallery,
National Gallery* by Tony Castle, 1927.
Image © London Metropolitan Archives (City of London).

Typeset by Tetragon, London
Printed in England by CPI Group (UK) Ltd, Croydon, CR0 4YY

CONTENTS

Introduction   7
A Note from the Publisher   11

MURDER AS A FINE ART   13

INTRODUCTION

*This introduction includes discussion of some of
the early plot points in the following novel, so new
readers may prefer to treat it as an afterword.*

Carol Rivett, who wrote detective fiction as Carol Carnac and as
E.C.R. Lorac, was a woman with a wide range of talents. In addition
to being an accomplished writer, she was a skilled needlewoman
and calligrapher, as well as being a capable musician. She was also
a gifted artist who studied at the Central School of Arts and Crafts
in London. Writing *Murder as a Fine Art*, which was originally published by Collins Crime Club in 1953, gave her the opportunity to
express her views on the art world while weaving a neatly contrived
mystery. In so doing, she had a great deal of fun; seventy years on,
the story remains a good read.

The novel opens at the premises of the Ministry of Fine Arts,
created "during that short era of optimism following World War
Two". Employing terms eerily similar to official jargon of the twenty-
first century, the author tells us sardonically that "'Co-ordination'
was the key-note", with representatives of "well-meaning and
expert bodies" working together under the same roof. The first
Minister of Fine Arts—in a tradition upheld by senior politicians
to this day—was keen to make sure that his own vast office was
decorated with paintings. However, financial pressures meant

that the room "was hung with works by obscure contemporary painters collected as opportunity arose by acquaintances of the Minister's. Some of these, painted in the early days of Picasso's cubist period, were real works of art. Some of them were not, but very few people were competent to judge these strange developments of art in the throes of transition. The typists called them 'the Minister's funnies'."

The current Minister is Humphry David, "a passionate addict of the arts" who had been on the opposition benches when the concept of the ministry was first mooted and had heaped scorn on the thinking behind it: "Government patronage of the arts is a mistake. It leads to every sort of abuse, and the artists, quite rightly, resent it." Now, ironically, he finds he has to find a *modus vivendi* within the department that is now under his oversight and which he privately regards as "the Ministry of All Fools". Humphry is a traditionalist, scathing about pretentious people who lavish praise on modern artworks simply because they are modern and different, and despairing of the notion that civil servants are equipped to act as connoisseurs of the fine arts. However, he is open-minded enough to recognise that in some instances he may need to overcome his own prejudices. My guess is that Humphry was to some extent a mouthpiece for the author's own opinions, and that, like many of her contemporaries, she was disgruntled about the failure of post-war government to live up to expectations.

Humphry is sceptical about the cost, scale, and value of the gargantuan public sector bureaucracy that has been created to serve the Ministry. A key figure in this mildly Kafkaesque establishment is Edwin Pompfret, deputy to the Permanent Secretary, and "one of those chaps who puts on a quasi-religious manner when studying works of art... He's got a slovenly mind, an unreliable memory and a colossal conceit of himself." This becomes significant when

Humphry consults a visitor from Scotland Yard. Henry Fearon is a friend who is an expert on forgery, including art forgery, and Humphry suspects that certain records and correspondence within the Ministry may have been falsified, with Pompfret a possible suspect. But when Pompfret is killed, crushed to death by the fall of a larger-than-life bust that stood at the head of a flight of stairs, the nature of the investigation at the Ministry undergoes a profound change. For although Pompfret's death appears to have been an accident, suspicion grows that in fact he was murdered.

CDI Julian Rivers, the principal series detective in the Carol Carnac books, leads the inquiry. Rivers is a likeable fellow who had previously served in the Royal Navy; pleasingly, his naval experience helps him to pick up an important clue to the plot. The emphasis on "howdunit" in this story is not unusual with this author; she clearly had a practical turn of mind.

Edith Caroline Rivett (1894–1958), to give her full name, began her career as a published novelist in 1931; *The Murder on the Burrows* appeared under the Lorac name and introduced Inspector Macdonald. The first Carol Carnac book, *Triple Death*, came five years later. An industrious author, she continued to write prolifically throughout her career while maintaining sound literary standards. Unlike many crime writers who produce scores of novels, she ranged widely in setting and storyline; far from flagging, she published some of her best work in the last decade of her life.

After her death, however, the books went out of print and were soon forgotten by all but a few enthusiasts. My parents had enjoyed her books (especially those set in Lunesdale), but when, in the 1970s, they encouraged me to seek them out, I found not a single copy in the local public libraries. Years later, I began to scour second-hand shops to seek out her novels in order to present them to my parents. After those books came back to me, I came to appreciate the range of her achievements. Happily, it proved possible to persuade the British Library to trace her estate and begin to reprint some of her best work.

The Lorac and Carnac books are now the bestsellers in the Crime Classics series. It gives me great pleasure to see how many readers across the world have come to appreciate her writing. Carol Rivett was a private and modest woman, and she would no doubt have been amazed by her posthumous fame. In 2024, public libraries in Lunesdale held exhibitions to celebrate her local connections, and on 19 August 2024, a blue plaque in her honour was unveiled by Lena Whiteley (who knew Carol personally) at her old home, Newbanks in Aughton. I was thrilled to be invited to attend, and I only wish my parents—who played a part, however unwittingly, in her revival—could have been there too.

MARTIN EDWARDS
www.martinedwardsbooks.com

A NOTE FROM THE PUBLISHER

FOR
PATRICIA

CHAPTER I

I

"NO, NO. NOT ACTUALLY PICASSO, MY DEAR CHAP. Influenced by—definitely influenced by, I think we might say…"

Humphry David spoke with the inveterate honesty which some of his subordinates deplored. After all, if a Minister has the good fortune to have in his department a picture which the majority of knowledgeable visitors recognised as the handwork of the greatest living painter, why need the Minister consistently contradict the knowledgeable?

But Humphry David was like that. He had not wanted to become a Minister at all. When the "project" of the Ministry of Fine Arts had first been mooted, during that short era of optimism following World War Two, Humphry David had voted against it. Of course, he had been in opposition then, and it was his duty to oppose, but happily his conscience and his political duty had been identical on that occasion.

"Ministry of Fine Arts? Rubbish! Leave the fine arts alone," he had declared. "Government patronage of the arts is a mistake. It leads to every sort of abuse, and the artists, quite rightly, resent it. And who on God's earth are they suggesting as Minister? I ask you—who? Look at 'em! I'll hand it to them as able administrators, as economists—(if you accept their premises)—as industrialists, but which of 'em knows a Duccio from a Simone Martini, or tempera from pure fresco?"

But the Ministry of Fine Arts had come into being. "Co-ordination" was the key-note: "Co-ordinate all these well-meaning and expert bodies," said old Higginson. "Get representatives of all of them under the same roof. Form Local Executives. The Divisional Executive idea should create the framework, local voluntary committees that is, to whom the Minister delegates..." and so he had prosed on.

The Ministry of Fine Arts had been born, and a home had had to be found for it. Happily (or unhappily, according to the way you look at it) a white elephant of a building had just been vacated by a sub-section of the Ministry of Food. Medici House, built by Decimus Burton in the spacious days of the Regency, stood on an island site conveniently near to the Green Park. Medici House was architecture in the grand manner. As a building it was beautiful. As a residence it had long outlived its usefulness. As a Ministry it was a nightmare. Its immense salons, its marble staircase, its spacious corridors and intricate basements, all ensured maximum difficulties in heating, in communication and in "co-ordination" (blessed word!) Moreover it suffered from being scheduled as a National Monument. There must be no alterations to the fabric. Even essential plumbing was regarded with suspicion.

"You might have smelt a rat when the Ministry of Food agreed to vacate it," said Humphry David bitterly. "Have you ever known those chaps take their claws off any property suitable to house typists? It's suitable for an Embassy. And if I had my way, I know which Ambassador I'd offer it to. I can't imagine anything more penitential than having to organise Medici House as a residence. Ask the Minister of Fuel and Power if he's going to make exceptions to his rationing laws in the case of National Monuments."

Among the galaxy of diverse talents commanded by the government of the day, the first Minister of Fine Arts had emerged. His name was Joyce-Lawrence, and he had had a liberal education in the Arts. (It was rumoured that he had been an art student in Paris when the first Surrealist Manifesto superseded Da-Daism.) He took possession of Medici House with a flourish of trumpets—at midsummer. He died of pneumonia the following winter. But he had left his mark on the Ministry. It was he who had decorated the Minister's office (fifty feet by thirty) with contemporary paintings. He had had great difficulty in coming to a decision about suitable embellishments for Decimus Burton's walls. "A Titian or two would look well," he had murmured. But Joyce-Lawrence was not then *au fait* with the regulations of the great national art collections. Governing bodies replied to his requests for loans with refusals solidly based on Acts passed when they came into being. They were in a very sound position to tell Joyce-Lawrence where he got off. Unabashed, he applied to the Chancellor for funds to invest in the purchase of works of art of National Importance. The Chancellor was sympathetic. He agreed that the Ministry of Fine Arts was deserving of special consideration at its inception, but—And here Joyce-Lawrence was favoured with a few cogent and extremely well-chosen words on the subject of Economics. In short, the new Minister must make do on the usual allowance for furnishing, equipping and embellishing his department.

It was then that Joyce-Lawrence showed the determination and spirit becoming to a new Minister of such a department. Titian, Vandyck and Velasquez were mentioned no more. The Minister's room was hung with works by obscure contemporary painters collected as opportunity arose by acquaintances of the Minister's. Some of these, painted in the early days of Picasso's cubist period, were real works of art. Some of them were not, but very few people

were competent to judge these strange developments of art in the
throes of transition. The typists called them "the Minister's funnies."
Some visitors knew enough about contemporary art to join issue
with the Minister in passionate pros and cons. But the experiment
was generally regarded as a success—it at least showed vitality, and
belief in living painters, though what Decimus Burton would have
thought about it is a different matter.

II

Humphry David was the third Minister of the new Department. He
had not sought office (particularly that one), but it was well known
that in his private life he was a passionate addict of the arts. He had
travelled, and his knowledge of paintings, periods and manners was
genuine and scholarly. He honestly loved pictures, and had spent a
large part of his life studying them. He was well known as a loyal
Parliamentary colleague, a good speaker, and a conscientious and
impartial Committee man. The lot of Minister of Fine Arts fell on
him almost automatically.

When he first saw his ministerial study, hung with Joyce-
Lawrence's collection, Humphry David stood and looked at them
unhappily. His real passions were for Holbein drawings and Dürer
engravings. He had never studied contemporary art. He said that it
aroused in him a sort of clinical distaste, because for some unknown
reason it reminded him of pathology, of operating theatres and
surgical instruments. After all, his abiding interests in art were all
pre-Elizabethan, and his chief enthusiasm as Minister was to forward the research begun on English mediæval wall paintings. But
Humphry David was an honest and conscientious man. He did not
condemn the "funnies" because he disliked them personally. He
simply admitted his ignorance of modern schools.

It was three months after he had become Minister that David invited Henry Fearon to come and pay him a friendly visit. Henry Fearon was employed at Scotland Yard, one of the many experts who serve the Police Commissioners so faithfully and unobtrusively. Henry had begun his career in the department dealing with forgeries, and he knew a lot about the composition of paper and inks, about handwriting, "engrossing," typing, and printed matter. Of recent years he had, by chance, been associated in inquiries (both here and on the Continent) into a series of forgeries of famous works of art, and it was during these cases he had met Humphry David, and picked the latter's brains for information on mediæval painting. The two men had got on well, and David both liked and trusted the rather disillusioned Yard man.

Fearon was shown into the Minister's study while David was telephoning, so Henry occupied himself (as many other visitors had done) by staring at the paintings on the walls. When David put down the receiver, Henry Fearon asked: "Are these your own choice, sir?" waving a hand towards the pictures.

"No. They're not. Joyce-Lawrence had them hung here. Quite frankly, they're the bane of my life, Fearon. I don't understand them. I know nothing about them, and I can't make head or tail of them. I know it's a shameful admission, but I haven't got to put on an act for you. Anyway, I hate putting on acts."

Humphry David got up from his desk and stared at an example of the cubist method, standing beside Fearon. "One of these days I shall begin to realise that thing has a beauty of its own," he said slowly. "I'm not dogmatic. I try not to be prejudiced, but I'm all at sea."

He rubbed his greying hair in a worried way as he tried to get his ideas into words. "This is said to be the heyday of the scientific expert," he said, "and I think it's true to say that evaluation of contemporary paintings needs more the quality of the expert than of the æsthete—if you'll pardon the much abused word. In order to apprehend these things, you need to have sat at the feet of the modern Gamaliels, the Surrealists and the Da-Daists and the rest. And I haven't, you know. I've just gone on studying things I like. It's a frightful admission."

"Why?" asked Henry Fearon. "It seems perfectly sensible to me."

Humphry David grinned, rather sheepishly. "It's the equivalent of saying 'I know what I like,' Henry. And that is the ultimate sole-cism. I'm going to start from first principles some time. You know those axioms. 'All vital art work is controversial. In any controversy, the majority are always the uninformed.' Well, that's me. So far as this stuff goes, I'm just that—uninformed."

"Does it really matter?" asked Henry vaguely. "Isn't specialisa-tion the climax of attainment these days? To know more and more about less and less?"

"Not in my department," said the Minister, and then he grinned again. "Between you and me, think of the fun I should have if I could only get to terms with these things. I could deal with some of these pretentious asses who come in and virtually genuflect in front of some of these... And I know some of them are liars. The pretentious asses, I mean, because what one says contradicts what another says. Picture A is significant. Picture B is a travesty—or the converse, according to the critic. You see, Joyce-Lawrence had a sense of humour. These pictures aren't signed. He didn't have the name of the painter attached to any of them, and his private list has been lost—if it ever existed. My own opinion is that they're all anonymous, for the best of reasons."

Henry Fearon began to laugh. "I think I get you," he said. "I should let them remain anonymous, and have verbatim notes taken when the pretentious asses get going: just as we do with witnesses.

You could publish rather a good book, complete with illustrations, for private circulation only, of course."

"This is all very heretical, but I know you won't quote me," said the Minister. "Do you like the way that one's hung?—the crystalline effect, I mean. It's called Meadow Grasses."

"Why?"

"I don't know. As a study of crystalline form it's rather attractive. When I came, it was hung the other way up. I had it reversed. It was my first decision as Minister: quite intuitive, you know. I'd nothing to go on. But I prefer it that way."

"Do you sometimes feel like turning the job up, sir?" asked Henry.

"No. At the moment, definitely no," replied David. "We're really getting to grips with the frescoes at Wyndford—that church in the Cotswolds you know. The stuff we've uncovered is a revelation: my own opinion is that the painter was influenced by the Fairford glass. You know the Fairford glass, Henry?"

"Well, I've seen it," said Henry Fearon cautiously, "but did you say you wanted to see me about a job, sir? I don't want to sound unappreciative, but my free time is up. Theoretically, I'm on duty again."

"Are you? Perhaps we'd better get down to it," said the Minister. "It may be all my eye—but it's like this."

III

They sat down, one on either side of the Minister's desk (it was a good late Georgian knee-hole writing-table, bought by Joyce-Lawrence for a song, on account of its dimensions, which were monumental. Being an individualist, Joyce-Lawrence had refused to tolerate Government furniture.) Producing cigarettes, Humphry David got going.

"As you know, Henry, this Ministry has suffered from what you might call infant mortality. Joyce-Lawrence died after six months in office. Of course, that was during the fuel crisis. Then they appointed old Higginson. He was a nice old chap, but the only pictures he really liked were the Chantry Bequest lot they keep in the cellars. Anyway, he died just before the General Election."

"Why did he keep these pictures up, sir?—or didn't he?" inquired Henry.

"Oh, he didn't interfere with them. You see, they didn't come within his experience and he didn't regard them as pictures at all," said David. "He regarded them as furnishings—Fine Arts: Ministry: for the use of. In any case, poor old chap, his main preoccupation was cheese-paring. If he could keep costs down he was as happy as a grig, and, as he said, if he'd taken these exhibits down, something would have had to be done about repainting the walls—but that's all by the way. The reason I mentioned the high mortality rate among my predecessors was to explain why I found things a bit disorganised when I got here. You see, this is a new department, and there's no tradition to steady it. It was bound to be a bit tentative at first, of course. Anyway, in order to get the hang of things, I thought I'd work through some of the files myself: not systematically, you know, but taking a sample here and there to get the climate, if you see what I mean: temperature prevalent winds, relative humidity and so forth."

Henry grinned. "Very conscientious of you, sir, and very enterprising. I dare say you came across some odd examples of the business attributed to Ministries by the general public."

"Did I not," replied Humphry David, "but there was a method of sorts in my researches. As you know, correspondence comes in from here, there and everywhere: suggestions, complaints, abuse, criticisms—some of the latter quite valuable. By reading samples of the letters and the answers sent, I thought I might get the feel of the policy my predecessors had followed—if they had any policy, which I rather doubt."

"One minute, sir," put in Henry. "I know M.O.F.A. is still in the making, so to speak, and generally speaking it's non-political: non-party, anyway, but I take it that you have a permanent secretariat, after the usual pattern?"

"Oh, yes," replied David. "Usual pattern about describes it. You probably know the set-out: there's the Minister and Parliamentary Secretary in the House. Here there's a Permanent Secretary; he has a private secretary with the rank of assistant principal, and, of course, a Deputy. Our more important branches—Museums, Awards, Acquisitions branch, and so on, have Under Secretaries and Assistant Secretaries at the head of them, together with the usual army of typists, filing clerks and the rest. I know people say it's a racket, and the size of the personnel involved sometimes appals me. Joyce-Lawrence started on the lavish side of course: apart from the branches I've mentioned, he set up a Public Monuments Branch, Artists and Architects, Loan Collections, Legal, Finance, Statistics, Information and External Relations, Establishments and Inspectorates. That's leaving out of account all the co-ordinating committees which bicker with the old-established governing bodies of Galleries and recognised Art Schools, and the branch which wages war with the M.O.E."

Henry Fearon grinned. "Thanks for telling me, sir. I'd no idea that ministries were so fearfully and wonderfully made. I take it that all these Permanent, Deputy, Assistant and Under Secretaries *are* all permanent? You inherited them, so to speak."

"Oh, yes. A Minister may die and the Government may fall, but the Ministry Staff endures. The Permanent Secretary here is Sir Charles Knott (they knighted him in the last Honours List) but he's been *hors-de-combat* with a duodenal for months, so my chief stooge, my prop-and-stay, is Knott's deputy—name of Edwin Pompfret. He was one of Joyce-Lawrence's appointments, and presumably he must be an able chap to have got where he has." Humphry David rubbed his hair unhappily. "Between you and me, Henry, and off the record, I can't abide Pompfret. He spells his name with a p in the middle, and I gather the typists call him Pompey. He's one of those chaps who puts on a quasi-religious manner when studying works of art. It's probably my fault, but he gets my hackles up. He started by treating me as a mental defective. You see…" The Minister looked round at his "funnies" and Henry said:

"I see."

"Very comforting of you, Henry," said Humphry David. "I was quite willing to admit that these things aren't my line of country, but I was not willing to be lectured by a pompous ass who's got all the jargon on the tip of his tongue, and no sound basis for any of his judgments. He's a window dresser, if ever there was one. Anyway, so far as is reasonable, I prefer to find my own way about, and not consult him more than I need."

"Look here, sir," said Henry. "This is off the record, so let's call a spade a spade. In your judgment, this bloke isn't trustworthy?"

"Personally I wouldn't trust him to order the weekly rations," said David. "He's got a slovenly mind, an unreliable memory and a colossal conceit of himself. And he tries to get other people blamed for his own mistakes. Well, about these files. My own opinion is that there's been some monkeying. You know the system we work on. All correspondence is filed complete, both letters and answers. As you can guess for yourself, all Ministers of the Crown get a lot of queer correspondence addressed to them personally. And the Minister of Fine Arts gets more than his share of letters from aggrieved parties. It's inevitable. Artistic judgment can't always be objective. We're not dealing with commodities like coal or steel or cotton, which have a basic commodity value. And artists, art committees, and patrons of the arts are all peppery customers. Anyway, all correspondence is, or should be, examined critically and replied to reasonably—or as reasonably as the circumstances warrant. Finally, all this guff is filed, and the files are open to examination by any senior members of the secretariat."

"Fun for them," said Henry, and David grinned.

"Quite. As a matter of fact, some of those files make better reading than any comics I've ever met. I've sat here evening after evening and got a lot of entertainment out of it. And so, to get to brass tacks, Henry. In my judgment, some of the files have been interfered with. That is to say, some of the original letters, or answers, have been suppressed and others inserted to make a reasonable sequence."

"What are you arguing on, sir? The matter of the letters? The manner of them? Or their superficial appearance?"

"Not the latter," said David. "They look all right—our replies, I mean. They're on the right paper and all that sort of thing. I'm arguing as a human being, Henry. I know the way these people's minds work, and I know the way the correspondence would go, and the amount of heat likely to be generated. If an aggrieved painter or an infuriated curator starts in with an indignant letter, he generally gets more heated and more unreasonable as the correspondence continues. He doesn't suddenly soft pedal and fade out with the equivalent of an apology. It's all out of character."

Henry Fearon made a non-committal sound, and the Minister went on: "Don't imagine I'm expecting you to tackle the job on the sort of lines I've been indicating. It's much too nebulous. I can only tell you that I, personally, have a feeling that there's been some jiggery-pokery. I may be quite wrong. What I suggest is that I give you some of the files to examine, and you can tell me if the letters seem consistent from your angle. Has the typing of them been done on our machines: has the same typewriter been used throughout? Are the fingerprints consistent with what you'd expect, and so forth."

"O.K., sir. Can do," replied Henry. "I expect we shall be able to tell you quite a lot about the documents. It's just our cup of tea. You see, it's much more difficult to produce a convincing alternative letter than most people imagine. These variations hardly ever stand up to expert examination."

"How lucky you are," said Humphry David meditatively. "You work from established facts. X always equals X in your equations. Evaluation of works of art is a chancier process: what is X to one critic may be Y to another."

Henry Fearon sat still, thinking hard. He knew Humphry David and respected him. It seemed to Henry that throughout the interview, the Minister had been stating a case: for all the seeming casualness of his conversation he had been neither vague nor trivial. He had got something to say, and he had chosen his own way of saying it. Henry glanced round again to the pictures on the walls. Then he asked:

"Is it possible to put a money value to these things, sir?"

"No. You see, they're not signed. They're worth just what anybody chooses to pay for them—in the sale room, that is. And there's not one of them which hasn't been commended by one critic and condemned by another."

Henry ploughed on. "I expect you've got to know them pretty well, sir."

"You mean I should know if one of them disappeared and was replaced by a copy? If I were asked to swear to it in a court of law, I should be very hesitant. You see. I don't know the manner, the technique."

Henry Fearon looked across at a canvas on which a seaside promenade was suggested rather than depicted. "It looks to me as though any clever kid could have done it as a leg pull, sir."

"Oh, no. No," expostulated the Minister. "I'm not so lost as that. Now that one, it might be... Well, never mind. But it's worth remembering that Joyce-Lawrence hadn't any money to play with. He couldn't have…"

"Lack of money hasn't mattered in some of the rackets we've encountered, sir," said Henry. "May I put it like this. You've lived with these things, and they're individuals to you. Because you've been used to thinking in terms of paint and line and composition you can see something in them I can't see, even though you don't love them. But your predecessor, the Chantry Bequest enthusiast, how real were they to him?"

"I don't know, Henry. I simply don't know," replied the Minister.

At that moment the telephone rang, and David picked up the receiver. "By all means," he said, "by all means. Bring him along now."

He replaced the receiver and said: "Don't go yet, Henry. Sit tight. I'll give you some 'projects' to study. Pompfret is bringing one of his *cognoscenti* along to see these pictures. They won't say much, they never do, not to begin with, but I think you'll be interested."

CHAPTER II

I

EDWIN POMPFRET WAS A TALLISH FELLOW, INCLINED TO OBE-sity, though Henry Fearon put his age at under fifty. In attire he inclined to the deliberately picturesque, and in contrast with the Minister's reticent dark suit and unobtrusive tie, Pompfret's corduroy jacket and flowing silk tie looked flamboyant. Suède shoes (rather good ones, noted Henry), voluminous flannel bags (cinnamon), brown corduroy jacket, tussore shirt, and a flaming tie knotted in a negligent bow: plus a ring suitable to a bishop (cornelian?) and a red silk handkerchief overflowing from a side pocket. His hair was sandy, his face rubicund, his eyes light blue and his horn-rimmed spectacles were angular and outsize. The man he brought in was small and grey, bowed as to shoulders, troubled in countenance, rather slovenly in dress, making no attempt at picturesqueness.

Pompfret led his visitor in and introduced him. "Dr. Weissonnier, Minister. You may remember his work on Braque."

"Delighted," murmured Humphry David and the visitor bowed silently. "Dr. Weissonnier was in Paris at the time Apollinaire coined the word 'Surrealiste,'" continued Pompfret expansively, but the small grey man gave him no encouragement. With a gesture towards the pictures, he said: "Permettez, Monsieur le Ministre?"

"By all means. Delighted," said Humphry David. The progress round the pictures was slow, and for Weissonnier's part, almost silent.

Once he said *"Par exemple."* Several times he grunted, whether in admiration, derision, or pain, Henry could not tell. Pompfret stood behind him and put in occasional disjointed words: Significant... Three-dimensional... Elimination... Selectivity... Derived... Decadent... Henry felt he could do the same thing himself now he had learnt the appropriate words. Pompfret waved his arms, made passes with his hands, narrowed his eyes. Weissonnier did none of these things. He approached one or two of the pictures so closely that Henry wondered if he were going to lick them, but he refrained. At the conclusion of his examination he made an abrupt bow to Humphry David.

"Infiniment reconnaissant, Monsieur le Ministre," he said.

"Not at all," murmured David, and the visitor walked straight to the door, followed by Pompfret.

"Well, you didn't get much out of that one," said Henry. The Minister was making a note on his pad.

"No. But he looked at them. Really looked. You can always tell. I must look into him. I've sometimes thought it would be a good idea to get an independent professional opinion on my own account. Pay for it, I mean. If I could only get hold of someone really trustworthy: someone, that is, who could be relied on to keep their own counsel."

"You don't want to get it in the papers," said Henry.

"That's it. This department is everybody's Aunt Sally already. Any brick's good enough to throw at us. 'Studio throw-outs at the Ministry.' You know the sort of thing—or even worse: 'Pictures worth a fortune in a government department. Details.' Well, we all have our small troubles but I must admit that Joyce-Lawrence's little joke is a weariness of the flesh to me. Now about those files, Henry. I don't want to send them out of the building, if I can avoid it. Not to begin with, anyway. If you smell a rat after you've given them the once over, it's a different matter. But I do want to avoid giving any grounds for gossip or surmise until I know what the probabilities are."

"Is there any feeling of suspicion, sir? Lack of confidence among your staff, or anything of that kind?"

"It's a bit hard for me to answer that one accurately. I haven't been here long enough to make real contact with people's minds, and they're still on their best behaviour with me—all save Pompfret, who doesn't indulge in such niceties. But we've got some interesting and worthwhile people here, particularly among the young ones. We've got an architect's department, and there are one or two very worthwhile young architects there, and the youngsters in charge of the loan collections are delightful people—they seem incredibly young to me, but I'm used to old fossils of my own age. I know they think things, Henry. I can see it in the wisdom of their serious young faces. And they try to spare me. When intelligent young people try to shield you from the colder blasts of contemporary thought, it's a crashing blow to the self-esteem of one who thought himself rather well-preserved."

Henry Fearon began to laugh. "I shouldn't have called you well-preserved, sir. Preservation hasn't occurred to you, but you don't seem old to me. You'd never have spotted the doings if your mind had started coagulating."

"Well, thanks for the kind words, Henry. Now I suggest that we leave the matter of these files until a convenient moment occurs for me to do some private digging. Then I'll give you a ring. I'm particularly anxious to avoid giving the impression that I'm snooping."

"You want to reverse the immortal phrase, sir, and work up to a bang and not to a whimper."

"Well, you do surprise me," said the Minister.

"Why? By the time a poet's phrase gets into a *Times* leading article even C.O. notices it. Look here, sir. Just give me the names of some of those intelligent young you were talking about."

"Why?" asked Humphry David bluntly.

"Because I sometimes go and chew a sandwich at the M.A.C., sir, and I might happen across them."

"What on earth made you join the Modern Arts Centre?" demanded the Minister.

"They make very good coffee, their premises are warm, comfortable and quiet, and I never see anybody I know there," said Henry Fearon. "We all have our private fancies: one of mine is to get right away from people in my own line of country occasionally, and the M.A.C. fulfils that qualification admirably."

"Very sensible. I wish I could say the same," said the Minister enviously. "I dare not go there myself. They know who I am, and they shrink away from me as though I were a leper. Well, thank you for being so understanding, Henry. I'll let you know when the occasion arises for operation files."

"Very good, sir," replied Fearon.

II

Humphry David, unlike old Higginson (his predecessor in office), did occasionally walk around the premises of his own Ministry as though his feet were made for walking, and not for permanent seclusion under a Georgian writing-table. When he first came to Medici House, his perambulating habits had caused consternation. The personnel of the place had got accustomed to a static Minister. The Right Honourable Alfred Higginson had gone straight to his desk when he arrived at the Ministry, and at his desk he had remained while he was in the building. Thither his secretaries, clerks, and

typists had brought him such papers as needed his personal attention. The consulting experts, the local representatives, the visiting
deputations, all these had found room for their business in the huge
apartment known as the Minister's office: the visiting curators, the
county architects, had brought their plans and elevations, their
"projects" and specifications to the Minister himself. "Old Alf" they
called him among themselves. Old Alf had glanced at plans drawn
across yards of double-elephant: he had cast an eye over blue-prints
which conveyed nothing at all to his conscientious but untrained
mind, and he always uttered the same question: "'Ow much is all
this going to cost, hey? 'Ow much is it going to cost?" But Old Alf
never walked about the building. The typists said he had corns, and
they were right. (Typists in Ministries are often well informed on
such small personal points.)

Humphry David not only had no corns, he had an inquiring
mind. And he was interested in Decimus Burton's building. (After all,
Decimus Burton had built the Athenæum Club, of which Humphry
David was a member, so he had a basis of comparison.) Up the
great marble staircase and along the spacious corridors the Minister
strolled in inquisitive contemplation, studying pilaster and capital
and frieze, moulding and enrichment, plaster panelling and niche,
elaborate ceiling and cornice. ("Robert Adam had this chap cold,"
he muttered.) Some of the original embellishments were left in the
building, being what might be described as monumental permanen-
cies. One of these was a marble bust of heroic dimensions standing
on a six-foot marble pedestal at the head of the state staircase. It was
a likeness of the last Earl of Manderby (or was reputed to be) and
had been executed by Canova after that sculptor's visit to London in
1815. Surmounted by a laurel wreath, the larger-than-life head of an
English gentleman of the Georgian era struck David as one of the
most dreadful objects he had ever seen. He hated Canova, anyway.

He had resented the amount of space—and marble—Canova's work occupied in St. Peter's. The one occasion on which Humphry David had found himself in sympathy with Edwin Pompfret was when, in his early days at Medici House, David had raised his eyes to the immense and flamboyant bust and said spontaneously, "But this is frightful… frightful."

"Too true, sir," replied Pompfret. "Couldn't it be moved elsewhere? The thing is too utterly revolting. It offends one's sense of values, and the sheer virtuosity of the treatment renders it the more deplorable. It should not be here at all. It labels us as Philistines."

"It's a work of art," said David unhappily. "One mustn't let personal prejudice intervene…"

"I've often wondered if it would topple off with a little encouragement," said Pompfret. "It'd be a wonderful sight to see it bounce down the stairs. It must weigh several tons."

"I like his warts," said David, studying the appalling white visage which glared out from under the profusion of laurel leaves. "They remind me of that lion's nose in St. Peter's. Well observed, as we used to say. But it couldn't be bounced off, you know. It must be pegged, or cemented or something."

"It isn't, Minister. I saw them put it back. It was dumped in the Piccadilly tube during the war, to safeguard it," said Pompfret. "John Joyce-Lawrence managed to temporise about its replacement. He was trying to get it shifted to Parliament Square. But after he died it came back here. Alfred Higginson admired it. It was the one thing in the building he really liked—until he got the bill for moving it back. London Transport supplied the tackle, and it was a very costly operation. It nearly broke the Minister's heart."

"Oh, God," groaned Humphry David. He wasn't generally a profane man, but he had stepped to the side to get the profile of the last Earl Manderby.

"I couldn't agree with you more, sir," said Pompfret, but the Minister turned on him sharply.

"Kindly refrain from using that expression to me in future," he said. "It is one of the more regrettable efforts in contemporary idiom."

"Too true," agreed Pompfret.

The Minister continued on his tour of the premises. Opening one of the double doors of the great ballroom, he heard a cackle and clatter as of a modern symphony in which the percussion players had got out of hand. The fortissimo died to a mezzo forte and then to piano as the instrumentalists saw their new conductor. In serried ranks, typists sat at their regulation tables, while additional trestle tables accommodated executants busy with card indices. There seemed to Humphry David to be hundreds of them, chattering, rustling and tapping beneath a painted ceiling from which amorini hurtled roses in a cloudless sky. The Minister withdrew, saying to himself, "What do they do? We're not a rationing body—or are we?" He strolled on, glancing in at heads of departments accommodated in unsuitable splendour, who were not even allowed to knock a nail in the walls to secure their inevitable notice-boards.

The only department in which Humphry David really enjoyed himself was the architects' section. Perhaps because of the fact that their double-elephant drawing-boards took up a great deal of space, they were housed in some of the few really small bedrooms on the top floor, but in comparison with the representation of Babel in the ballroom, they looked sane, purposeful and serene.

"How nice to see somebody really doing something," said David.

The room had three occupants, two lasses and one lad. The former were seated at their drawing-boards, with impedimenta of long T-squares, set squares, rulers, compasses, springbows and the rest. The boy was merely lounging—but he looked a nice boy, David thought, with an open, eager face and intelligent eyes. The girl near-est to the door got up: she was very tall, very fair; serene and sensible looking; and she had no make-up on her face. Her smooth pale skin was innocent even of powder. The Minister was old-fashioned, and this break away from over-ruling feminine custom pleased him a lot.

"Who are you and what are you doing?" he asked.

"Patricia Oxton, sir—and Ruth Kenton. We are both working on the Small Towns Gallery Project."

"Project… How I do loathe our jargon," he said, "but tell me about the galleries."

The other girl—Ruth Kenton—was slim and dark and shy, but Patricia Oxton explained their task as calmly as though she were used to seeing Ministers bobbing into her drawing office.

"It has been suggested that small market towns which serve a large rural area should be provided with galleries to house local works of art, loan collections and exhibitions by local painters, amateur and professional," she began.

"A very good idea. Who started it?" said David.

"Mr. Joyce-Lawrence, sir. He was very keen on the idea, but the buildings he asked us to plan were too ambitious. They were too big and too costly, and we have produced various plans since, always trying to cut the unit cost and reduce the areas. In fact every space is dual or triple purpose and the specification can't be cheapened any further." She raised her head and glanced across the room. "This is John Dunne. He has been investigating sites for us."

"It seems so hopeless, sir," burst out the boy. "I go along and try to find a site: then I'm told it's either building land and therefore too expensive, or agricultural land and mustn't be built on, or scheduled as an open space and sacrosanct. What they really want is a gallery suspended in space."

"I know," agreed the Minister, "but let me see the plans and the elevations. I like this sort of thing. It's concrete."

"It isn't," burst out the dark girl.

David glanced at them in turn. "Do you all go and inspect the sites?" he inquired.

"We have done once or twice, sir," replied the fair girl.

"What fun you must have," said David.

He sat down at the drawing-desk, perched on a tall stool, and spent a happy half-hour examining elevations, plans and materials. Somehow he found the fact of dealing with designs produced in his own department was refreshing after the amount of purely clerical work with which the place was inundated. He knew he was being illogical, but he enjoyed it all the same. As he got up to go he said:

"What do you think of the last Earl Manderby?"

"The Casanova Minotaur?" inquired John Dunne, and then got very pink. "I mean Canova, sir."

"Do you? I don't somehow think you did," said Humphry David. "While agreeing with you that the noble countenance does suggest the writer you mention, I should be obliged if you could let your little joke die."

"Couldn't we get rid of the thing, sir?" inquired Patricia Oxton. "It's a lovely staircase, and that object spoils it. I've often thought it'd be a wonderful idea to exchange the bust for the Dutch candelabrum which used to hang at the top of the staircase. That really is lovely. I've got a picture of it somewhere."

"You're better informed than I am, young woman," said the Minister. "Where is this candelabrum now?"

"In Chicago, sir. But if Earl Manderby was really done by Canova, it must be worth a lot, and they like large things in the States."

"Bad for international relations," murmured John Dunne. "They'd label it 'Portrait of an English gentleman.'"

Patricia Oxton was rummaging amongst a pile of Architectural Press publications in a drawer of her desk, and she passed one over to the Minister.

"That's the candelabrum, sir. It's a lovely design—just a slight variation on the traditional Dutch pattern. It must have looked grand hanging above that landing."

David studied the photograph. "You're quite right," he said. "It's very fine indeed. A pity it was sold—but I suppose they had to realise everything they could to cover death duties."

"Why didn't they sell Manderby?" asked the irrepressible John Dunne.

"Filial piety, perhaps," suggested the Minister. "It couldn't have been shortage of shipping space because that candelabrum is an immense thing. I've never seen one with so many sconces."

"Perhaps good taste operated for once," said Patricia Oxton. "The one thing is beautiful. The other isn't."

Humphry David would have joined issue with her over her arbitrary pronouncement (Earl Manderby was a horror, but Canova was Canova, and discipline must be maintained), but the door of the room opened abruptly, and a dark fellow glared in, saying sharply: "You've gone to the wrong people for those roofing estimates, Miss Oxton. If you could leave off chattering for a moment…"

Then he suddenly observed the Minister and his dark face flushed. "I beg your pardon, sir," he exclaimed.

"No need. No need," replied David. "I *was* chattering, I admit it, and I've learnt something I didn't know. Are you acquainted with this picture, Welles?"

The dark fellow was Roger Welles, head of the architectural section, and a modernist of the post-functional school. What post-functionalism was David did not know, but he regarded the name with suspicion.

Welles looked down at the picture of the candelabrum. "No, sir, though I am aware that there were some very fine examples of candelabra in this building. Not that this one ever hung on the staircase. That's preposterous, of course. It was probably in the great drawing-room."

"The one in the great drawing-room was a glass one," said Patricia Oxton. "It was bought by Atheneon Cinemas, and it is now in the Tottenham Court Road Atheneon, adding lustre to the foyer."

"How do you know?" demanded Welles irritably. "Are you specialising on the function of the candelabrum in interior decoration?"

"I hadn't thought of doing so, sir," replied Miss Oxton, with unmoved serenity. "I read about the lustre effect in an article on the Atheneon. Jon Vanderlag won the competition award for the building."

"Well, I don't think there's the least chance we shall get either of the candelabra back here: we can't compete with either Chicago or the Cinema in the matter of expenditure," said the Minister, and turned to Welles. "I'm very interested in this idea of small town galleries," he said. "It's a good idea. How can people learn anything about pictures if they never see any?"

"It depends on what it is proposed to hang in the galleries, sir," said Welles, and his voice was acid. "Mr. Higginson was in favour of disinterring some of the narrative pictures of the early 1900's—what might be called the death throes of the Academic movement."

"Oh come, we could do better than that," said the Minister cheerfully. "I'm quite prepared to loan the pictures in my study. However, we can argue that out when we've got one of your galleries built."

John Dunne looked more pessimistic than ever. "'Murdering impossibility, to make what can not be, slight work,'" he murmured.

"I ought to know where that comes from," said Humphry David thoughtfully. "Don't tell me. I'll remember it sometime." He nodded to the three young people, repressed a desire to say "God bless you," and turned to Welles. "Come to my office sometime and give me your opinion on that design for the new cathedral at Hudderstown," he said cheerfully.

It was a good exit line. The design in question was pure Gothic revival, and to Welles the Gothic period was dead, buried, and again dead. "Rightly so: too true," as Pompfret would have said.

On leaving the Architects' Branch, the Minister (who had not got a well-developed bump of locality) turned to his right along the passage instead of to his left, and soon realised that he was completely lost. He eventually came to a staircase very different in design from the grandiose structure by which he had ascended: it was steep and twisting and David descended it with caution. On the floor below there was much chattering and a certain amount of giggling and scuffling around a tea trolley which was being wheeled along the passage by a decorative young chit in a smart white coat, attended by some messenger boys. The guardian of the trolley called to David: "Cupper tea, ducks?"

"Not at the moment, thank you very much," replied the Minister politely. The girl stared at him as he passed her, and then gave a squawk of alarm. "Crikey!" she gasped, and fled in confusion, followed by the two messengers.

Humphry David descended another flight to the ground floor. Here, to his relief, he saw a large notice. "Loans collection Branch." He knew where he was now. Persisting in his private inspection, he opened a door and looked into what had been the Music Room of Decimus Burton's mansion. All round the walls tall narrow pigeon-holes had been erected, calculated to contain canvases of various dimensions. In the centre of the room the inevitable clerks worked diligently, and filing cabinets occupied the platform. A group of superior young women were having an argument with two young men, one dark and morose-looking, the other fair and perplexed.

"I think this arrangement is much more intelligent," said one of the young women. "Chronologically it makes sense." She began to read the notices above the pigeon-holes, and the Minister listened, entranced: "Post-Impressionists, Expressionists, Neo-Realists, Fauvistes, Cubists, Neo-Cubists, Futurists, Vorticists, Constructivists, Purists—"

"It's much too arbitrary. You can't reduce art-movements to systematic planning," said one of the men, and the other put in:

"We haven't any real Vorticists. It was a one-man movement anyway, and nobody here is qualified to distinguish between Cubists and Neo-Cubists, and the examples we have of either school would disgrace any one-horse gallery in the provinces. If I had my way I'd burn the lot."

A horrified "Sh... sh... sh..." from one of the girls focused attention on the Minister. He came forward as the sound of typing died away.

"Can you define a Vorticist for me, please? I'm afraid I'm very ignorant about contemporary art. It's not my period."

"Wasn't the Vorticist school founded by Wyndham Lewis, sir?" put in the girl who had been pleading for an "intelligent arrangement," and the disgruntled man said:

"We haven't a Wyndham Lewis here. The things labelled 'Vorticists' are geometrical designs collected from Paris junk shops. The signatures on them mean nothing. They were probably added by the agents who sold them."

Humphry David studied the speaker thoughtfully. "I don't think I know your name, although your face is familiar," he said courteously.

"Paul Weston, sir. Admittedly I'm no expert, but I'm very much interested in modern painting."

"I wish I were," said David with his usual simplicity. "I gather you don't think very highly of our loan collection, so far as present day painting is concerned?"

Paul Weston flushed, but he stood his ground. "I've only my own opinion to go on, sir. I don't think we're doing modern painting justice. If I had my way, I'd scrap the lot and start again with a few examples by first-rate painters."

"And how would you share out 'a few examples' between all the provincial galleries who want a loan collection?" asked the intelligent arranger sweetly.

"It's quite a problem, isn't it?" put in David urbanely. "Meantime, may I say how much I admire the lettering of the notices? They're really beautiful Roman capitals."

"Mr. Weston did them, sir. He studied architecture at one time," replied the girl.

Paul Weston flushed again. "Isn't that typically English, sir— decent lettering to denote bad paintings?"

"Is it?" asked Humphry David coldly.

He left them to their discussion and returned thankfully to his study to consider the latest report on the Cotswold wall paintings.

After the Minister had left, Ewart Blackwell (the younger of the two men), turned on Paul Weston.

"Look here, aren't you being a bit exhibitionist?" he demanded indignantly. "It may be true that we haven't got a Picasso or a Paul Klee, and our post-impressionists are all small beer, but we've a decent representative collection, and I don't see why you want to tell the Minister we've got a collection of duds. It's enough to make him shut down the whole branch."

"It'd be an excellent thing if he did. Then I should join the R.A.F. again and tinker with engines, and you could go into a bank and do some painting in the week-ends," said Paul Weston unkindly.

Before Blackwell could retort, Weston went out of the room, and Pamela Barton (who had been rearranging the canvases) turned quickly to Blackwell.

"Don't take any notice of him. He just has these moods of despondency and there's nothing you can do about it."

"Well, he needn't be so damned superior," said Blackwell, "all because he was brought up in Paris and thinks he knows. After all, he's not an artist himself."

"I was awfully interested to learn that you paint. I hadn't realised that," said Miss Barton.

Blackwell flushed. "Oh, I'm pretty dud. I know that. Weston saw one of my canvases once and told me I was a born plagiarist. I suppose I am—but he needn't be so superior."

"Oh, never mind. He's probably got indigestion," said Pamela. "Do you really think we ought to label this 'Vorticist'? It might be anything."

"Too true," said Blackwell, and they both giggled.

Pompfret's expressions were common currency in Loans when anybody felt flippant.

CHAPTER III

I

BOB TITMARSH WAS NIGHT WATCHMAN AT MEDICI HOUSE. HE came on duty at ten o'clock every evening, relieving George Smith, who was one of the housemen. The housemen worked in two shifts, from six in the morning until two in the afternoon, and from two until ten o'clock in the evening. It was their job to supervise the cleaners, to stoke the furnaces, to bring in crates and other heavy packages, and otherwise to assist in jobs which demanded brawn rather than brain. All were ex-servicemen, and Titmarsh and Smith were particular cronies, having shared the glories and tribulations of service in the Far East. Consequently Titmarsh generally arrived at the Ministry about half an hour before Smith went off duty, and they enjoyed a pot of char together somewhere in the dim recesses of the dreariest basement in London. One of the good points about working in a government department was that no one was too particular about the amount of tea that went into the pot, and tea, as the grocers said, was "tight." They could have made their tea in the more hygienic canteen (house staff, for the use of), but as old soldiers they liked privacy. In the basement they could at least say just what they meant.

Both men knew the habits of those who made up the Ministry staff. Some of the "high ups" kept their own hours: "poppers in and out" George called them. The large mass of employees, the typists and filing clerks and their fellows, had all left the building by five-thirty, going to swell the queues (and scrums) at bus stops, tubes and main line stations. At five-thirty George organised his evening shift of charwomen, who dealt with marble staircase, tessellated pavements, parquet floors and miles of drugget. But in the evenings, when the building was quiet, a few eccentric and conscientious V.I.P.s occasionally came back to their offices in Medici House to deal with problems whose nature was a mystery to George. Among these eccentrics was the Minister himself. "'As to pop in and out when he can," said George, "along of them divisions in the 'Ouse. Ministers 'as to vote same as common or garden M.P.s, or the (blue pencilled) government'd be in queer street. But what chaps like that Pompey wants to come snoopin' around in the evenings for I just don't see."

George had had more than one shock when, ambling about in the comfortable "undress" of an old soldier, he had come face to face with the Minister or the Deputy Permanent Secretary. The result of these meetings had caused George and Bob to take cover while enjoying their evening char. "Keep out of the officer's way" was a natural reaction for such hardened warriors.

On this particular March evening, George was giving Bob a private and personal opinion on the old furnaces which were still the *fons et origo* of the central heating in Medici House. Joyce-Lawrence had died (of pneumonia) before he had had time to get these abominations replaced. Alfred Higginson, who had been brought up "hard," had said that these were no times to squander money taking out boilers which still had a lot of work left in them, and if the housemen couldn't do that much extra to help the government which helped the working man, they didn't deserve the Welfare State. Humphry David was working hard to get through the divers problems he had inherited in Medici House, and he hadn't got down to the boilers yet, though he had given permission for open fires to be lighted in some of the very adequate fire-places which Decimus Burton had designed before central heating was practical politics. In the remoter wings of the Ministry, as Pompfret liked to say, the central heating lived up to the first part of its title—doubtless it was central, but at the extremities it was not heating.

The essential of this problematical heating installation, the furnace proper, produced heat in more senses than one. George said that it was calculated to make a naval stoker's blood boil, and he couldn't put it stronger than that. He told Bob a few of the troubles the abomination had caused that day, warned him that a fresh consignment of totally unsuitable fuel had been delivered that evening, and finally left Bob to get on with it, with a few additional words of sympathy.

Bob went straight to the cellars. It was always his first job on night duty to stoke up for the night—keep the qualified thing going somehow. He went and examined the new lot of fuel and swore vigorously. Instead of small nuts, or coke, or small anthracite, the contractors had left big stuff, suitable for the enormous fire-places which were not allowed to be used, but impracticable for shovelling into an awkward boiler fire. With a few appropriate epithets, Bob got busy with a coal hammer, and the cellar resounded with the vigour of his attack. After that he raked the fuel into convenient heaps and got busy on raking out the fire, knowing full well what sort of time he would have if the ancient horror choked itself, as it was only too liable to do. It took a full half-hour of noisy, dirty, back-breaking work before he had got things to his liking. In spite of his perpetual grumbles, Bob was a good worker. He stoked conscientiously and left the cellars ship-shape for his mates on the morning shift.

Having washed the marks of stoking from hands and face and brawny arms, he resumed his coat and went up to the ground floor for the next item of his routine—a general inspection of the ground

floor. When he reached the great entrance hall he found it in darkness: this was contrary to regulation, which ordained enough pilot
lights for the night watchman to see if things were in order. Flicking
down the nearest switch, Bob grumbled again. "Fuse gone," he
muttered. He knew where the fuse boxes were, and using his torch
went and got a step-ladder to inspect the boxes above a door at the
back of the hall. He soon found the faulty one which controlled the
lighting circuit of the hall: the ends of the fuse shone in the light of
his torch. He replaced it carefully and saw the pilot light come on,
went and put the ladder away and continued his tour of inspection.

Shuffling along comfortably in his old slippers, Bob moved
across the marble floor of the entrance hall and then stopped dead,
one brief inevitable word of profanity choked back by a shock of
astonishment. A man's body sprawled at the foot of the great staircase, his blood spreading in grim runnels on drugget and marble:
around him were white lumps and blocks and splinters, as though the
plaster ceiling had fallen on him. But the plaster seemed to gleam,
and Bob suddenly recognised it for what it was before he raised his
eyes and saw the empty plinth at the top of the first flight of stairs.
The larger-than-life bust of the last Earl Manderby had fallen from
its place: it had crashed down the marble staircase, and, judging by
the evidence, it had fallen on Edwin Pompfret's head and hurled
him down, too. Together they lay at the foot of the noblest state
staircase in London: both with broken necks. Earl Manderby's
neck had severed below the chin; detached from its monumental
shoulders, among chips and blocks of laurel leaves, stylised curls
and fragments of outsize features, the marble head lay grotesquely
close to Pompfret's, while Pompfret's blood clotted on the black
and white blocks of the pavement.

Bob Titmarsh had seen grimmer casualties than this one when
he served in the Armoured Corps, but there was some quality of

horror in the contrast between the civilised dignity of the great hall and stairway and the sorry mess of blood and body and broken marble on the floor which kept the ex-serviceman stock still for a few seconds as he stared incredulously. Then he went forward and bent down to see if he could do anything for Pompfret, knowing all the time that there was nothing anybody could do. With a muttered profanity which really expressed sheer pity, Bob turned quickly to the porter's box by the front door: there was a telephone there, and Bob dialled 999 for the first time in his life, wondering if it "worked." It worked all right. The voice at the other end was a competent voice, and no time was wasted. "Stand by. We'll be along in a few minutes," came the assurance.

II

Just as he put the receiver down on its rest, Bob heard the click of a key in the lock of the front door, and before the night watchman could do anything, one of the great inner doors opened, and the Minister stood on the mat and looked across the palatial entrance hall to the foot of the stairs. He stood and stared as though he were petrified, and then turned with a jerk of astonishment as Bob moved forward.

"Sorry, sir," said the night watchman. "Afraid it's a nasty accident. I rang 999, sir. Thought it was the best I could do. He's... well, he's dead, sir."

Humphry David said sharply, "And who are you?"

"Night watchman, sir. Name of Titmarsh. I was just starting my round, sir."

"You mean you saw this... accident... happen?" asked David.

"Not me, sir," said Bob quickly. "I've been down in the cellars, stoking the furnace. Always my first job of an evening here. And then one of the fuses went..."

"All right," cut in the Minister. "Are you sure he's dead? Isn't there anything we can do?"

"You take a look at him, sir," said Bob. "I've looked once, and that was enough, begging your pardon."

Humphry David went forward, conscientiously. He knew even less about casualties than he did about contemporary painting, and what he saw sickened him. He felt Bob's hand under his arm.

"You come and sit down, sir. The Yard'll be here in a minute. They'll see to it."

Very firmly, Bob led the Minister away from the stairs and supported him to a chair. "Put your head between your knees, sir. I'll get you some water. Enough to turn anyone up, that is."

"All right, thanks very much," said David. "I'm not much good at that sort of thing... not used to it."

"I've seen worse in my time. H.E. and that," said Bob. "That'll be the Yard, sir. I'll go and let them in. Don't waste much time, do they?"

III

The group of C.I.D. men were led by Detective-Inspector Lancing. Quickly, quietly, without any fuss, they got busy on what was to them a routine job. In a few brief inquiries, Lancing got his essentials: spoke with courteous respect and a brief word of sympathy to the Minister, shepherded him to his study, gave one quick stare at the "funnies," and said he would rejoin the Minister after he'd got the main facts from the night porter, adding: "Can I get you a drink, sir? You've had a shock, coming into a thing like that."

"Yes. Not used to it," said David. "All right, officer. I can find myself a drink. You get on with your job. I'll stay here."

Bob Titmarsh stood in the hall and watched the C.I.D. men appreciatively. He recognised competence when he saw it, but he felt a queer unaccustomed stirring of fear. Constable on the door: constable at the rear, plain clothes men round the body: all very sensible, no fuss, no bullying, but a feeling of being closed in. Then Lancing came into the hall again.

"You came on duty at ten o'clock, Titmarsh. What time did this happen? It's ten fifty-five now."

"Some time between ten o'clock and ten-thirty," said Bob carefully.

"Can't you do better than that?" asked Lancing. "Where were you when you heard it?"

"I didn't hear it," said Bob.

"You didn't *hear* it?" asked Lancing, glancing from the empty pedestal on the landing, down the now chipped marble stairs. "Are you telling me you were in this building and you didn't hear a ton or so of marble bouncing down those stairs?"

Bob's chin went up. "Yes, that's what I'm telling you," he replied stubbornly. "Say if you come and see where I was, and what I was bloody well doing when that there happened. May save us both a lot of trouble later."

"All right," said Lancing. "Go ahead."

Bob Titmarsh led the C.I.D. man from the magnificence of the entrance hall through the quiet dignity of a panelled passage: through a doorway to a less dignified passage: through another door and down a flight of awkward stone steps to the one-time kitchen quarters, of no dignity at all. Down again by a stone spiral stair to the cellars (with a laconic "Look out for your head") Bob led on through a series of archways to the furnace cellar. Wasting no words, he seized the coal hammer and began to smash some of the big lumps of coal, his blows echoing like artillery in the confined space. He opened up the furnace, produced his long tools and began to rake, making about as much noise as a tank on cobbles. Then he clanged the furnace door to and turned to Lancing.

"That's what I was bloody well doing, mate, and if you think I'd have heard a V.I while I was at it, well, I begs to differ."

"O.K.," said Lancing cheerfully, "I get you." He glanced at the antique furnace. "Hell of a thing, isn't it? What time did you arrive here this evening?"

"Nine-thirty as near as makes no difference. George Smith and me (houseman, George is, second day shift) we made a cuppa and had it just upstairs in the cubby-hole by the store room. Ten o'clock I come down here, George having gone home. I broke up about half a ton of that there qualified fuel. Then I raked the old b— out and got rid of the cinders and dust and raked that pile of coal up. About half an hour that lot took me."

"Right—and then?"

"You come along and I'll show you. Seeing's believing." He led the way up from the cellars to the basement.

"I washed some of the muck off in that sink there—call it three minutes. Then I set out for my first round, same as I always does."

Bob told how he had found the entrance hall in darkness, tried a switch, got a step-ladder and opened the fuse box. All the time Lancing followed Bob from place to place, but checked him as he was opening the fuse box.

"Don't touch it now. They don't want the lights doused in the hall. Can you remember if the fuse box showed any black, as though the fuse had blown?"

"I don't remember any burn marks, but the wire was parted. I chucked the ends down somewhere. Don't like no whiskers on my fuses."

"Quite right. If you threw the ends down they'll be there some-where. Just two questions. Do you always go straight down to the cellars to stoke when you come on duty?"

"Yes. Always."

"Do those cellars continue right under the building?"

"All the way," replied Bob. "Fair catacombs. I been through most of 'em. Took some of them architects from upstairs for a tour one night. Miles of 'em there is, enough to give you the blooming jit-ters to think this great whale of a place is built on 'ollow cellars, if you take me."

Lancing grinned. He rather liked the description. "What's your next job of a night, in the ordinary way?"

"After I gone me round, I carries coal up to the rooms of them that's important enough to be allowed it. No lifts in this place. And I does the fire-place in his nibs' office—the Minister, meaning no offence. Wood, he burns. Sends up 'is own lorries with it from his country place. He's a decent honest bloke, our Right Honourable."

"So I'm told," said Lancing. "What about deceased—off the record?"

"Pompey they call him. Pompey the Great, if you 'appen to know who 'e was. A funny thing that. They called that there statue wot caused all the trouble Pompey. Not that I had anything to do with either of 'em. So it's a case of nothing to report."

"Right. When do you have a meal?"

"After I done with the coal and that."

"Well, you go and have your meal now. Then you'll be free if I want you. Where do you eat?"

"In the cubby-hole I showed you. They leaves the victuals on the canteen hot plate, but I don't fancy it in there. Too blooming big."

"O.K. I'll send for you if I want you."

IV

By the time Lancing got back to the entrance hall, his superior officer
had arrived. Chief Detective-Inspector Julian Rivers was standing a
short distance from the body, his shoulders slightly humped under
his greatcoat, his hands thrust into his pockets. The police-surgeon
was still there, and the photographers were packing up their gear.
Rivers was looking up and down, from the pedestal on the landing
to the body on the marble pavement, as though he were measuring
the distance.

The surgeon was saying: "Within the hour: it's eleven-ten now.
They got the phone call at ten forty-six. I'd put death at ten-thirty,
with a margin of five minutes either way. His skull's crushed like
an egg shell and his neck's broken. The thing hit him from above.
But I'll get all that buttoned up in appropriate language when I've
had a proper look at him."

"Thanks. That's all I want for the moment," said Rivers. "Made
a proper mess of him, didn't it? Our chaps will be moving him right
away. We want to be careful over the bits and pieces. You never
know, you know."

"As you say. Tell me what happened when you've worked it out.
It looks a rum go to me. Oh—one other thing. He'd lowered some
whisky shortly before he copped it. I'll tell you how much later. I
could smell it. May be relevant. But he'd have had to be fighting
drunk to have knocked that thing sideways."

"He doesn't appear to have knocked it sideways," murmured
Rivers. "They both travelled direct."

The case-hardened police-surgeon looked at his "subject" with
interest not unmingled with diversion. "It's a variation on the usual
pattern," he observed. "Good night—though I doubt if you'll have
what is generally called a good night."

Lancing came and joined Rivers and gave him a brief resumé of what he had learned from Titmarsh. "All quite interesting, not to say suggestive," said Rivers. "We'd better watch out while they move the body, Lancing. There may be something which'll give us a lead. I can't see how this happened."

"It beats me, sir. If it was an improvised effort they must have got a strong man on the premises. That thing must have been a colossal weight, and the greater part of the weight's in the base—the chest and shoulders."

"Doesn't look as though there was much improvisation about it to me," said Rivers.

"That's why I had you called, sir," said Lancing. "It looked all nice and accidental at the first glance—but not the second. Struck me somebody had worked out a nice line in dynamics."

The two detectives watched closely as the body was moved on to the waiting stretcher, but no unexpected object caught their eye—just the chips of blood-stained marble and the horrid mess of what had once been human brains.

They lifted the heavy body on to the stretcher and the bearers moved stolidly away, young Brady marching beside them to do his part of the job—to collect and list every item of interest in Pompfret's pockets and upon his person. Rivers gave an order to mop up the floor and to scrutinise every chip and sliver: to throw nothing away. Then the Chief Inspector got his hands on the great piece of marble which Canova had fashioned with such detailed skill into the armoured shoulders of a Roman noble. Rivers was strong, but he couldn't raise the carven mass from the dent its weight had made in the pavement.

"What was it? A gladiator?" asked Lancing. "Not my idea of interior decoration—even here. They ought to have put him in the British Museum among his fellows."

"Nothing Roman about this, barring the décor," said Rivers. "Monumental masonry, made in Italy when this house was built, more likely. A proud reminder of some grand tour. Nothing to repine over in this breakage—to my mind. But then this sort of thing always left me cold. Judging from what remains of the chap, his countenance was no treat in normal dimensions: with the cubic capacity doubled, his offensiveness was quadrupled at least. Let's go and have a look at that plinth up there."

"Right. I'll just measure his depth so to speak, to see how much clearance there was behind him."

"Well, one thing's quite clear. Nobody could have got behind the thing and shoved that way," said Rivers a moment later.

The massive plinth stood almost flush with the wall behind it. From his own observation and Lancing's measurements Rivers could see that there had been only a few inches of clearance behind the back of Earl Manderby's laurel wreath and the wall.

"Can you see anybody, drunk or sober, being lunatic enough to raise their arms round that monstrosity of a bull neck in order to tug the thing forward?" asked Rivers.

"It's surprising what drunks will do," mused Lancing, "but we don't know that he *was* drunk. It's true the bust wasn't fixed in any way, not pegged or cemented. It just stood there on the plinth."

"And came down on Pompfret's head," mused Rivers. "It's a teaser. It wasn't shoved from the side: it came straight down those stairs."

"Galileo," murmured Lancing; "meaning which got to the bottom first?"

"Search me," said Rivers. "They'll do the sum for us at C.O. Just the sort of thing that experts love doing, but I always fancy my own theory of probabilities. Leaving out *how* the thing was shifted, let's try to visualise what followed. It fell forward, giving Pompfret a glancing blow, so that he'd have been flung back and hurtled down the stairs to the bottom. Did he bounce... yes... so did the thing. You can see the blood and the dents."

"Anything against him having been killed with a sledge hammer up here and then chucked down, like Jezebel, with the thing bouncing down afterwards to supply corroborative evidence of painful accident?" inquired Lancing.

"It's an idea," agreed Rivers, "though no one used a sledge hammer on him just here. A cosh, perhaps. There's no blood up here. But he bled on the stairs."

"So would you, sir, if I chucked you down them head first," said Lancing. "Jack fell down and broke his crown. Marble's very hard."

"Very hard. So's this. It's such extraordinarily good bowling," said Rivers. "Hallo. There's the Minister come to take a look round. I'd better go and pay my respects, leaving you to ponder over Galileo and the leaning tower."

"According to the evidence, both the apples got to the bottom at the same time," said Lancing. "But does that apply here? There must have been a lot of momentum..."

"Acceleration of gravity," murmured Rivers. "Increment in velocity being about thirty-two feet a second... if that's relevant, which I doubt. We'll leave that one to the back-room boys."

CHAPTER IV

I

RIVERS WENT DOWN THE STAIRS AND ACROSS THE MARBLE floor to where Humphry David stood waiting quietly. "I apologise for keeping you waiting, sir. My name is Rivers. I have been trying to puzzle out how this thing happened."

"So have I, Chief Inspector. Come along to my room for a few minutes. I might as well tell you everything I can that's likely to throw any light on it."

The long room was brilliantly lighted, and Rivers had some ado not to stare as his eyes met the incongruous pictures: Cubist, abstract form, Surrealist fantasy, landscape and seascape expressed by vivid splash and eccentric line, they hung in the dignified room as unexpectedly as the figments of a dream, clear and yet incomprehensible, at once naïve and sophisticated, child-like yet mature.

The Minister switched off the overhead lights, leaving only the shaded desk lamp alight. "It'll be easier to talk if we can't see them," he said. "I find them intrusive."

Rivers laughed. "A very apt word, sir. All the same, I should like to look at them sometime."

"I know. One does. But they're intrusive," said David. His face was pale and tired, but his smile was a friendly one, and Rivers liked him instinctively. He knew the Minister by sight, of course, and knew his reputation for kindliness, integrity and fairness.

"Do you accept this shocking occurrence as an accident, Chief Inspector?" asked David.

"If it was an accident, I find it extremely difficult to grasp how it happened, sir. And if it wasn't an accident, I still find it exceedingly difficult to grasp how it happened."

"If I were poor Pompfret I should say 'I couldn't agree with you more,'" said David, "but I'd better tell you the one thing I know which may be relevant. That marble bust of Earl Manderby, a very brilliant piece of sculpture by a famous sculptor, was deplored by most of us. I disliked it extremely. Pompfret disliked it even more extravagantly than I did. A primitive piece he would have admired and venerated, a Henry Moore he would have worshipped, but Earl Manderby was of a period he execrated and anathematised. Don't think I'm being merely verbose. What I have stated is relevant. You see, Pompfret knew that this piece of sculpture wasn't fixed to the plinth in any way. He'd seen it replaced on the plinth, after it had been moved to safety during the war. He actually conjectured to me about the chances of engineering an accident which would destroy the thing—in exactly the way it has been destroyed."

"That's interesting," said Rivers. "What sort of a chap was he, sir?"

"He was a First Class Civil Servant, and he had been Deputy to the Permanent Secretary here since the Ministry was inaugurated," replied Humphry David.

"I know those facts, sir," replied Rivers quietly. "I wasn't being either impertinent, flippant or familiar when I asked you 'what sort of a chap was he?' I used those words deliberately. May I put my question another way, meaning no disrespect to you, sir, or to deceased. Was Mr. Pompfret capable of being a very silly ass when he was not occupied in being a First Class Civil Servant?"

"I can only give you my own opinion in reply to what I regard as a cogent, if colloquial, question," said David. "A man of your rank doesn't use colloquialisms to a Minister of the Crown inadvertently. I understand exactly what you mean. You are asking me if I think that Pompfret was fool enough to have tried to tip that mass of marble down the stairs, without realising what a dangerous thing he was doing. I think it's just conceivable. He was, in my opinion, a very conceited fellow."

"Thank you, sir. That's what I wanted to know," said Rivers equably. "Next: the police-surgeon said that deceased smelt of whisky. Have you any comment to make on that?"

"No, because I didn't know him apart from his work," said David. "He didn't strike me as the sort of man who would drink to excess, and I have never thought of him in that connection." He sighed wearily. "I didn't really like him, Chief Inspector. I don't say that as a reflection on Pompfret: I say it to explain why I know so little about him. I avoided seeing more of him than was necessary to the efficient working of this monstrous machine we call a Ministry."

"It occurs to me that the whisky may be relevant, the more so if deceased were of temperate habit," went on Rivers. "Whisky can affect a man's judgment more than is generally believed, especially when he's not accustomed to it. But while I'm willing to believe that a man made optimistic by alcohol might have been foolish enough to try to tip that bust off its plinth by tugging it forward, I can't imagine that he would have succeeded in the attempt. The thing was a tremendous weight, its centre of gravity was low, and it stood on a very adequate plinth. In addition to that, it was too high up to give a satisfactory grip."

"Then how do you explain what happened?" asked David.

"I'm not trying to explain it, sir. I'm only trying to determine what didn't happen, but it does look to me as though more than one person was involved in the matter. Which brings me to the inevitable question—was anybody else known to have been in the building at the time, barring the night porter?"

"I know of none," replied the Minister. "I myself am in the habit of coming to work here in the evenings occasionally, especially when I have had to be in the House a lot. I have a key and can come here any time. Pompfret also had a key. I know he was very busy. We have been under fire in the House in the matter of ways and means, and Pompfret was preparing a statement for me, dealing with policy and expenditure previous to my taking office. But as to whether he had anybody else here with him, I can't tell you." Here he broke off abruptly, and then asked, equally abruptly: "Did you know that I had had Henry Fearon here, discussing a matter on which I wanted an expert opinion—I might also add, an unofficial opinion?"

"No, sir. He has mentioned nothing of the kind to me."

"Henry's a very trustworthy fellow," said David. "He knew that I wanted to avoid any official action until I knew whether what I vaguely suspected had any basis beyond my own guesswork. But you will have to know all about it now. I had a feeling that some letters in the files, previous to my own appointment, had been doctored; that some had been removed and been replaced by others. I still don't know whether I am right. I was intending to get Fearon to examine some of the correspondence for me; I have delayed doing so because I didn't want any of my staff here to get the impression I was snooping unfairly, nor yet starting a post-mortem on events which were dealt with before I came here."

Rivers nodded, and then asked, "Did the letters in question pertain to Mr. Pompfret's department?"

"No. He had no specific branch or department. He was more like a general liaison officer. Some of the letters in question were from the Loans Collection Branch. Joyce-Lawrence, the first Minister, inaugurated this branch. Incidentally, it was he who sanctioned the purchase of the paintings in this room. He had various agents, both here and on the Continent, who purchased on commission examples of different periods and schools to make the nucleus of the Loan Collection. As you will have gathered, these works of art were loaned to various galleries and educational establishments throughout the country. The correspondence which attracted my attention began with a complaint from a private individual that some of the pictures thus loaned were not authentic: they were either copies, or were wrongly attributed to the painters named in the catalogue."

David paused here, and lighted a cigarette, holding out his case to Rivers. "I want to be careful here, Chief Inspector. This Ministry has attracted a lot of criticism and abuse, particularly at its inception."

"I know that, sir," put in Rivers quietly. "It often seems to me that in the realm of painting and sculpture the cleavage between the traditionalists and the experimentalists is deeper than in any other subject. Even the poets are more tolerant, more willing to bridge the gulf, than are the academic painters on the one hand and the modernists on the other."

The Minister nodded. "It's a great help to know that you take an interest in the matter, Chief Inspector. It makes my explanation less laborious. The first Loan Collections were greeted with a spate of abuse from the traditionalists. That was only to be expected, as the first Minister was mainly interested in the moderns. A lot of the abuse was from uninformed persons, but it was complicated by criticisms of extreme acerbity from some painters of the modern school who resented their own non-inclusion." Rivers' lips twitched, and Humphry David suddenly burst out, "I *knew* it would happen. I foresaw it all. You can not organise creative artists. You can only infuriate them by trying to do so. I know you won't quote me, Chief Inspector, but the inception of this Ministry was one of those mistakes made by the well-meaning."

"I will never quote you, sir, and I hope you won't quote me when I say that the most terrifying thing in what is called modern civilisation is that the worst mistakes *are* made by the most well-meaning people."

"Perfectly true," said the Minister in a voice of profound melancholy. "Where had we got to, Rivers?"

"Loan Collections, authenticity of various exhibits and complaints from persons unspecified, sir. Now I propose that we leave the examination of these files to Henry Fearon. I should like to ask one specific question of you, personally. You suspect that certain files have been tampered with. Do you connect this with deceased?"

Humphry David took his time before replying: at last he said: "I have no evidence of any kind. I can only say that I thought it was my duty to tell you of any irregularity which I had suspected in this organisation."

"You wouldn't like to tell me what's at the bottom of your mind, sir?"

"No. I can't tell you. I don't know. I can't even make up my mind about these pictures in here. They're not signed. Why aren't they signed? What was Joyce-Lawrence up to? Was he merely economising by buying pictures which he liked personally, but which had no market value? Or was he being hoodwinked by agents who were using him for their own ends? In short, did he, all unknowingly, give an opportunity for a racket which has gone on from that day to this?"

Rivers got up and switched on the overhead lights and moved deliberately round the walls, looking at the pictures.

"I'm right out of my depth here, sir. I can only say that I like some of them and dislike others. But you must have heard these pictures discussed by people who have visited you here, people with the knowledge to assess these things in expert terms."

"I have heard them discussed all right," said Humphry David. "The trouble is that those with a claim to expert knowledge have disagreed in their judgments. In this matter I speak merely as an interested onlooker, and I may be quite wrong in my opinions, but it seems to me that, in the absence of a signature or attribution to any particular studio or clique, the pundits of to-day disagree as to the merits of paintings such as these. In short, their opinions are perilously near to your own, Chief Inspector, and to mine: they like some and they dislike others, but the ones which are commended vary as much as the reasons for commendation." The Minister got up from his place and walked to a canvas which seemed to blaze with authentic sunlight. It suggested, rather than represented, a french window opening on to an iron balcony, with sunlight gleaming through transparent curtains: involved in the intricacy of the foreground was a great mass of cerise flowers, a plate holding a flat fish and a straw hat.

"Speaking from the heart of an uninformed person," began the Minister contemplatively, "I should have guessed that this was painted by Matisse. Other persons have hazarded the same opinion, until informed that such cannot be the case. I'm beginning to wonder if other painters of to-day have emulated the contemporary artist who produced Vermeers. It's a fascinating line of thought."

"It certainly is," said Rivers. "Fortunately for me, I have not got to work on such intangibles. My immediate job is concerned with the physical problems involved in shifting an exceedingly heavy mass of marble from a substantial plinth six feet high. It will also involve questioning a large number of people as to their whereabouts between ten and eleven o'clock this evening."

"Of course," said the Minister, turning away from the gaiety of the pseudo Matisse. "You'd better start on me. I was in the House until 10.15. I walked across here, slowly and peacefully, by way of

Storey's Gate, past the Foreign Office, across Horse Guards Parade to the Mall, up Marlborough Gate and St. James's and across Piccadilly to Dover Street. I arrived here just as the night porter had telephoned for the police. As to corroboration of my movements, I doubt if anybody noticed me from the time I left Old Palace Yard until the time I entered this building."

"You'd be surprised how much our point-duty men notice, sir," replied Rivers. "Now I don't want to keep you here indefinitely, but I should be much obliged if you could find the filed correspondence you mentioned to Henry Fearon. I think that should be examined first thing to-morrow morning."

"I'll go and get it for you immediately," said David. "And I've no intention of going home for the time being. It's just possible that I may be able to help you in the event of questions cropping up. It's true that I'm virtually a newcomer and don't know so much about the workings of the place as I should like to know, but I've wandered round a bit."

"Thank you very much, sir," rejoined Rivers. "I'll report to you if anything interesting turns up."

II

When Rivers left the Minister, one of the attendant C.I.D. men told him that Detective-Inspector Lancing was in Waiting Room A with the two housemen who had worked the second shift. George Smith and Alec West had been routed out of their beds shortly after retiring to them; sleepy and somewhat tousled, they were answering questions with commendable common sense and helpfulness.

George was of the opinion that no one else had been left in the building after normal working hours save Pompfret himself. The latter had told George that he would be working late, and that the cleaning of his office would have to wait until the morning shift. Pompfret had also sent to the canteen before it closed, and asked for a tray to be sent to his room with something in the way of a cold supper.

"Mr. Pompfret said he never got a chance to do his own work during the day time, sir. He had no end of visitors, delegations and that, as well as overseas visitors who wanted to see the British playing at the Fine Arts—his words, sir, not mine. Anyway, he'd worked here in the evenings several times lately."

"Do you know how late he generally stayed here?" asked Rivers.

"No, sir. Not my business, but I do know he never had no visitors after the place shut. It was my job to listen for the doorbell. We sometimes get letters or packets delivered in the evening, and the bell's as loud as a fire alarm. Needs to be in a place this size."

George went on to explain about the evening cleaners. "We try to get the sweeping and vacuum cleaning done in the evening, sir; two hours, the shift is. Then the dusting's done in the morning. Alec and I always go the rounds while the cleaners are here, keeping an eye on things. That means I go through most departments of an evening, and I always try to glance round the heads' offices—heads of departments, that is. Apart from Mr. Pompfret's room, I reckon there wasn't anybody in the place."

"Same with me, sir," put in Alec West. "I go round the canteen and offices, the filing room, waiting rooms, Loans Collection, store room and library. General inspection, and an eye on the cleaners so to speak."

At eight o'clock the two housemen had had their supper, which was left ready for them in the staff canteen: after that, one or other of them did a final round of the ground floor, while the other filled up the inevitable daily form detailing the hours worked by the part-time cleaners, together with a report on any breakages, damage, articles lost or found. It was Alec West who had done the final round of the ground floor, inspecting doors and windows and pronouncing everything in order—Earl Manderby being safely on his plinth. He admitted cheerfully that he had spent his last half-hour on duty (all tasks being completed) in reading the newspapers, of which he always found a large variety in the wastepaper baskets which were emptied into salvage sacks. George Smith had admitted Bob Titmarsh by the basement door which they always used, had his cup of tea, and left (also by the basement door) at ten o'clock. Bob Titmarsh had already given his evidence to Lancing. It was the latter who said to Bob:

"How many people would be likely to know that your first job when you come on duty is to rake and stoke the furnaces, Titmarsh?"

"Search me," said Bob. "Nobody that I knows of."

"Half a tick, mate," put in Alec West. "You're down there in them cellars, and you wouldn't know, but I can tell you this. When you rakes out that hell of a contraption down there, everybody in this here building knows it. I've often noticed it when George is on the job. The noise travels along the hot pipes: leastways, that's what I always reckons it is. You get a sort of vibration, so's you'd think there was an earthquake. Fact is, all them fixtures is loose: they rattle like the coachwork of an old car rattles, and Bob, 'e goes for that bastard good and hard. I've still been here some evenings when Bob gets busy, and he makes row enough to shake the whole bag o' tricks to blazes."

"That's right about the vibration, sir," put in George. "There's been complaints about it. Complaints! That so-called central 'eating's given rise to more complaints than the pictures they send round on loan, and I can't put it fairer than that, seeing as I keeps an album of press cuttings about the goings on here."

Lancing began to laugh and made an effort to choke back his unofficial mirth, but Rivers put in:

"Show me your album some time, George. It'll help me get the atmosphere. But about the complaints: who complains?"

"Everyone, sir, barring the Minister. I never known a gentleman who complained less. Now the Museums branch, they're nearest the target, so to speak. That set of rooms gets so hot you could roast chestnuts in them—and the fumes when we stokes—well, the language them Museums use is something shocking. And then the Public Monuments and Architects up on the top floor, they call it 'Token 'eating' seeing they've got pipes for the look of the thing but they're not even warm to the hand."

"Them Public Monuments has a poor time," said Alec. "No sense they haven't got, but the Architects, they've got some snappy girls up there. What they can't do with a yard or two of flex isn't worth doing. I reckon they've got their private central heating all right, but luckily they're sensible and don't leave nothing about, so I haven't had to report."

"Well, you don't seem to be dull here," said Rivers. "Now I should like an opinion from any one of you who'd care to risk one: do you think that Mr. Pompfret could have shifted that marble head himself, without any assistance?"

There was dead silence for a moment or two; then Bob Titmarsh spoke: "Speaking for meself, I reckon he did. He had to. George and Alec say there wasn't nobody else in the building. Well, that leaves me. I didn't help him. So he must've done it himself."

"Now don't you take me wrong, mate, but he didn't do it himself," said George. "I'll tell you why. He was a big chap, but his heart was no good. Athlete's heart he called it. Used to row or something. He couldn't move a crate weighing twenty pounds and that's a fact. Always got one of us chaps up when there was any shifting or lifting. And I reckon that thing weighed between ten and fifteen hundredweights. Look at the size of the base."

"That's all very well, but what about me?" demanded Bob indignantly. "I was here. You weren't."

"Now don't you talk silly," said George. "You took the Inspector down to the cellars and showed him the coal you'd broken up. You raked out that there furnace and you stoked it. Likewise you put a new fuse wire in. No one's going to suggest you went and obliged Pompey with a bit of strong man stuff. You hadn't the time."

"That's a fact," agreed Alec, "but somebody helped him. He didn't shift that thing by himself. I saw it put back a coupla' years ago. Nice bit of tackle they brought to lift it—sort of derrick and crane outfit. No end of a job it was. It's no good, Bob. He never shifted that there by himself. And what's more, I don't reckon you could have done it neither."

"It's a fair puzzler and no mistake," said George.

CHAPTER V

At two o'clock in the morning, Rivers and Lancing sat down in the canteen to tea and sandwiches, provided by Bob Titmarsh. They needed them. In the interim they had made the grand tour of Medici House, including what Lancing called The State Apartments—ballroom, great drawing-room, small drawing-room, music room, gallery and library: great dining-room, family dining-room, breakfast-room, morning room and study, all now coming under the common denominator "offices." From here they had progressed to the main bedrooms and finally to the servants' bedrooms (more offices), and descended again to view the intricacies of the basement, with kitchens whose acreage had to be seen to be believed, servants' hall, servants' dining-room, pantries and store-rooms.

During this effort of pedestrianism they had been accompanied by one or other of the junior C.I.D. men who were each in charge of one floor of the formidable mansion and who were endeavouring to master its intricacies, including cupboard space, connecting stairways, corridors and fire escapes. A constable had been on duty at each of the three outer doors of Medici House since a few minutes after Bob's telephone call had warned the C.I.D. that a death had occurred on the premises.

Rivers had outlined his first impressions to Lancing: "It seems improbable that Pompfret could have pulled that weight off its plinth:

there was either another man helping him, both being inspired by the same irresponsible idea of smashing the thing up because they despised it, or else somebody else engineered the smash in order to smash Pompfret."

Lancing nodded. "In either case, there was nothing to prevent the second man going straight out of the front door and getting clear away."

"That we don't know," said Rivers. "We don't know precisely when it happened. I'm pretty sure it was timed to coincide with the night watchman's activities in the cellars. If it was done just as Titmarsh was finishing off his job with the coal hammer, it's possible that the second practitioner realised that all noise from the cellars had ceased, and that there was a fifty-fifty chance the night porter would come rushing up to investigate. In which case, number two may not have dared to risk running down the staircase and crossing the entrance hall, but preferred to take his chance of hiding himself in this building, and emerging to join his own department after the crowd arrives to-morrow morning. But it's up to us to ascertain, as far as it's possible, that there's no one concealed in this building."

Lancing nodded. "Sounds easy, but it isn't," he said. "What with the number of secondary staircases and rooms which open one into another, it's the dickens of a business to ensure that no one is hiding here, although I think it would be very difficult for anyone to get clear of the house unobserved. Then there's that business of the fuse going."

"Yes. We don't know for certain that it was part of the plan— if plan there was," said Rivers. "The wiring in this house is old. Sometimes a sudden vibration causes a fuse to blow, because the nature of the vibration makes an old bulb go phut, and a bulb burning out can affect the fuse wire. I've known that happen. However, the back-room boys will tell us if the fuse burnt out or has been snipped with scissors. Walter found the bits which Titmarsh removed."

"I still go back to the original question," said Lancing. "How was Earl Manderby shifted? We've got plenty of man power here. Can't we get the shoulders back into position?"

"No. We can't," said Rivers decidedly. "We may be willing, but we're none of us skilled in lifting weights of that kind. If we bungled it, it'd mean that somebody might get crushed underneath it. I don't want a practical reconstruction. But we've got the measurements and we know the space it occupied. Let's go and see if we can think it out. After all, somebody did it. It's not reasonable to suppose they had a gang of weight lifters on the job."

They went up the marble staircase again after a further inspection of the fragments of what Lancing called the doubly-defunct Earl, and they stood on the landing with measuring tapes and rules.

"The obvious thing to have done would have been to lever him out from behind," said Rivers. "House breakers use long iron bars and the force they exert is terrific, but that wasn't done here for a variety of reasons. Look at the wall. It's plaster, and there isn't a mark on it. To use a lever you've got to have a fulcrum. And you've got to have something to stand on. The thing's too high to lever out while you're standing on the floor. Can you see a chap on a step-ladder levering away at that object? He'd have levered the step-ladder from under him before he got the thing moved."

"Could he have stood on the edge of the plinth?" hazarded Lancing.

"Bestriding Earl Manderby like a colossus," said Rivers. "No. He couldn't. When the Earl was in place there's only an inch on either side to stand on."

"Get a cable of sorts round the noble neck and tug from a suitable distance?" said Lancing.

"While Pompfret stood on the top stair and waited for the Earl to fall on him?" asked Rivers disgustedly. "He must have been very drunk to oblige. In any case he'd have been in the way of your hypothetical cable. They both fell straight down the stairs."

They both stood and stared, until Rivers said: "How it was done I don't know, but Pompfret couldn't have done it by himself. Standing on the floor he couldn't have reached high enough to get a serviceable grip on the thing. There wasn't a cable, there wasn't a step-ladder or platform and there wasn't a levering iron."

"You believe what Titmarsh said?" inquired Lancing.

"Yes. I do. Until I find any reason for disbelieving him," said Rivers. "Titmarsh was alone in this building according to his own computation. He didn't go and commit a murder when he was the only person on the premises: neither do I believe he aided and abetted one, for the same reason."

"I agree with you about Titmarsh, but for a different reason," said Lancing. "I believed he was telling the truth when he said he didn't hear the thing fall. On the face of it, it seemed such a crazy thing to say that I don't believe any guilty man would have risked saying it: the guilty man would have said that he did hear the crash when he was in the cellars, and have given us the time that was convenient to himself."

"I'm disposed to agree with you there, unless we find reasons for revising our judgment," said Rivers. "Incidentally, I've had a message from the man on duty in the House of Commons. The division was earlier than expected, and the result was given at 10.15. The Minister of Fine Arts left the Chamber immediately after the result of the division was known, but he was button-holed by a backbencher and stood chatting for five or ten minutes before he finally left the House. He crossed Old Palace Yard at half-past ten."

Lancing grinned. "That simplifies that—but if the backbencher
hadn't intervened, the Right Honourable might have arrived just in
time to see what happened to Earl Manderby and Pompfret. It must
have been a dramatic sight."

The two men stood and stared at one another for a few moments,
lively speculation in the eyes of each. Then Rivers said: "We'll go and
study Pompfret's room in detail before we pack up for the night."

II

Edwin Pompfret, Permanent Deputy Secretary, had had for his office
the "Small" Drawing-Room on the first floor of Medici House. In
comparison with the "Great" Drawing-Room this apartment could
have been described as small: it was a mere twenty-eight feet by
twenty, twelve feet high, and lighted by three magnificent long windows which overlooked the one-time garden. (The air-raid shelters
built during the war still stood in this derelict space and were now
used as storage room by the Establishments branch.) The Small
Drawing-Room was panelled in white, with gilded mouldings, but
paint-work and gilding had long lost their beauty. The furniture was
regulation. Desk, chairs, cupboards, filing cabinets and typist's table
all looked inadequate and mean in the once beautiful room. The
picture above the white marble mantelpiece was an abstract work. It
was not a painting, for it consisted of an appliqué of various papers
and fabrics, including hessian and ordinary newsprint, superimposed
by coiling lines of string. To Lancing's uneducated eyes, the notice-
board was both more attractive and better composed, showing
some lively colour in the pamphlets which had been designed for
the enlightenment of the public. These had been pinned up, presumably by an enterprising typist, to make a well balanced ensemble.

Rivers disregarded both work of art and notice-board: he pulled on rubber gloves and began to open all the cupboards and drawers, leaving them open. In one cupboard, behind the desk, were some bottles of Sherry (Amontillado, post-war), sherry glasses, tumblers, a siphon and a modest flask of whisky. On a side table was the supper tray sent in from the canteen: on the mantelshelf was one tumbler which held a drain of whisky and soda. The writing-desk was tidy, the blotter had no papers on it: the ashes in the grate were still not cold, and had been glowing when the police first entered the room. Rivers stood and looked round the room.

"Presumably he had finished work for the evening: his desk is tidy, his papers put away. There's nothing to indicate that anybody else was in the room with him or that he'd been expecting a visitor. Rather the reverse: if he'd been expecting a visitor he'd probably have had the supper tray taken away. It looks undignified and inartistic, and I gather Pompfret liked to work for effect. Since he kept sherry here, presumably he offered a glass to his friends. The sherry glasses haven't been used."

"It looks to me as though he'd finished his job, tidied up, and had his whisky and soda standing by the fire-place before he went home," said Lancing.

"But he wasn't going home, because he hadn't got his hat and coat on," said Rivers. "Where's his cloakroom?"

"Across the passage," said Lancing. "His hat, coat, gloves and umbrella are still there, likewise his brief-case, but there's nothing in it except *The Times* and a book on Expressionist Painters."

"He had finished working and tidied his desk," said Rivers, "but he didn't go and get his hat and coat. He walked to the landing at the head of the grand staircase. Why?"

"Did he walk?" queried Lancing. "Mightn't he have been carried? What's against coshing him in here, private like, and then carrying him to the landing?"

"There are various arguments against that course of action," said Rivers meditatively. "The first was his weight. He was a big chap, an athlete run to fat. I'd put his weight at fourteen stone at a guess. You and I have been trained to lift and carry heavy bodies: we know the handiest way of doing the job. Most men don't—particularly Civil Servants. And neither you nor I would have been enthusiastic about carrying Edwin Pompfret from this room to that landing. It's quite a long way, past the length of the ballroom."

"Yes. There's that," agreed Lancing, and Rivers went on:

"Moreover, there would always have been the risk of meeting somebody, or being seen from below. It was known that the Minister sometimes came and worked here in the evenings. Other less exalted persons may have done so on occasion. From what I know of Ministries, it is always possible for those who work in them to have access to their offices, either in the week-ends or in the evenings, before or after hours. There was no guarantee that some zealous Under Secretary or Assistant Secretary or Deputy Secretary wouldn't take it into his head to come back and do a spot of overtime, especially in view of the Ways and Means purge that's going on. And what explanation could a chap give if he were discovered staggering past the ballroom laden with fourteen stone of coshed Pompfret?"

Lancing grinned. "Too true—to quote deceased's favourite form of affirmation. But following up your line of thought, sir, the motto must have been 'if t'were done, t'were well it were done quickly.'"

"It seems so to me," said Rivers. "Whatever the mechanics of the thing were, it must have been some arrangement whose working parts could be disposed of rapidly. I'm toying in my mind with two different tableaux. One shows Pompfret by himself, standing on the landing, brought to a halt by something or other: standing there just long enough for Earl Manderby to shift forward and hit him. The second tableau shows Pompfret standing in the same place as in tableau one, but with another chap standing beside him saying 'Just look at that'... whatever 'that' might be."

"I prefer tableau two, sir," said Lancing promptly. "I think you've produced the evening's great thought. 'That' was the contraption, lever, mechanism, or whatnot which shifted the thing. How would this work? The unknown operator goes along to Pompfret's office and says 'For the love of Mike come and look at this contraption on the landing: someone's fixed up the most fantastic job of work on our Manderby,' and Pompfret toddled along to inspect and stood gaping. No, that won't do. Not quite. Manderby hit the back of Pompfret's head, didn't he? Pompfret must have been standing with his back to Manderby."

"I think we've got to assume he was standing with his back to the thing," said Rivers. "Otherwise he'd have had time to side-step when he saw it shift. But the objection's easily met. If number two had exclaimed 'What's that lying at the bottom of the stairs?' it's probable that Pompfret would have obliged by turning round to look." Rivers broke off and glanced at the tumbler standing on the mantelpiece. "Of course it'll make things a bit clearer when we know how much whisky Pompfret had lowered. Number two may have come in here, as you suggest, and talked to Pompfret for a bit, and induced him to put down a stiffer whisky than he was accustomed to. If he were a bit fuddled he might not have realised that the contraption wasn't a mere comic. In fact it might have been rigged as a comic."

"Or, finally, was Pompfret in on the joke?" hazarded Lancing. "Pompfret hated the thing. Would he have connived at an accident for the liquidation of Manderby without realising he was to share in said liquidation?"

"Personally I don't think so," said Rivers, "not unless he was drunk. First-class Civil Servants who have reached Pompfret's age and position aren't prone to irresponsible monkey tricks with the nation's property. My assumption is that Pompfret was murdered, and that his murder will prove to be connected with some racket or irregularity the Minister has been nosing out in his private researches. Well, we'd better get down to it. We'll have the fingerprint men in later, but first we'll go through everything in the room and see if we can find anything other than official matter. This is where we have reason to be grateful to Civil Service methods. He was a very tidy bloke."

III

Rivers and Lancing had been at work for less than half an hour when the door opened to admit the Minister. Rivers looked at him in surprise.

"I thought you'd gone home hours ago, sir."

"I thought I'd collect those files I was talking about," said David, "but it looks as though I'm too late. They've gone."

"Well, that's illuminating," said Rivers, but Humphry David put in:

"It may be—or I may be jumping to conclusions. The letters may have been taken for some legitimate purpose, in which case they'll be on the premises somewhere. It's permissible for any senior employee to study correspondence, past or present, pertaining to his department. In fact, the answer to a letter of to-day or to-morrow may depend on an answer given the year before last."

Rivers pulled forward a chair for the Minister and another for himself. "Since you are still here, sir, are you willing to stay a bit longer and go into this matter of the files?"

"I'm only too willing," said the Minister. "I take two things for granted: that you will respect my confidence and that you understand that what I say is surmise, and rather hazardous surmise, at that. Obviously, if my half-formed suspicions have any basis, the whole thing will have to be discussed between the Cabinet and the Commissioner." A half smile flashed across the Minister's tired face. "It occurs to me that you may think this Ministry should have been called the Ministry of All Fools rather than Fine Arts. I've been disposed to think the same thing myself. It originated in a period which I can only call Cloud Cuckoo land, when we were all in a state of irresponsible optimism. The Welfare State was to be a hundred per cent achievement, in which all the benefits of civilisation could be shared by every citizen." He broke off and added: "I don't want you to think I'm embarking on a political polemic at this very unsuitable hour. The only way I can make you understand the confusion of policies in this establishment is by reminding you of the optimism which gave birth to it, the initial extravagance following that optimism, and the curtailment and retrenchments which followed, salutarily if haphazardly, after the first fine careless rapture."

Rivers settled himself back into his chair. "I have noted your provisos, sir, and I ask nothing better than to listen. You are offering us what is a rare gift to detectives: an understanding of the background against which the events of this evening occurred. I realise very fully that this is a complex background: our first business, after the obvious routine measures, is to grasp the background."

CHAPTER VI

I

"FORTUNATELY FOR US BOTH, THIS MINISTRY HAS BUT A SHORT history," began Humphry David. "Joyce-Lawrence, the first Minister, was a brilliant fellow—though no administrator, I fear. He was an artist and a humanitarian, and I believe him to have been passionately sincere, however much I disagreed with his politics. You may remember some of his speeches: he was an orator and he could dominate a working class crowd as well as inspire respect in the House of Commons. But by the very nature of the man, he was, I fear, gullible. And to be a successful Minister in this department, you need to be cautious, watchful and hard-headed. This problem of the files I've been worrying about—it involves the two most thorny branches in the Ministry—the Loans department and the Acquisitions department." With his diffident smile, Humphry David studied Rivers' intent face.

"You might call them the deep-end," he went on. "Joyce-Lawrence plunged. He wanted to bring Art to the Masses—to the market towns and villages: to the miners and the factory workers, to the butcher and baker and candlestick maker. Hence the Loans department and its ancillary. Joyce-Lawrence began to buy pictures. I needn't enlarge on that. If he started out in the grand manner, he was soon corrected by economic realities. He then started on a less grandiose project: he bought examples of the many schools of to-day when and where he could, using his own judgment as to painters, obscure and otherwise. Then he died. And, in confidence, he left a considerable confusion of contracts as well as canvases, of promises as well as pottery and sculpture. His successor, and my predecessor, Higginson, was appointed because he was a good administrator and a sound economist. He brought method and business ability to the job. But what could he make of the chaos of acquisitions the first Minister had amassed?"

"Expert advisers?" queried Rivers, and Humphry David laughed.

"If there was one body of men Higginson distrusted, it was the art experts. He said the country had paid through the nose for them already, and look at the result. In a sense, I sympathised with him. Art criticism to-day, as an eminent writer on the subject has stated recently, 'has its peculiar frailty.' Look through the reproductions in that excellent and authoritative handbook on Contemporary British Art which you will find on all the bookstalls. Find me the common denominator, the underlying impulse, between the classic representationalism of the first illustrations and the abstractions of the last ones. I beg your pardon, Chief Inspector. I'm getting off the point. But when old Higginson said that modern art criticism was only a high falutin' way of saying 'I know what I like,' I admit I had some sympathy with him."

"So have I," agreed Rivers promptly, "but what did Mr. Higginson do about it?"

"Joyce-Lawrence plunged. Higginson surfaced," said the Minister. "He put a stop to all buying to begin with. He did consult with a few elderly and conservative academicians. They said 'Burn the lot.' Higginson was horrified. He said they'd cost the country good money. If Puddletown-in-the-Pool wanted an exhibition of modern art, they could still have it, if they'd pay packing and transport. But what Higginson really did was to prune the over-luxuriant growth he found here. There were far too many advisers, too many passengers, all given temporary Civil Service status. Every department was cluttered up with advisers and experts on this, that and the other. Just as Joyce-Lawrence plunged into buying, so also he plunged into collecting experts. Higginson axed them. In one sense he did a good job of work: many of them were redundant; some, I believe, were mere eccentrics, to put it charitably. But perhaps Higginson was too drastic. He got the Ministry a bad name among artists and dealers: he also left us without a single reliable authority on the Loans collection branch and Joyce-Lawrence's 'Acquisitions.'"

"A question here, sir, if you'll forgive the interruption," said Rivers. "In the period under discussion, who was head of the Loans department?"

"There have been quite a number," replied David. "Vernon Dawson was the first. He was a strong supporter of Joyce-Lawrence and found life hard when Higginson became Minister. Dawson did a very unusual thing for a senior Civil Servant; he resigned from the service. I was told he inherited property in Canada and went to Vancouver to live. Higginson promptly took the chance of economising by putting the Loans Collection and Acquisitions branch under one head. Patrick Byrne was given the job. He wasn't interested in art, but I believe he did a lot to clear up the muddle inherited from Joyce-Lawrence."

"Byrne... wasn't he killed in that plane which crashed in the Peak district?" asked Rivers.

"Yes. He was. That was last September, four months before I took office. Byrne's successor is James Dellison. He's a thoughtful, business-like chap, of a studious disposition. He read Economics for his degree, but studies Anglo-Saxon land tenures for his pleasure. Higginson, of course, valued him as an economist, and I know him to be an able and conscientious administrator, but I suspect that as a judge of modern painting he's even more at sea than I am myself. Because he has a conscientious mind, he doubtless studies the dicta of distinguished critics, from Roger Fry and Clive Bell to Herbert Read, but to what extent his reading influences his æsthetic judgment I cannot say."

"Does reading ever influence one's æsthetic judgment?" murmured Rivers.

Humphry David gave the least shrug of his shoulders, and raised his eyes to gaze pensively over Rivers' head at the "appliqué" picture above the marble mantel.

"You're a man of parts, Chief Inspector. Can you tell me anything about that? Do you find it beautiful, or satisfying, or inspiring? Would you think it valuable in terms of money? Do you even regard it as a good design or composition?"

"It means nothing to me at all, sir. I don't even dislike it. I can't see why anybody was moved to do it, nor why anybody wanted to buy it. In fact I agree with Lancing that the notice-board is much pleasanter to look at. But presumably Mr. Pompfret liked it and saw something significant in it."

"Perhaps," said the Minister sceptically. "On the other hand he may have kept it here because he knew that it was the sort of thing he ought to like. So far as Pompfret was concerned, he knew all the jargon about contemporary stuff of this kind, but he couldn't recognise an authentic work of art of any other period."

"You're telling me that you didn't trust his judgment, sir?"

"Not regarding works of art, or what I call works of art, but kindly remember that the converse was true. Pompfret considered that my judgment was negligible. Well, I've given you an outline of the teething troubles of the M.O.F.A., Chief Inspector. First Minister, a fanatic modernist with no sense of economics but a profound compassion for humanity. Second Minister, a competent

administrator and economist who wielded a pruning hook with
vigour. Third Minister, myself. I know something about mediæval
wall paintings, about etchings and engravings, and I'm acquainted
with the classics of painting and sculpture. I'm ignorant about
contemporary art and repelled by much of it. And I find myself in
charge of a government department which has collected a considerable number of contemporary paintings whose value as works of
art is controversial."

"Might I add that during Mr. Higginson's term of office, there
was nobody left in this establishment whose judgment on contemporary art was worth having?" asked Rivers blandly.

Humphry David nodded. "That's terribly near the truth, Chief
Inspector. Higginson was appointed as an economy measure: it
was his job to check the lavish expenditure Joyce-Lawrence had
embarked on. Higginson made his economies by cutting down
Acquisitions, by dispensing with advisory experts, many of whom
had been very highly paid, and by concentrating on careful administration. He did a good job, considering the economic difficulties
of the nation. His motto was 'mark time until better times come
along.' In short, he saw to it that the administrative machine worked.
But in the meantime there may have been some serious oversights
due to lack of expert inspection. To put it baldly, there may have
been some frauds perpetrated which no one in this building had the
knowledge to spot. The number of canvases in the Loan Collection
is the right number. What I have been wondering is whether the
canvases are the original canvases."

"That's a very interesting conjecture, sir. It may have been that
some of the packers were got at. Or it may have been dishonesty on
the part of other personnel in this building. And so to the inevitable
question: how much did Mr. Pompfret know, or guess, of the pos-
sibilities you have thought out for yourself."

"Let's get this quite clear," said the Minister. "I hold, and always have held, very strong convictions on the integrity of our Civil Servants. There is a tradition of honesty among them which we have every right to be proud of. I've told you I disliked Pompfret. I thought his æsthetic judgments were clap-trap, mere kow-towing to fashion and a lot of verbiage. But that doesn't mean I think he was corrupt. I don't think anything of the kind. Nevertheless, I think he was foolish and I know he was conceited. If he had become aware of any irregularities, or smelt a rat in the Loans department, I don't think he would have reported it direct to me. He might have tried to investigate it for himself. And I suppose that is the point I had in mind when I came in here to talk to you."

"A very cogent point, sir. So far as I can judge, Mr. Pompfret was murdered. I don't think there's any possibility that he could have shifted that block of marble by himself. Moreover, what you have said about him has reinforced my judgment, as far as I am in a position to make one. A man who had attained the degree of seniority which Mr. Pompfret had attained cannot have been devoid of a sense of responsibility. He wouldn't have played childish tricks with national property, and neither do I think he would have jeopardised his own career by indulging in them—unless he was drunk."

Lancing spoke for the first time here: "He couldn't have got drunk on the whisky that was taken from that flask, sir. If they find he had swallowed enough whisky to intoxicate him, he was given the whisky by somebody else, and that somebody was careful to remove all traces of the fact."

"Agreed," said Rivers, and turned to the Minister again.

"Can you tell me if there are any formalities about entering this building, sir? Do visitors have to sign a form stating their business when they enter the building, and do they have to produce any exit-form on leaving?"

"Not to my knowledge—though admittedly I'm the last person to have exact information on the subject," said David, his face lighted by the diffident smile which made him so likeable. "We're not on the Official Secrets list, or anything of that kind. It's my impression that if anybody knows their way about, they can walk in without let or hindrance and go to the department or individual they seek. Not to the Minister's office, of course. Ministers are—well—feather-bedded, in that respect. And I'm pretty certain there's no exit-permit. There are porters, of course, and the usual inquiry desk. But the war-time precautions about entry and exit had been given up before this establishment came into being. But you'll check up on all this. I admit I'm very ignorant of domestic details." Suddenly the Minister chuckled. "My dear chap, I'm sometimes appalled at the amount I don't know about this machine I'm officially in charge of. I'm like the average motorist: I drive the thing while having no knowledge of what's going on under the bonnet. I know there's something called a big-end in my car. I also know there's an Establishments branch here, but if asked for details of either, I'm sunk. That's where old Higginson was good. He knew nothing about Art, but what he didn't know about the Establishments branch wasn't worth knowing." He broke off. "I'm babbling, Chief Inspector. If there aren't any other questions you want to ask, I'll get home to my bed."

"Well, sir, after your refreshingly frank disclaimers of knowledge of domestic detail, it's hardly fair to interrogate you on this line, but do you think it would be possible for any unauthorised person to penetrate into the Loan Collections or Acquisitions branch?"

"I think it's conceivable they might get there," said the Minister. "In fact I walked in there myself before anybody in the building knew me by sight, but I was very properly challenged as to my authority. Have you any idea of the number of employees there are in even quite small Ministries? I believe Higginson found two thousand on the pay-roll here when he took over. That included the annexes in Bryanston Square, of course. But if you penetrate to the Loans Collection, you'll find it's swarming with personnel. They're all very busy, very earnest, very serious: they catalogue and check. They file and report. They analyse and systematise. They number and compute. They have an enormous amount of correspondence, some of it being from earnest persons in pursuit of what they call 'culture,' some of it being sheer abuse, some of it being really valuable criticism. And they answer it all most conscientiously. There's nothing casual about them, believe me." He broke off, and looked again at Pompfret's picture. "And if you asked every member of the department to write you a critique of that preposterous object up there, they'd do it *au grand serieux*, and the sum total would be—a set of opinions. No more. No less."

Rivers turned round and stared at the composition as though he expected to find enlightenment there.

"I'll leave you to it," said Humphry David. "I'm afraid I haven't been very helpful. You may even consider that I've been excessively flippant, in view of the horrible thing that happened here, but dwelling on its horror doesn't do any good."

"There you're perfectly right, sir. I can only tell you we are very grateful to you. You have helped us a lot," replied Rivers.

II

"If ever I happen to die a sudden and violent death, I should like to think my papers will be as orderly and business-like and generally meticulous as the late Edwin Pompfret's," observed Rivers some half-hour later.

"I take leave to hope they won't be," said Lancing promptly. "There's nothing for us here. No personal papers at all: no correspondence that couldn't be published as an advertisement for Civil Service methods. No muddle, no controversy, no rancour; it's all as neat and feelingless and aseptic as a chemist's dispensary. The chap must have had a private self, but he didn't keep it here."

"He couldn't have been merely negative or he wouldn't have been murdered," said Rivers. "Hallo, who's that? Come in."

It was Sergeant Gray who came into the room. "There's a Mr. Danvers here, sir. He was Mr. Pompfret's assistant, a co-ordinating secretary I think he's called. There was nobody at Mr. Pompfret's flat. He lived by himself. One of the housemen here mentioned Mr. Danvers, and we rang through to him and he drove here to see if he could be of any assistance."

"What zeal," sighed Rivers. "All right, Gray. Send him up."

It was quite a young man who came into the room a few minutes later: a fellow with bright dark eyes and a face naturally lively and cheerful. He wore a dark overcoat and white muffler over his dinner-jacket and despite the melancholy morning hour (it was half-past three) he looked very wide awake.

"Mr. Danvers?" said Rivers, as he rose to meet the visitor. "It's very public spirited of you to come here at this forbidding hour."

"Not all that," replied Danvers. "I'd been to a dance, and I hadn't gone to bed when your phone call came through, so I thought the least I could do was to come along and see if I could help. I'm all at sea. They told me that Mr. Pompfret had been killed by falling downstairs. Is that right?"

"He fell downstairs, and he was killed, but not by his fall," said Rivers. "The marble bust of Earl Manderby fell on top of him. How it happened I can't tell you—"

"But, good Lord, he loathed the thing," burst out Danvers. "He was always saying he'd like to tip it off. We even discussed ways and means of doing it. Not seriously, I mean. Just as a joke."

"And do you think that Mr. Pompfret was serious when he said he wished to destroy it?" asked Rivers.

"No. That's to say I'm quite certain he'd never have attempted it," said Danvers. "He was always talking about the things he'd like to blow up—the Albert Memorial and the Wedding Cake and the Central Hall and St. Pancras Station and most of the London statues, but that didn't mean he intended to do it. It was just his way of saying he disliked them."

"Yes. I follow that," said Rivers, "but I'm interested in the ways and means discussion for destroying the bust. Can you tell me some of the suggestions put forward?"

"It was all hot air," said Mr. Danvers deprecatingly. "The only practicable project was my own—employ mining technique. Drill a hole in the base, plug it with explosive and detonate by a time fuse. Lord—you're not telling me that's what happened?"

"No. I'm not," said Rivers. "There's no indication of an explosion. We don't know how it happened, but it's difficult to believe that Mr. Pompfret shifted that weight by himself. I must ask you if you knew of anybody who was at enmity with Mr. Pompfret, or who had a grudge against him?"

"Good lord, no. Of course not."

The reply was of the automatic, thoughtless sort, such as any good-natured man would give when speaking of a colleague with whom he had been on friendly terms, but both Rivers and Lancing sensed the sudden wariness in dark eyes which were naturally frank and cheerful, and the quick turn of the head as Danvers shifted his position a little. "Pompfret had been here ever since the Ministry began," he added. "He was my chief. We got on rather well. He was a bit overbearing, you know, and put people's backs up by his manner, but nobody took that very seriously."

"Did you know him personally, as a friend, apart from office work?"

"A bit. We ate together occasionally, and went to a few shows—ballet and art exhibitions—but I didn't know him well. He was a lot senior to me, and had ideas of educating me about contemporary art. All quite wasted, but I had to learn a bit of the patter. You know, it's awfully difficult to realise he's dead. It was only a few hours ago he told me he was making an evening of it with a wet towel round his head, working out a justification of our existence as he called it. He really did believe in this show, you know; he said that this Ministry was a real contribution to civilisation."

Rivers recognised the subtlety in this sentence: quite unobtrusively Mr. Danvers was steering the conversation away from personal topics. With deliberate avoidance of subtlety Rivers returned to the personal inquiry.

"I gather that Mr. Pompfret lived by himself in bachelor chambers. Was he a bachelor?"

"I never asked him," replied Danvers. "I don't really know anything about his private life."

Rivers allowed a deliberate pause. Then he said:

"I get a good deal of practice in assessing answers, you know. I think what you really mean is that you'd rather not repeat anything which you do happen to know about Mr. Pompfret's private life. If that is so, why did you come here? You said that you came 'to see if you could help.' To help whom?"

Some people said that Julian Rivers was sleepy looking. His grey-blue eyes were fringed by rather thick fair eyelashes, and generally speaking he didn't open his eyes wide—hence the sleepy look. But as he spoke to Danvers, Rivers looked at him with eyes that were wide open and deliberately observant and his change of aspect was remarkable.

"You can stick to it that you don't know, if you like," he went on. "It won't make any difference in the long run. It will only mean that we shall get the needed information from somebody who has no reluctance at all about giving it."

Danvers flushed. Then he said: "All right. I suppose I asked for all that, but it goes against the grain to gossip about a chap who's just been killed. Pompfret was married, but he and his wife had separated."

"Separated or divorced?" asked Rivers.

"Separated—I think. I never heard of a divorce."

"Do you know where Mrs. Pompfret is living now? We try to avoid letting next of kin learn about things like this from the morning newspapers, or from some journalist out for copy."

"Yes. I see. I hadn't thought of that. But I'm afraid I can't give you her address off-hand. I don't know it. I can tell you about his family, though. His mother and sister live in Sussex, near Uckfield. I've never been there, but I know he used to go there for week-ends."

"Thanks. I will see to it they are informed. Now I think that I have indicated to you that we must consider the possibility that Mr. Pompfret was murdered. Have you any comment or suggestion to make?"

"No. I'm afraid I haven't," said Danvers slowly. "It seems unbelievable."

"It's rather a difficult question to jump at you," said Rivers quietly. "Say if you go home and think it over. If anything occurs to you which you want to tell us there'll be plenty of opportunity to-morrow. We shall be here."

Lancing saw Danvers' slight movement of discomfort. "It's percolating," thought Lancing. "Sudden death can seem quite animating at first, exciting and unexpected. It takes time for the implications to ring a bell."

"Yes... oh, well, that'd be best," said Danvers. "It's been a shock, you know, and I feel a bit muddled."

"That's all right," said Rivers evenly. "Go and take advantage of what's left of the night. Sleep on it, in short."

Mr. Danvers had only gone out of the room a few seconds when Rivers lifted the telephone and spoke to the Sergeant on duty downstairs. Lancing looked disappointed. "You might have let me do it, sir. He hardly looked at me."

Rivers shook his head. His instructions about following Danvers had been terse and to the point.

"You never know… Bailley can pick him up outside. Quite a nice chap, this Michael Danvers, but inclined to be one of those rushers-in. My own feeling is that he came here because he expected some information. But he didn't get any."

Lancing grinned. "Is this where the Scandal of the Files becomes the Figment of a Minister's Imagination?" he inquired.

"No. I don't think so," said Rivers meditatively. "But I don't think we can do any more to-night. Four o'clock. Four ack emma. You can get just four hours' sleep if you don't dilly-dally."

He got up and stared at the abstract composition above the mantel. "There's an idea in this thing," he said.

Lancing cocked an eye at the composition.

> "… the intellectual Quixotes of the age,
> Prattling of abstract art,"

he quoted.

"I don't object to your quoting contemporary poets, but I do object to your hacking bits out of them," retorted Rivers. "You weren't thinking of Pompfret as an intellectual Quixote, by any chance? If so, think again."

CHAPTER VII

I

ABOUT HALF-PAST TEN ON THE MORNING FOLLOWING Pompfret's death, Chief Inspector Rivers, accompanied by Sergeant Brady, knocked on the door of a studio near Hampstead Heath. Rivers' instinct to have Michael Danvers followed when the latter left the Ministry had borne fruit. Danvers had got into his car (which he had left parked at the side of Medici House) and had driven up to Hampstead. Sergeant Bailley had followed Danvers' car (an M.G.) on its progress northwards: first in a police car, later in a taxi, with the police car keeping a discreet distance in the rear, ready to co-operate with Bailley by radio signals if Danvers' small M.G. eluded the following taxi.

It was a nice easy chase—Berkeley Square, Grosvenor Square, Portman Square, and then full speed ahead up Gloucester Place, Park Road, and Wellington Road to Swiss Cottage, thence up Fitzjohn's Avenue to Heath Street, Hampstead, and eventually to some little known, and surprisingly rural, back streets, where little brick houses which were not much more than cottages stood in pleasant gardens. Some of the gardens had been built over, and the studio to which Michael Danvers had paid a visit in the small hours was a rather decrepit Victorian structure, long since due for demolition, but surviving until town planners were no longer held in leash by recurrent financial crises.

Rivers stood waiting at the studio door, his shoulders hunched against the chill wind of the March morning, his eyes taking pleasure in the crocuses and snowdrops and winter aconites which flowered in the shelter of an old south wall.

He was here because he was following a hunch; in part guess-work, the guessing based on experience of human behaviour, in part the result of the reports which had come in from the divisional police during the night.

The door was opened to him, after a longish wait, by a tall woman dressed in a loose painter's smock and dark slacks, the coat much daubed with paint. At a first glance she looked young: she had crisp curly red hair, a creamy skin and blue eyes, but the line of her jaw and setting of her eyes were not those of a young woman. In her left hand she held a palette and brushes. Rivers followed his hunch.

"Mrs. Pompfret?" he inquired.

He saw her mouth and jaw tighten, while her blue eyes stared at him arrogantly.

"My name is Virgilia Hill. What is your business?"

"We are officers of the Metropolitan Police, and I am in charge of the inquiry into the death of Mr. Edwin Pompfret," said Rivers quietly. "I have reason to suppose that you have already heard of his death and I apologise for troubling you at such a time, but the inquiry had to go forward. May we come in?"

The blue eyes which met his had no sorrow in them, but some degree of anger mingled with their scornfulness. Rivers had known at a glance that there was no unhappiness in this woman's mind: exasperation seemed nearer the mark.

"Very well. Come in. Not that I can tell you anything about Edwin Pompfret," she retorted.

She led the way into the studio and went and put her palette and brushes down on a table which stood beside an easel. Brady stayed unobtrusively by the door and Rivers went up to the easel. The paint box was open, and beside it was the usual mess of jars and bottles and rags. One end of the long room was curtained off, and a settee and chairs stood in front of a gas fire. The painting on the easel was a flower study in the modern manner, a great mass of red tulips swaying above a skull, crudely but vividly depicted. There were red tulips arranged in a "corner" nearby, and the skull stood below them. Rivers had stared at a number of paintings in the Minister's study during the course of the night and had observed afresh what very occasional visits to modern galleries had shown him: that some painters still use brushes to apply their paint, others use palette knives and leave their surfaces "like morainal detritus" as Rivers expressed it—rough and angular, with the marks of the knife making a sort of modelling. The tulips had been put on with a palette knife, likewise the skull and background, but the brushes which Virgilia Hill had held were charged with the vivid red of the blooms.

As though irritated by Rivers' deliberate observation of the canvas, Virgilia Hill swung the easel away, so that he could no longer see it, and she then came and stood by the gas fire, her hands in the pockets of her smock, and faced him with a curtly inquiring: "Well?"

"You have told me that your name is Virgilia Hill, madam. I addressed you as Mrs. Pompfret because I have reason to believe that you were married to Mr. Edwin Pompfret, and that you are now his widow. Is that correct?"

"I don't see what business it is of yours, or of anybody else's," she replied. "I was married to Edwin Pompfret in 1945. I left him in 1948. Since then I have had nothing to do with him. I have neither seen, spoken to, or heard from him for over three years, and I know nothing about him. He did not support me. I had no interest in him, and I know nothing about the way he lived or the way he died."

"The probability is that he was murdered," said Rivers quietly, and she flashed back:

"I am not in the least surprised. He was the most maddeningly irritating person I have ever known. But I did not murder him and I know nothing about his death. When we separated, by mutual agreement and with mutual relief, we ceased to take any interest in one another." She jerked her head back, tossing away the red curls from her forehead and Rivers reflected that she was beautiful in her own way, though her beauty was marred by the hardness and ill-tempered expression of eyes and mouth.

"I bore him no ill-will," she added. "Once I had left him, I ignored his existence, and he did mine."

"You say that you took no interest in your husband," said Rivers, "yet his secretary thought it desirable to come and acquaint you with the news of Mr. Pompfret's death in the middle of the night."

"Michael Danvers?" she asked scornfully. "So I have to thank him for this pointless visitation. I met Michael Danvers by chance, only a few months ago. Why he thought it necessary to come out here in the small hours to tell me about Edwin's death I can't imagine."

"Can't you?" asked Rivers. "I don't think a great deal of imagination is needed to supply an explanation, and it seems foolish to pretend to unnecessary obtuseness, either for you or for me. You must be aware that when the attention of the police was drawn to you, madam, inquiries about you would naturally follow. It is assumed by your neighbours that you are not living here alone."

"The assumptions of my neighbours don't interest me," she retorted. "I live here alone, earning my own living. I am independent, beholden to nobody, and I entertain such visitors as I wish." She stared at Rivers, her blue eyes angrier now. "Oh, let's get down to it," she cried, as though in exasperation. "Michael told me the way

Edwin was killed. That preposterous Canova thing fell on him. Ask anybody in that pantomime of a place how often Edwin said he was going to smash the thing up. It wasn't that he knew good sculpture from bad: he didn't. He just paid lip service to the moderns. But he was quite stupid enough to try to play tricks shifting the Canova monstrosity and to get caught out because he hadn't the wits to realise what he was about."

Her words came quickly, spoken in a rush, but Rivers sensed that there was something besides anger in her voice. Was she piling on scorn and bitterness because she did feel something of the wretchedness of that undignified death? Rivers disliked her: he thought that she was another of the aggressive products of the modern school, deriding pity and constancy and the decencies of reticence, but he wanted to get at the essentials of the woman, at what underlay the "nail varnish" as he put it, of modern outspokenness.

As though reading his thoughts, she went on: "You'd respect me more if I put on an act, wouldn't you?—if I'd shed a few tears, asked for sympathy and played the part of heart-broken widow. I could have done it, you know. But I'm not like that. At least I've told you the truth. When I left my husband, I left him. I wasn't interested in what he did or who he did it with, and his death means nothing to me. And I suppose you're sitting there, thinking I pulled the Canova down to pay out old scores."

"You couldn't have: not by yourself," replied Rivers. "Neither could your husband have done so. It was too heavy. But if you like to tell me what you were doing yesterday evening, it might tidy things up."

She looked at him as though surprised by the quiet unemphatic voice, not knowing what to make of him. It occurred to Rivers that quietness and lack of emphasis were alien qualities to this angry-eyed woman.

"I was rehearsing a play at The Barn," she said, "if that conveys anything to you. The Barn is a sort of shack down in the Vale of Heath, where a small company produce plays as a try-out before an invited audience. I was there from eight o'clock until eleven. The stage manager is Paul Staunton. If you don't believe me, Staunton and a dozen other people can tell you where I was."

"Thanks," said Rivers. "Did you yourself write the play which was being rehearsed?"

"What on earth's that got to do with you?"

"I think I have heard of Virgilia Hill as a writer," said Rivers, "but not as a painter."

She flushed. "I don't believe you. Nobody's heard of me as a writer or anything else."

"I thought that you wrote a play called *Puppets in Paradise*," said Rivers.

"Information received," via the divisional police, the milkman and the newspaper men, had put the C.I.D. in possession of the fact that Virgilia Hill, tenant of the studio in Heath Passage, had written the play Rivers mentioned. It had been produced at the Experimental Theatre in Camden Town and had run for four nights.

"So what?" inquired Miss Hill, her eyes sullen and resentful.

"As a detective, it is my duty to check any information given to me," said Rivers. "You volunteered the information that you earned your living and that you were independent. In view of that statement, would you tell me how you earn it?"

"When and how I can," she retorted. "As a freelance journalist, as a designer, as a painter."

Rivers moved across the studio and went and stood in front of the easel. Then he looked among the brushes and gear, and at last he said: "Am I to understand that you are painting this picture? You had a palette and brushes in your hand when you opened the door."

"For the obvious reason, that I was painting," she replied.

"Didn't you overlook the fact that the paint on this canvas has been applied with a palette knife and not with a brush?" inquired Rivers evenly. "There is no palette knife among this gear, and the paint is not wet. It's tacky. It has not been touched since yesterday." He turned and faced her. "Isn't it true that you have never painted?" he asked, "that you know so little about painting that you forgot that a palette knife is always in evidence among a painter's tools? In short, that your entry on the scene as a painter was a stage entry rather than a practical one?"

She stood perfectly still, saying nothing at all, while her face flushed red and then the colour faded away, leaving her face pallid save for rouge and lipstick. At last she found her voice.

"You seem to think you know a lot about painting. The way I paint and the tools I use are my own business."

Rivers spoke again, patiently and evenly: "You claimed that you were speaking the truth. To some extent you may have been, but I think you tried to fool me by pretending that you were painting this picture. There could be only one reason for the pretence, that you don't want me to know who the painter really is. Can't you understand that when you are interrogated in a murder case, if you are innocent of complicity in the crime, the only wise thing to do is to speak the exact truth."

"I have told you the truth. I told you that I left my husband four years ago: that I had ceased to have any interest in him, or he in me, and that his death means nothing to me. I don't know anything about the way he died except what Michael Danvers told me. I know that I had nothing to do with it. As for what you say about my painting, it's just an assumption of your own and you don't know what you're talking about. If you're going to arrest me on a charge of killing my husband, you're just making a complete fool of yourself."

"Had I had any intention of arresting you, I should have been bound by police rules to caution you that anything you said could be written down and used in evidence," said Rivers. "I have not so cautioned you. I have warned you, as an individual as well as a policeman, that you would be wise to speak the exact truth. You must have the knowledge to realise that, in a case of this kind, you will be the focus point of a detailed inquiry. I'm sorry, but it's no use trying to hide anything. It may be just bad luck on you—I don't pretend to judge—but the circumstances of your life here, your friends, your income and your work, are all going to be inquired into. If you refuse to answer questions, or answer them inaccurately, you only assure that those questions will be put to the proof elsewhere."

"Then go and ask who you like anything you like," she flashed back. "I've told you everything that you need to know, and I've got nothing more to say. I have not seen my husband, or had any communication with him, since I left him four years ago. I know nothing of his death, and I've told you where I was yesterday evening."

"And you won't tell me who painted the tulips?" put in Rivers.

"I have told you. I painted them myself," she retorted.

"Are there any other paintings of yours I could see?" he asked.

She stared at him, her eyes baffled and weary, but she answered swiftly.

"No. There aren't. When I do paint, I sell my work. If what you want is to poke round the studio and look for canvases, get on with it. The quicker the better, and leave me to get on with my work."

"Thank you very much," said Rivers.

He walked quietly round the studio: he looked behind the curtain at the sleeping quarters and kitchenette. It was all surprisingly tidy and freshly swept and dusted. There were some unused boards and canvases, some uncovered stretchers and rolls of canvas and paper, but no other pictures. Neither was there any sign of any personal belongings save those which presumably belonged to Miss Hill.

While Rivers wandered round, Brady stood stiffly by the door and Virgilia Hill stood by the gas fire. She had lighted a cigarette and smoked it furiously, but she took no notice whatever of Rivers. When he came back towards her, she suddenly spoke again.

"I realise you think I've behaved abominably. I suppose I have, by your standards. I'm not apologising or withdrawing a word I've said, but I'm so exasperated I can't keep my temper. I—we—made a hash of being married. The only thing I asked was to forget all about it and do the things I wanted to do—writing, producing and painting. As you've reminded me, I haven't made much of a success of any of those, either. My play last night was another flop. Then, in the middle of the night, Michael Danvers came rushing in to tell me that Edwin was dead and the police raging round at the Ministry. I'd tried to forget all about him. He nearly drove me mad when I lived with him and now he's dead I'm suspected of murdering him. It's all crazy—I don't know anything about it and I don't want to know. And all you're doing here is wasting your time."

Rivers stood opposite to her and studied her worn face. Then he said: "It is often regrettably true that a police inquiry brings distress to innocent persons as well as guilty ones, but it has to go on. This one will go on. If an individual be innocent, the only thing for him to do is to answer questions put to him and leave the police to sort out the relevant facts from the irrelevant ones. To try to protect somebody whom you fear is guilty results only in being regarded as suspect yourself."

"If you must make assumptions, I can't stop you," she retorted, "but you're wrong, wrong in every guess you've made."

"It is my duty to ask you to stay here, or if you intend to leave, to notify the police of your intention," said Rivers.

"Oh, I shan't go away. Why should I? I've nothing to fear from you," she retorted.

II

As Rivers and Brady drove back from Hampstead, Brady asked: "What did you make of her, sir?"

"I disliked her exceedingly," said Rivers, "but whether she'll turn out to have anything but nuisance value I'm uncertain. In any case, she was in such a temper that we didn't get a chance to judge her fairly. I think I see the reasons for her fury—she told us quite a bit in her final outburst. She has fancied herself as a dramatist. Her first play was an utter failure. She had another tried out at this Barn place and that also appears to have been a dud. After coming home from a rehearsal of her own hopeless play, she was woken up in the small hours to be told of her husband's death. If my guess is worth anything, she wasn't alone in the studio. Her companion, having heard the news of Pompfret's death, decided to go while the going was good and leave Virgilia Hill to face the music. The combination of events wrought on an unstable temper and by the time we arrived she was in such a rage that she could only be abusive. But whether all this indicates that she knows anything about Pompfret's death is questionable."

"But what about the painting, sir? Do you think she *did* paint it?"

"I'm pretty certain she didn't," said Rivers. "It was a clever vigorous thing in its crude way. A painter doesn't deliberately use a palette knife as uncompromisingly as that and then smooth it over with a brush. No, I think she put on an act there all right, but not of necessity for our benefit. She wasn't expecting the C.I.D. to walk in. It may be that she's been in the habit of marketing somebody else's painting under her own name. The one thing I'm convinced of is that she's silly and unobservant: silly with the sort of obtuseness that assumes equal stupidity in other people, and her pose of complete indifference to her late husband was an affectation which is very prevalent to-day among people who like to think they're 'modern' in outlook. To be superior to all old-fashioned virtues and sentiment is the aim. You'll find plenty of demonstrations of the manner in modern fiction as well as modern painting. Violence is strength. Stridency is sincerity. Well?"

Rivers shot his final monosyllable at Brady with such an abrupt note of interrogation that Brady got quite pink. He was still in his twenties.

"I don't know, sir," he said slowly. "I admit the violence, or exaggeration, but isn't some of it a reaction against the pose of virtue and sentiment which used to pass muster as goodness? I agree with you about disliking Miss Virgilia Hill, but not because she said that when she left her husband she didn't take any further interest in him and didn't care whether he lived or died. That was probably true."

"Then why did you dislike her?" asked Rivers. He always liked to find out what went on in the minds of the younger men at the Yard, for in spite of his own conservatism in some matters, he was aware enough of the change in outlook between his own generation and Brady's.

"Well, sir, she's an educated woman and she'd no need to be rude and abusive, and then I disliked the way she spoke of Pompfret. She said he was a fool and an irritating fool. She could have left that out."

Rivers laughed. "You're being inconsistent, Brady. You're basing your argument on taste, and the taste you're upholding is old-fashioned, the sort of quality your mother would have valued."

Brady grinned. "I suppose I am, sir. I expect that I respect very much the same things that you do, but I don't agree that all modern thinking and modern taste is bad. I didn't dislike Miss Hill because she's modern, but because she's hard and selfish and pretentious. And I thought you made the real point, sir, when you asked her how she earned her living. It so often comes down to that."

Rivers chuckled a little. "You're not a very sound exponent of modernism, Brady. You're going back to the oldest motive of all—to whose profit? I think it's improbable that Virgilia Hill makes a living out of her plays, and freelance journalism isn't very profitable in these days of newsprint shortage. Whether she stands to profit from her husband's estate we don't yet know. But the person I'm most interested in at the moment is Michael Danvers."

"If he'd been involved in the crime, sir, do you think he'd have gone up to that studio?"

"No. I don't. But he withheld evidence which it was his duty to have given and I want to know why."

"The answer to that one seems to stick out, sir," said Brady.

"I don't think anything really sticks out in this case," said Rivers. "Things overlap and intertwine and are generally involved, just like an abstract painting."

"Meaning you can't see the reason for any of it?" hazarded Brady.

"All the reasons depend on other reasons," replied Rivers.

CHAPTER VIII

I

RIVERS LEFT HAMPSTEAD WITH AN IRRITATING FEELING THAT he had been wasting his time. He knew that his visit to the studio had been essential, for in any murder investigation the victim's next of kin and immediate associates have to be investigated.

Rivers had delegated to the county police the business of interviewing Pompfret's mother and sister in their home near Uckfield. Mrs. Pompfret senior, widow of a solicitor, and Miss Natalie Pompfret, came under the heading of "nice people"—a pair of unostentatious gentlewomen respected by their country neighbours, busily occupied in the day-to-day business of housekeeping and gardening. Neither knew very much about Edwin: they thought of him as brilliant, and admired (while not sharing) his understanding of the fine arts. Natalie Pompfret, aged fifty, grey haired, weather-beaten and plain spoken, had spoken of her sister-in-law as an "impossible person." "Their marriage was a disaster. I always knew it would be," she had said. "My brother should have married someone gentle and sympathetic and quiet, not that opinionated, red-headed bohemian who contradicted every word he uttered. Neither my mother nor myself approve of broken marriages, but we couldn't help being relieved when Valerie left my brother." Miss Pompfret did not know where Mrs. Edwin Pompfret now lived. "We haven't heard of her since she left my brother, and I don't think he knew where she lived, either. She may have resumed her maiden name—Hislop."

Further inquiry evoked the fact that before her marriage Miss Valerie Hislop had been secretary and manageress at a small gallery and art dealer's establishment in Chelsea, since closed down. The county C.I.D. man who went to see Natalie Pompfret and her mother reported to Rivers: "I think they are just what they appear to be, kindly conventional folk. Miss Pompfret disliked her sister-in-law very much, but as the brother had lived with—and probably in part supported—his mother and sister previous to his marriage, the latter's opinion may not be unbiased."

So the red-headed Valerie Hislop had become Virgilia Hill, still red-headed, still opinionated, still "bohemian" (in Miss Pompfret's use of the word), and Rivers would have to investigate her mode of life and resources.

Owing to Edwin Pompfret's admirably orderly habits, and the business-like filing and labelling of his papers, it had been very easy for the C.I.D. investigator to discover the size of his estate: about £5,000 invested in good industrial concerns: £2,000 in National Savings and government stock: £2,000 life insurance. With sundries totted up, Edwin Pompfret left about £10,000, and this was bequeathed in his will in equal shares to his mother, his sister and his wife, provided the latter had not remarried, to which proviso was added another—"living a chaste life." However advanced Edwin Pompfret's views on art had been, his views on behaviour evidently had still coincided with those of his unadvanced mother and sister.

With a feeling that honour had been satisfied in the matter of routine, and that further investigation of Virgilia Hill and her painting could wait until more immediate problems had been considered, Rivers sent for Michael Danvers as soon as he (Rivers) returned to Medici House from Hampstead. Danvers came into the waiting-room which the C.I.D. had taken over as an office and looked at Rivers with a calm cheerfulness that was almost too good to be true. Without asking him to sit down, Rivers began:

"You told me last night that you could not give me Mrs. Edwin Pompfret's address because you did not know it, yet when you left here you drove straight out to see her."

Michael Danvers did not lose countenance and he looked Rivers straight in the face.

"Perfectly true, all of it," he said. "I could not then have given you her address: I knew neither the name of the road nor the number of the house where her studio is built. I had been to the studio once only. I thought I could find my way there, and I did. Your only complaint against me is that I did not offer to take you there. Well, I admit that, and I'm prepared to take the consequences. I'd do the same again for anybody I cared about."

"Are you aware that if you withhold evidence from the police, you may risk being charged as accessory after the fact?" asked Rivers.

"If you say so," replied the other. "Look here: you're a man in addition to being a policeman: I'm a man, in addition to being a Civil Servant. There's a human problem here, and one that matters to me, personally. I went to the studio last night on impulse. After I'd left you, I realised that I'd got to find out for myself if Virgilia Hill knew anything about Pompfret's death. I was certain that I should know if she had. She gives herself away more easily than most people. I'm perfectly certain that she knew nothing about it at all. I was so sure of it that I was prepared to give you her address this morning as soon as I saw you."

"Which is tantamount to saying that you'd have helped her to get away if you thought her guilty," said Rivers.

"I don't know about that. I can't tell you. I might have done—though I'd have known it would be pretty futile," said Danvers. "I'm only an average size in fools, not an outsize. And there's one other thing I'd better tell you. If you think I'm her lover, you're wrong. I've no feelings about her that way, nor she about me."

"Did Mr. Pompfret know that you knew his wife?" asked Rivers.

"No. I only knew a few days ago that she was his wife. I met her as Miss Hill, and accepted her as such. She told me quite suddenly, after I'd mentioned my boss by name, that she was married to him. I'd heard Pompfret's wife had left him—most people know that. I was amazed when she told me she was his wife." He broke off, and then added: "I know just what it must look like to you. You probably think it's all over bar the shouting, because V. H. and I together thought out a cunning way of killing Pompfret. But you couldn't be farther from the truth."

"I don't need you to interpret my thoughts for me," said Rivers, and there was an edge to his voice. "Neither do I propose to ask you any further questions for the moment. Your idea of responsibility and of telling the truth do not tally with my own."

Michael Danvers stood very still, as though considering the sharp words he had just heard. Then he said:

"You must, inevitably, be single-minded. To you, black is black and white is white. To you, there is only one sort of responsibility, but I have the right to ask myself 'Responsibility to whom?' Is it better to be an objective witness or to keep faith with a friend? I don't pretend to know." Suddenly he grinned at Rivers. "I know I've landed myself in a mess. Government servants aren't expected to use their own judgment, but I'm still glad I used mine. You see, I know that I had no hand in killing Pompfret, and I know now that his wife hadn't, so I can afford to keep calm. If you'll kindly tell me whether I'm under arrest or whether I go on dictating letters of delaying tactics 'pending the Minister's decision,' it'll save government money. The typists are all flapping around like penguins."

"So far as I am concerned, you can go back to your department—pending the Minister's decision," said Rivers.

II

Rivers then went to see the Minister and put to him the decisions made by the C.I.D. in consultation with the Commissioners.

"It is better for the normal routine of the establishment to continue as far as possible, sir. Certain departments must be interrupted, but I will deal with those later. We are assuming that Mr. Pompfret was murdered, and the murderer must have been in the building when death took place. In my judgment the murderer must be a man well acquainted with this building, and most probably a man employed in this building. The number of persons so employed makes investigation a slow and difficult process, but it is better to have everybody on the spot so far as is possible. Absentees will be interrogated separately."

"Yes. I agree with all that," said Humphry David quietly. "As you can imagine, the place will be seething with gossip. It is possible that among the rumours and suggestions that are flying around there may be some grains of truth. I should like to make it known that anybody who thinks they have any vestige of information can report to me, personally, if they would rather do that than report directly to the police. I don't know if you will agree with that. Some people are very unwilling to report to the police, particularly the less well-educated. They have unreasonable fears of getting involved more deeply than they consider warrantable."

"We shall be very grateful for your co-operation, sir. I know that you are respected and trusted here, and I think it quite possible that information might come your way which would be slow to come ours. Now I think it might be helpful if we tried to work out priorities: it seems plain enough that Mr. Pompfret had direct contact with the personnel of some branches, and very little contact with others."

The Minister nodded. "Yes. At risk of wearying you, I will repeat the general structure as it were. Certain branches are grouped together under the direction of a Deputy Secretary or of a Chief Inspector. The Deputy Secretaries report on the branches under their supervision to the Permanent Secretary, who is in direct contact with both the Parliamentary Secretary and the Minister. Pompfret, as you know, was deputy to the Permanent Secretary, who is on sick leave. Now as to the branches, those in which Pompfret took the greatest interest and with which he was most in contact were the group under Mr. Dellison: that is, Acquisitions, Loan Collections, Architects, Artists, Public Monuments and Museums. Those branches in which he tended to accept expert opinion were in the group under Mr. Bonnington, including Legal, Finance, Statistics, Education and Inspectorate. The Establishments branch tends to be self-contained—it deals with such matters as staff training, recruitment, transfer, promotion, as well as the maintenance of this building, office arrangements, cleaning, catering and so forth. Pompfret called it the 'chores' department, and left it to its very competent administrator."

"Thank you, sir. I'm beginning to get a mental picture of the set-up. I gather that Mr. Pompfret's personal preferences were in the direction of spreading the arts, as he understood them, as widely as possible."

"Yes. It's my opinion that the older he grew, the more he fancied himself as a sort of director of public taste. I don't want to be unfair to the man, Chief Inspector. I'm groping—as you are groping—towards an understanding of a man to whom I'm afraid I didn't behave very well, and whom I did not know as well as I ought to have done. To begin with, he was one of those potentially able administrators we get from the universities. He took a good degree—a second in Greats, incidentally, and passed high up on the list in the Civil Service exams. He was at the Ministry of Education— or Board of Education—from 1925–39, then was promoted to Assistant Secretary in the Ministry of Supply during the war-time years, and it was during this period he met and was influenced by Joyce-Lawrence. Pompfret came here when Joyce-Lawrence was appointed first Minister, and together they enjoyed the first opti- mistic months of the M.O.F.A. To put it as fairly as I can, he started by being an able scholar, grew into a first-rate administrator, and then slightly lost his balance when he was introduced to the heady wine of contemporary art. It will be obvious to you that there was very little understanding or sympathy between Pompfret and my predecessor in office. Higginson tended more and more to concen- trate on purely administrative and economic aspects of the Ministry, leaving what he called 'the frills' to Pompfret. I have given you this outline to assist you in your assessment of priorities, but I should be interested to learn if you have any particular line to follow up."

"As I see it, sir, there are two lines to be followed. First, there is your own conjecture: that some fraud has been engineered in one of the departments directly concerned with either the purchase, transport or housing of works of art, and that Mr. Pompfret was murdered to prevent the discovery or reporting of the fraud. The second approach deals with Mr. Pompfret's private life. His wife left him some years ago, but there was no divorce or legal separation. It may be that Mr. Pompfret refused to agree to a divorce, or that the portion of his estate bequeathed to his wife tempted someone to take action. We can't disregard that possibility. Finally, his wife may have formed an association with somebody employed here who was concerned in the hypothetical fraud you yourself postulated."

Humphry David's kindly face looked distressed. "I can't help hoping that's not the case," he said. "I didn't even know that Pompfret was married, or had been married."

"I've got a suggestion here, sir," put in Rivers. Briefly he told the Minister of Michael Danvers' activities. "I'm not trying to make trouble for him, sir, and I am certainly not suggesting that he was here when Pompfret was killed. I know that he wasn't. But it's possible that he might tell you more than he was willing to tell me. I've no means of making him talk. If a man says he's prepared to face the consequences of refusing to give evidence, that's that. But there's at least a possibility that he might tell you a great deal more than he's prepared to tell me, at the moment, anyway. And I think he knows a number of things which might clear away misunderstandings."

"Yes. I see. I'll do what I can," said David. "I know Danvers a little, and I like him. I should have described him as a straightforward fellow. Perhaps I can help him to straighten out his complex of personal loyalties and civic duty. I'm prepared to realise that it may have seemed an insoluble dilemma to a young man."

"I'll leave him to you, sir. Now we have already put our own men on duty in certain departments, and we have arranged for expert investigators to examine those exhibits in the Loan Collection which are in the building, and the files of the Acquisitions department. These investigators will also come to examine the pictures in this room. Henry Fearon is already working in the Files department, with the assistance of some of your staff. For the rest, I repeat that we believe the murderer must have been employed in this building. We hope, by patient elimination, to get the inquiry down to reasonable limits. At first sight, it looks an interminable job, but we nearly always collect some relevant information as we go along, and the inquiry may focus itself more quickly than seems possible at a first survey."

Humphry David nodded. "Yes. I suppose that out of a welter of surmise and gossip, small rancours and jealousies, something will emerge and take shape, as crystals form in an evaporating dish. Somebody always notices something—if only they can recognise and report the something—"

"Finally, sir, a word of advice if you can give it. I want to get to know this building. Whom do you recommend as guide?"

"The official surveyor would be the most appropriate person, but I believe he is up north somewhere, surveying another 'stately home' which is suggested as a regional museum. I commend you to the Architects' department. They have some very intelligent young people up there who have studied the fabric to good purpose." He paused, and then added: "It goes against the grain with me to realise that we are all suspect, but as a matter of common sense I would hazard that it wasn't a woman who chose that particular method of killing Pompfret. You'll find some very knowledgeable young women in the Architects' department who would act as guide and answer questions as well as any of the men."

"Thank you very much, sir. Now, with your permission, I will go and find out what sort of progress my men have been making."

III

After Rivers had left him, the Minister sent for Mr. Charles Bonnington, the Deputy Secretary who was co-ordinating director of the branches dealing with Education, Legal matters, Finance and Statistics, Information and External relations.

Bonnington was a man approaching sixty, grey-headed, serious of aspect, impeccably neat in attire. He had been a Civil Servant, dealing mainly with administration, for over thirty-five years. He was an able and conscientious man, but years of office work, of committees and their inevitable atmosphere of expediency and compromise, had damped down any spontaneity and originality he might once have possessed. His lode star was precedent, his abiding hope was compromise, but within these limits he was a man of integrity and loyalty.

Humphry David asked him to sit down, and then said: "As you will agree, it is very necessary that Mr. Pompfret's place should be filled. The Treasury does not wish to make a permanent appointment without due consideration, but we should be grateful if you would supervise the work of his office until further notice. As you know, Pompfret acted as the final adjudicator of matters which were to be brought to the Minister for personal consideration. With your own long experience of government departments, and your knowledge of the working routine of this Ministry, I feel you could be a great help to me at this difficult time."

"Thank you for your confidence in me, Minister. I shall be happy to do my utmost to assist, but I fear that there may be matters not within my competence. My work has dealt with problems of administration rather than problems pertaining to the fine arts."

"You can bring direct to me any matters on which an immediate decision may be necessary," said David, the hint of a smile in his eyes, for no one knew better than he did how "immediacy" can be translated into "pending the discussion of" by any self-respecting Civil Servant. Suddenly the Minister spoke again, his voice keen, his words incisive:

"This matter of Pompfret's death is in a sense a challenge to us all, Bonnington. It demands that we should put aside all the reticences and evasions which are a comfortable adjunct to ordinary working conditions and social contacts alike. I ask you, personally, as I shall ask all your senior colleagues, is there anything you know which throws any light on the matter? Have there been, to your knowledge, any dissensions or enmities or stresses in the inner workings of this place?"

Bonnington looked aghast. He smoothed his neat grey head and pursed up his lips, as troubled as a conventional man could be.

"I find it hard to answer, Minister. I can say without reservation that I know of nothing which would explain the tragedy: nothing, that is, beyond Pompfret's known dislike of the Canova work. But if you ask me have there been dissensions…" He broke off and David put in:

"You would reply that there have never been anything but dissensions since this Ministry began?"

"That is to some extent true, sir, but differences as to policy, as to artistic values, as to expansion and finance, none of these could promote the bitterness and antagonism which might lead to personal violence. No, no. I cannot believe that. But if there *is* a problem for the police to solve, my own belief is that the solution is not—er—integral to this establishment. It lies elsewhere. It is with repugnance that I mention the private life of a colleague, but I understand that Pompfret made a disastrous marriage. His wife, I believe, left him. It was alleged that she was a woman of violent temper and held extremist views, on politics as well as on art. If there be a mystery to solve, I feel very strongly that its roots lie elsewhere."

The Minister did not alter his attitude of courteous attention, his expression of grave inquiry, though it flashed across his mind that he was being handed the inevitable departmental answer to difficult problems: *"passed to you, please."* Passed, in this case, to the world beyond the walls of the Civil Service citadel: "not integral to this establishment… not within our terms of reference; external to our policy; depending on extraneous circumstances beyond our control."

For once the Minister dispensed with departmental punctilio and the nicety of ministerial questions.

"Do you imagine that Mrs. Pompfret gained access to these premises and tilted the Canova bust on to her husband's head?" he inquired, speaking with intention to shock. But Mr. Bonnington's reaction was in the nature of evasion.

"It sounds in the highest degree improbable, Minister. But all the circumstances can be said to be in the highest degree improbable."

"Yes, we have never had a murder in a Ministry before," murmured David. "In the light of this unprecedented happening, I ask you all to make unprecedented efforts to search your minds for any incident that may be relevant. And now, you will wish to make arrangements in your own department, so that you may be free to take Mr. Pompfret's place."

Mr. Bonnington's face was a study, but he only bowed silently. David added: "Would you be good enough to ask Mr. Danvers to come and speak to me? I will explain to him that you are taking over for the moment."

Again Bonnington bowed, as though to relieve himself of the necessity of speaking. As he went out, the Minister thought to himself unhappily that until the problem was solved, it would be impossible to look any of his staff in the face without a tacit question in his own mind: "What does he know...?"

CHAPTER IX

I

"Yes, I've been here since the ministry started in the Loans Collection department," said Paul Weston to Chief Inspector Rivers. They were sitting in Weston's small office, once the music library of Medici House. It opened off the big music room, now emptied of its usual staff. A group of three men, one the curator of a famous gallery, one an art dealer of international reputation, one a painter, were now in the big music room, considering the canvases stored there. The staff of the Loans Collection had been accommodated temporarily in a room in the basement; feeling entirely disorganised and exceedingly embittered, they were doing more talking than typing and more tea drinking than administration.

One of the first people Rivers had talked to after leaving the Minister was Mr. James Dellison, the Deputy Secretary in charge of Loans Collection, Acquisitions, Architects, Artists, Museums and Public Monuments branches. A man of forty-five, cut to pattern and urbane, Mr. Dellison seemed not at all overpowered by the wideness of his responsibilities. He was, as he explained at once, an administrator, and his interpretation of his office was to keep the wheels turning smoothly while in low gear.

"Owing to economic pressure we are not able to develop any ambitious projects at present," he explained. (Rivers had heard that one before.) "The Loans Collection is fairly representative, and we have only added half a dozen small works in the past financial year. Acquisitions can be said to be in cold storage at present: the work of that department is almost entirely consultative and advisory at the moment."

"Saying what it would be advisable to do when it becomes advisable to do it," murmured Rivers, and the other agreed. Then he added:

"As you know, I have only been here for a few months, and we had a change of Minister in November: then the financial crisis practically forced our projects to a standstill, so it may be said that we've just been ticking over as it were, and sticking to routine."

"Yes. I rather gathered that," said Rivers. "Now I think for the purpose of this inquiry, I should like to see some members of the Loans Collections and Acquisitions branch who have been here from the word go—the start of this Ministry. Who would you suggest?"

"Well, in Loans I suggest Paul Weston and Ewart Blackwell: both were appointed by the first Minister. Blackwell entered the Civil Service through the usual channels, but Weston was attached as it were. I think the then Minister judged him to be knowledge-able about contemporary art. We have a number or people working here—the architects, for instance—who are Civil Servants by virtue of working for the Ministry, but did not enter through examination."

"In fact this Ministry is a law unto itself," said Rivers, and the other cocked an eye at him, but he replied with departmental discretion.

"A new department has to make its own traditions and prec-edents, and you wouldn't expect this Ministry to conform to the pattern set by the Ministry of Fuel and Power or the older Post Office tradition."

Deciding to return to Mr. Dellison later, Rivers asked to see Mr. Weston. He was a dark lean young man, with a pleasant voice and some quality which suggested the word "artistic." Trying to define that vague word for himself, Rivers decided that it involved a greater degree of sensitivity than the normal. This young man wasn't actually nervous, but he gave a faint impression of tension, and Rivers noted that he was the first witness in the Ministry who looked personally concerned about Pompfret's death. Having assured Rivers that he had been in the Loans Collection branch from its inception, Paul Weston waited for the next question.

"Would you tell me how you got your job here?" asked Rivers. "I'm pretty ignorant about the Civil Service. I only know that the examination for the higher grade would be quite beyond me."

"They'd be beyond me, too," said Weston. "I got in by the back door, so to speak. I was in the R.A.F.—glider squadrons—until 1945, and when I came out I was twenty-five. I didn't want to start as a student, or go to a University, so I just worried round among people I knew and got an introduction to Mr. Joyce-Lawrence. He was looking for people who'd fit in this department—it's not the usual Civil Service routine—and it happened that I was interested in modern painting, so Mr. Joyce-Lawrence gave me a job here with temporary status, and here I've stayed."

"Quite an interesting job," said Rivers. "To what extent did it bring you into contact with Mr. Pompfret? I ask you that because I've been told he was particularly interested in this department."

"Yes. I think he was," agreed Weston, "but he wasn't interested in personnel, only in exhibits. I don't think I've ever had what I should call a conversation with him. I've heard his opinions and received his instructions. Higher grades don't chat to lower grades, if you see what I mean."

Rivers smiled. "We might get on faster if I say I've heard a bit about Mr. Pompfret," he said. "What I want to know is this. To what extent was he an expert on art?"

"To no extent," replied Weston. "He had opinions, but they were mostly second-hand ones." He broke off. "This is a bit awkward. I didn't know him very well: I don't think any of us did. But I don't want to run him down. He was a very able man, I believe, and he did want to make this department a success. He'd got the right ideas about that, because he caught the enthusiasm of Mr. Joyce-Lawrence. But he didn't really know very much apart from what he'd been told by critics and what he'd read. However, his death probably means the demise of this department. It's been hanging between life and death for some time, and now I think it'll be quietly interred. Which is rather a facer for me." He looked at Rivers apologetically. "Sorry. My woes are off the point."

"Not altogether," said Rivers, "but can you tell me why you prophesy the demise of Loan Collections Ltd.?"

Paul Weston suddenly laughed, and broke off into a fit of coughing. "Sorry," he said when he'd recovered. "I've got a foul cold. I ought to have stayed at home out of consideration for other people. About Loans Collection. It was one of those inspired ideas. If Joyce-Lawrence had been able to carry it through, it would have been a tremendous thing: it might have led to something like a people's Renaissance. But you must know what happened. He wasn't able to carry it out. The Treasury wouldn't let him. So the whole thing became a sham. Instead of a collection of great works of art it became a collection of mediocrities. The majority of the canvases are by painters nobody has ever heard of: they're labelled in schools or styles or movements. We try to put their names on the map, so to speak, but I'm afraid it's all rather second-rate."

"I gather there's been a certain amount of dissension about this branch of the Ministry," said Rivers, and Weston replied:

"If by that you mean we've come under fire from critics in every quarter, you're right. If you're asking if there's dissension in the staff here, you're wrong. It's true that we bicker a bit over the canvases, but that's only to be expected. You couldn't find a pleasanter group of people to work with. And though Mr. Pompfret was what I call arbitrary in his opinions and a bit overbearing in manner, he didn't interfere with us. As for Mr. Dellison, he's just administrative—not interested in art movements and so forth."

"You were here when the branch began," said Rivers. "Did you have anything to do with buying the pictures, either in an advisory capacity or any other?"

"Oh lord, no," replied Weston. "Mr. Joyce-Lawrence either acted on his own initiative or through advisers chosen by himself. All of us here are merely administrative, like librarians. We see the stuff is circulated and returned, advise local galleries as to what we've got, and see that canvases and other works in stock are in good order, safely stored and reasonably arranged."

"Who does the checking when canvases are returned?"

"Whichever of us was responsible for advising and issuing. We check our own lists."

"Did Mr. Pompfret ever interfere in this circulating business? override your decisions as to what was sent out or give definite directions?"

"No, except…" He broke off, and Rivers said:

"Well, except what?"

"Except when he wanted to show a canvas to a visiting expert or something of that kind. There have been occasions when he's asked for our lists and sent them back with a direction to replace such and such a loan exhibit with another of a similar genre."

"On these occasions, did he bring his visiting expert here, to the department?"

"No, not of necessity. Sometimes he had the picture sent up to his room. Once or twice I've taken them up myself, if asked to do so."

"Why did he ask you to do it?"

Weston's mobile lips twitched a little. "I think he liked to pretend some of the exhibits were very valuable, and a messenger or porter wasn't quite to be trusted."

"Well, are they very valuable?"

"Not to my knowledge. I don't think there's anything here which would even command a good sale room price."

"And did you go upstairs again to retrieve the exhibit?"

"Not always. In fact very seldom. He sometimes kept them quite a while, and sent them back by one of the upstairs messengers."

"You say that Mr. Pompfret kept some of them quite a while. Do you know if he ever took any of these pictures out of the building?"

"Well, yes. He did on occasion. At least, I think he did. We use green wrappers to protect the surfaces of canvases when they're shifted. I once saw Mr. Pompfret carrying something to his car in one of our wrappers, and the parcel was the size of one of the exhibits he'd had sent up to him—an abstract by Lemoine, quite a small thing." The young man broke off. "If you'd only tell me what you're getting at, I might be able to help a bit more."

"The trend of my questions makes it fairly obvious what I'm getting at. Has there been any fraud or theft from this department, and if so, did Mr. Pompfret become aware of it, consciously or unconsciously?"

"I shouldn't have thought there was anything here of sufficient value for a crook to be interested in it," said Weston slowly, "and the marketing of works of art is a chancy business. If there was any funny stuff connected with this place—which I think is extremely improbable—I should connect it with some of the so-called experts who came to see Mr. Pompfret. But I'm only guessing and the whole thing seems quite haywire to me."

"Never mind what it seems to you. What do you mean by 'so-called experts'?"

"Well, I think Mr. Pompfret was a bit gullible on the subject. I'm only giving you my own opinion about this, and I may be quite wrong, but if a foreigner wrote to him, with a lot of impressive-sounding verbiage and some compliments about the artistic enterprise of the Ministry of Fine Arts, I think Mr. Pompfret tended to take the writers at their own valuation and was prepared to spend quite a lot of time on them. He had some very odd birds to see our exhibits."

"What made you think them odd?"

"Well, they didn't really seem to us to know very much about anything. If you talk to Miss Barton—she's in Loans, and works with me—she'll tell you the same thing. She's taken a lot of trouble to read up her subject and she does know her stuff, so far as names of painters go. She talked to an Italian visiting expert, and mentioned Nicholson and Bacon, and the chap not only hadn't heard of them as painters, he thought she was talking about writers. And he was supposed to be studying British contemporary painters. But look here, sir—" and Weston's voice became suddenly eager, "I know it's not my province to make suggestions, but isn't your theory a sort of contradiction in terms?"

"Don't imagine I want to debar you from making suggestions," said Rivers. "Tell me any ideas you have. I know no more about this Ministry than you do about Scotland Yard, and considerably less about the fine arts than you do about police procedure. I'm here to pick your brains, and I admit it frankly."

"I haven't many brains to pick," said Weston, with the disarming grin which lit up his sensitive face, "but you suggested just now that a fraud or racket had been worked in this department, and that Mr. Pompfret had become aware of it. If such a thing had happened,

I don't think Mr. Pompfret would ever have become aware of it. You've told me to say what I really think. Well, in my opinion, he didn't know a picture from a boot. Without his book of the words he was all at sea." A fit of coughing interrupted his quick speech, and then he went on: "It does sometimes happen that a middle-aged man takes to the arts for a hobby. Rich men become art patrons. Some of them do develop a sensitive judgment, some don't. Mr. Pompfret was a bit like a convert to a new religion: but he hadn't got a seeing eye."

"Yes. I get your point," said Rivers. "About this 'seeing eye' as you call it, awareness or ability to judge. To what extent do *you* know these pictures in your charge? You evidently don't think a great deal of them. Are you going by your own innate judgment, by experience, or by the book of the words as you call it?"

Weston sat and pondered. "You're asking me if I know a first-rate picture from a mediocre one," he said slowly. "If I could pick out a Graham Sutherland portrait from a pretentious daub—"

"I'm not asking you if you could tell a Graham Sutherland portrait from a daub," interrupted Rivers. "I'm asking you if you could tell a Cezanne still-life from a skilful copy of a Cezanne still-life?"

"I don't know," replied Weston slowly. "I just don't know. I'm not a painter. But I do know the exhibits we've got, and I know them much better than Mr. Pompfret did, and I know that they're the same ones we've always had. Some of them are works which show an original mind and an individual approach as well as skill in applying paint, but a lot of them are what you can call 'derived,' that is they imitate manners rather than originate them. And not one of them is worth the attention of a thief."

Rivers sat silent for a moment. Then he said: "As you can assume for yourself, what we are looking for is a motive. We are here because we believe that Mr. Pompfret was murdered, and we must search for a motive both in his professional and his private life."

"But can you be certain he *was* murdered?" expostulated Weston. "It was common knowledge that Mr. Pompfret hated Earl Manderby—and it wasn't only because he considered it the done thing to hate nineteenth-century Italian sculpture, either."

Rivers cocked an eye at him. "What other reason had he for hating it, then?"

Weston flushed. "Ask any of the typists, sir, or the messengers."

"I'm asking you," replied Rivers.

"Very well. It's not a dignified answer, but it's true. Mr. Pompfret was nicknamed Pompey. So was Earl Manderby. Some giggling little idiot of a typist swore that Manderby resembled Pompfret. It was one of those idiotic suggestions that catches on, and Mr. Pompfret heard about it. He was livid. It may sound silly, but he cherished his dignity. It got him on the raw."

"If you're suggesting that Mr. Pompfret demolished Earl Manderby to salve his own dignity, can you tell me how he shifted such a weight off the plinth?"

"I don't know. I can't imagine," said Weston. He looked weary and depressed. "It's a beastly business, all of it. Everybody here is discussing it—you can't blame them. I don't think anybody believes Mr. Pompfret was murdered, not the serious-minded ones, anyway. They believe that he made up his mind to get rid of Pompey the Second, and that he thought out some clever trick for shifting it and got caught as it fell. As for how he did it, I'm not going to quote people's ideas: some of them sound too jolly possible. It's up to them to produce their own theories."

"That's fair enough," said Rivers. "In any case, I've made you talk until your voice is almost non-existent. If I were you, I should go home to bed and get rid of that cough."

"Bed doesn't seem to help. I went home early yesterday and got to bed, and barked myself hoarse all night. My landlady's about sick of the sound of me."

"Where do you live—have you got a long journey?"

"No. I've got digs in Marylebone, just off the High Street."

"Well, why not go back and keep warm," suggested Rivers. "We've upset your routine for to-day and somebody else can continue the delaying tactics in which I'm told that Ministries excel."

"I think our routine, delaying tactics, and all that, have been side-tracked for good," said Weston. "We've been regarded as a nuisance by everybody. The artists regard us as a laughing stock, the Treasury regards us as waste of money, the public considers us perverse and the Minister thinks that we started at the wrong end of the stick, chronologically. He's a very nice courteous, conscientious Minister, and he'll intone the funeral service over us beautifully."

"It's an inclusive Jeremiad," said Rivers, "but perhaps the visiting experts will give you a dose of restorative."

"The visiting experts will disagree. They always do," said Paul Weston.

II

Mr. Ewart Blackwell, also of Loans department, was Rivers' next visitor. Blackwell was fair-headed, his pink face ornamented with impressive horn-rims, through which his blue eyes looked startled and apprehensive. He hastened to disclaim any expert knowledge of art, but was very emphatic that the system for checking works which had been out on loan was practically foolproof. He was very guarded in everything he said, particularly about Pompfret, whose judgments, he insisted, he had never thought of querying.

"Did you know that the typists called both Mr. Pompfret and Earl Manderby, Pompey?" inquired Rivers.

Blackwell got very pink. "Yes. I do know that... it's just one of those silly things that happen in places like this. It doesn't really mean disrespect, or anything like that. People do tend to exaggerate so."

Rivers regarded him thoughtfully. "I see that you've always done clerical work, even in the Army."

"Yes, sir. Rotten eyesight," replied Blackwell nervously.

"Perhaps short sight isn't always a drawback in this department," suggested Rivers.

Blackwell got pinker than ever. "I'm all right if I get close to them," he said ambiguously.

Rivers laughed. "I wish I could say the same," he replied. Blackwell looked completely mystified.

CHAPTER X

"A MURDER ON THE PREMISES," MURMURED PATRICIA OXTON. "It's like a catalytic agent: it expedites reactions."

"Don't try to be epigrammatic about it," said Ruth Kenton, and John Dunne put in:

"It's only a hypothetical murder at present: it doesn't become an official murder until the Coroner's jury has given its verdict, and I'll lay my last bonus on the probability that they'll say accidental death; but would you like to explain what you mean by a catalytic agent, or were you just experimenting with words, like you do with handwritings?"

The three junior members of the Architects' Branch were having their lunch together in the Ministry canteen. Normally speaking they did not sit at the same table, they found it better to separate and avoid talking shop, but to-day they had congregated by tacit consent, and it was this fact that had evoked Patricia Oxton's remark. She replied to Dunne:

"We're crystallising into groups in this canteen. The Architects are sitting together, Loans Collection is sitting together, Museums are sitting together. It's as though an external agent had made us all branch conscious. Perhaps it's a sort of herd instinct, flocking in face of danger."

"No, it isn't that," said Ruth Kenton. "It's the urge to talk. Typists talk anyway, but people who claim professional status have to try to behave as though they are above such human weaknesses as gossiping. We three have been working solemnly all the morning, when we were really all panting to exchange views. And of course it's much more satisfactory to exchange views with people you know, who're not likely to misunderstand you."

"I agree about the urge to talk," said Dunne. "It's because people want to talk that so many of them have gone out to lunch elsewhere, where they can gossip their heads off without fear of being eaves-dropped: that's why this place isn't so full as usual and there's been a choice of tables. What are you two eating? I'm for boiled ham and pease pudding: I need something sustaining."

"I'll have ham, too," said Patricia. "I believe ham is regarded as a suitable dish after a funeral. Funerals seem to make people hungry. Exhaustion following emotion, perhaps."

"I don't feel any emotion," said Ruth Kenton. "I'm very ashamed of the fact, but it's true. Mr. Pompfret was once just somebody I passed on the stairs, never knowing whether I ought to stand at attention because he was a Deputy Permanent Secretary. Now he's become a sort of piece in a problem."

"That's what he's become to everybody," said Dunne. "After all, he wasn't a chap who inspired devotion, not even the most sentimental typist can screw out a tear, and they wept in floods over Corny—the late Right Honourable Alf. Anyway, I'm interested in problems, and I've been picking up all the ideas about how it happened. Everybody thinks he did it himself and got copped being too clever."

"How could he have moved it?" asked Patricia Oxton. "The base of that bust was over two and a half feet across and the shoulders about the same and it was over twelve inches deep from front to back: concrete weighs 125 lb. a cubic foot and marble is heavier. I make it that the shoulders and chest alone must have weighed between three and four hundredweight without that monstrous head and curls and laurel leaves. He could never have moved it."

"Not with his own fair hands," agreed Dunne, "but one or two of the packers have thought out some very cunning ideas. Bill Carter said if he'd been challenged to shift it he knew how he'd have done it."

"How?" demanded Patricia.

"By fitting one of those small motor jacks between the wall and the shoulders or neck and working it horizontally instead of vertically. A jack that can raise a car would be strong enough to shove a few hundredweights outwards."

"The jack's quite an idea," said Ruth Kenton, "besides which, Pompfret had got one of those small jacks in his car. He used to park his car by the air-raid shelter, and I've seen him get one of the housemen to change a wheel for him."

"The idea may be a good one, but there wasn't a jack on the landing," said Patricia Oxton. "There wasn't anything. All the housemen know that."

"I know, but Carter's got an idea to cover that. If Pompfret *did* do it, he'd have made careful plans to get out of the way before the night watchman came up from the cellars, and he'd have been particularly careful not to have any of his own tools left in evidence. Carter suggested that the bust could have been jacked forward until it was only just stable, half of it off the plinth, and then the jack was removed and concealed, because a good shove from behind would have sent Manderby toppling. Only Pompfret didn't realise he'd got the centre of gravity too far forward, and when he came back to give the final shove, Manderby obliged too soon and came crashing forward on his own."

"Bert—you know, the porter—" put in Ruth Kenton, "he said that Titmarsh, the night watchman, was smashing up coal down in the cellars, and there would have been a lot of vibration."

"What, in this place?" said Patricia Oxton.

"Well, there were one or two near misses in the blitz and you never seem to get to the end of what blast does to a place," said Ruth Kenton. "You know as well as I do that some houses are still springing cracks and masonry's coming down in some places and the reason is that foundations or walls got shifted during the blitz and it's gone on deteriorating until something went."

"Yes, this house got a packet round it," said Dunne. "That's rather an idea. I wonder if they surveyed the vaulting down in the cellars. If Titmarsh was using a coal hammer and Pompfret was busy with a jack they might have set something going. D'you think the C.I.D. would let us go round with a spirit level and plumb lines?"

"Look here, I think the jack idea is pretty smart," said Patricia Oxton, "but I do not believe, and I will not believe, that Pompfret was the sort of irresponsible maniac you're making him out to be. We all know he loathed Manderby, and he was livid when he tumbled to it that the typists called both him and Manderby Pompey. I admit all that, but I can't swallow the idea that Pompfret worked out a scheme to destroy the Canova thing. It's true that he took to dressing like a Bloomsbury æsthete, but he was a high-up Civil Servant. There's no type in the world which is more averse to wild cat tricks: circumspection's as much in their bones as circumlocution is."

"That's rather well put," said Dunne, "but some chaps do alter as they grow older. There's such a thing as 'getting religion.' I maintain there's a similar variation from the norm when a man 'gets art.' You know Weston, in the Loans asylum: he saw a bit of Pompfret. Weston says that Pompfret took to art as some chaps take to religion, and that it went to his head."

They were all leaning forward over the table, voices lowered, glancing round occasionally to make sure they weren't overheard, for all the canteen waitresses were agog to pick up any gossip. Ruth Kenton said:

"You're just saying he went crackers. I know it can happen, even to the most stable and academic of mankind. The psychologists say it's due to some conflict in the subconscious. Perhaps his ego suffered a jolt when his wife walked out on him and he had to compensate by developing an addiction to the arts."

"Took to contemporary painting as other men take to alcohol," murmured Dunne, but Patricia Oxton put in:

"I should think that's rotten psychology, because according to all accounts his art addiction was only superficial. But I didn't know his wife left him. Were they divorced?"

"No. Just separated," said Ruth Kenton. "I once saw her at the Modern Arts Centre. It was when they had that exhibition of East Africa native art—soapstone carvings and such-like. I took old Rosie Burke—she'd been personal typist to Pompey for donkey's years, and when he came here, she came too, and she wanted to learn about 'Art,' poor old trout, and somebody wished her on to me. Anyway, Rosie knew Mrs. Pompfret—I believe she was asked to their wedding as old Faithful—and both Pompey and Mrs. P. happened to synchronise at the M.A.C. show and Rosie was frightfully upset because it was after they'd separated, and she didn't think it was quite nice. I took her into the members' room and gave her coffee—"

"Who? Mrs. P.?" demanded Dunne.

"No, you idiot, Rosie. She was all of aflutter and sort of poured it all out to me. I was frightfully interested, but unfortunately Welles came in, and he gave us a very dirty look. I think he overheard a few words and didn't approve. Anyway, he handed me a raspberry next day about not gossiping to the typists."

"I say, you're frightfully well informed," said Dunne. "What's Mrs. P. like?"

"Oh, very advanced. Contemporary art writ large all over her. She's been a howling success as lookers go, but a bit sere and yellow now. She's one of the red-headed sirens—real red, not henna, and good at that. But I should think she'd have been hell to live with, so perhaps poor old Pompey was well quit of her."

"Aren't we being loathsome?" said Patricia Oxton. "Just because Pompfret's been killed, we're all chewing over his private life. We'd never have gossiped like this when he was alive."

"Look here, it's no use going high-minded over it," said Dunne indignantly. "Being killed makes a chap interesting. Human nature's like that. While he was alive, Pompey wasn't interesting. He was just a Civil Servant plus a pompous manner. Now he's perished from a surfeit of Manderby he's become very interesting. And you were listening just as hard as I was, anyway."

"Oh, I know I was. I'm panting to hear more: that's why I said we were being loathsome."

"Well, I think you've got it all wrong," said Ruth Kenton. "I wasn't interested in Pompfret, but I was very interested in seeing his wife. I can't think how they ever risked getting joined in holy matrimony. He was a static bore, while she has a sort of dynamic quality."

"Oh lor!" groaned Dunne. "I don't like the sound of that, much. Novelette-ish, in the dated sense of the word. Anyway, she couldn't possibly have shifted Manderby. Oh, look, there's Weston. Let's see if he's got any beans to spill. The C.I.D.'s been concentrating on Loans."

Dunne got up and stopped Weston, who was making for the door, saying: "Come and have coffee with us."

"Well, I've got a foul cold, so you've been warned," said Weston. "I'm going home early. Do any of you know any infallible cold remedies?"

"Such a thing doesn't exist," said Patricia. "All you can do is to stay in bed until it's better and take aspirin at intervals to make you feel less foul."

"Get someone to rub your chest," suggested Ruth.

"Not on your life. My landlady came and rubbed it last night and she's got hands like hoofs," groaned Weston. "She nearly skinned me and then wanted to apply a mustard plaster afterwards. Talk about a remedy being worse than the disease, don't I know it!"

The waitress came and served their coffee, and then Weston turned to Dunne. "I know what you button-holed me for—to hear about the Grand Inquisitor. Sorry I can't oblige. We're being asked not to recap. But he's a very nice sort of chap: name of Rivers. Chief Inspector. Not in the least what I'd imagined a C.I.D. officer could be like."

"He was in the Navy once," put in Ruth Fenton.

"How do you know?" demanded Dunne.

"Because they have architects at Scotland Yard. Rather funny to think of. I suppose somebody's got to design police stations and prisons. Anyway, John Melbourne worked there for a bit, and he told me about Rivers. Why is it the Navy produces more likeable people than the Civil Service? Nobody would ever say 'He was once a Civil Servant' if they wanted to imply he was rather glamorous."

"Oh, can that!" said Dunne, and then turned to Weston. "Are you allowed to answer this one—do the C.I.D. think Pompfret was murdered?"

"Yes. They say he couldn't have shifted that weight himself. I didn't repeat anything I'd heard, but I rather think Rivers will waffle round picking up projects, so you'd better make up your minds if you're going to tell him some of the dotty ideas which are floating around."

"I think it's up to everybody to tell him their own ideas themselves," said Patricia, and Dunne put in:

"Look here, Weston. What do you think yourself? After all, you can pass on your own ideas. Do you think Pompfret was murdered, or that he was killed by accident?"

Weston was silent for some seconds, his sensitive face troubled: then he said, "If it was impossible for him to have moved that weight himself, I suppose one's got to admit that he was murdered: but I don't see how anybody else could have moved it, either."

"Well, it was shifted all right, wasn't it?" said Dunne, "and I'm more prepared to believe he moved it himself than that anybody else did. Weston, you saw more of Pompfret than we ever did. What sort of chap was he? Do you think it's possible he went odd in the upper storey? If he did, he might have got a thing about Manderby. You see, Pompfret had begun to think he was important, hadn't he? The way he dressed, and his pompous manner, indicated a sort of dramatisation of himself."

"I think there's something in that," said Weston slowly. "I suppose he altered a lot after he came to this Ministry. When he was at the Ministry of Supply he seems to have been true to type—the administrative type—with just a few frills of picturesqueness because he'd taken to studying modern art. But it wasn't until he came here that he blossomed out into corduroy jackets and coloured shirts and suède shoes and an almighty manner."

"And you've got to remember that he'd got married shortly before he came here," put in Ruth Fenton, "and that his wife was one of these advanced art addicts. She probably influenced him and encouraged him to be picturesque, so that she shouldn't get ragged by her own gang because she'd married a Civil Servant."

"Look here, I think we're getting beyond the limit," put in Pat Oxton indignantly. "I admit that we're bound to puzzle over what happened. It was such an utterly improbable and melodramatic thing to happen, but we're going beyond the bounds of decency when we try to bring his married life into it, and then suggest that Pompfret was weak in the head."

"I quite agree with Miss Oxton," said Weston promptly. "We've got to draw the line somewhere. I think I'd put it like this. I believe that Pompfret did shift that bust himself. Any other suggestion seems so madly improbable. The preparations would have had to be too elaborate. If anybody had wanted to murder him they could have done it with the usual blunt instrument without going to all that trouble. And if Pompfret *did* do it himself, well, his mind must have been a bit deranged, because it was a crazy thing to do."

He broke off suddenly, and Dunne looked up a bit guiltily when he saw Robert Welles, the head of the Architects' department, advancing towards them.

Welles spoke acidly: "When you have quite finished your lunch, I should like to go over your figures for that extension to the Stockpool gallery, Dunne. Your estimate's based on out-of-date prices. Weston, you're broadcasting that filthy cold bug you've got. Pack up and go home to bed."

"I'm just going," said Weston hastily.

Welles went on out of the canteen and Dunne hastily signalled to the waitress for bills, as Weston got up with a grin and a brief "Good-bye."

Ruth Kenton calmly lighted another cigarette and said to Pat:

"Don't go yet. That was a tick-off and I'm not prepared to be ticked-off for sitting over lunch. Provided we put in the specified time, which we always do, our working hours are our own business. And it's not to be expected we shan't discuss an event like Pompfret's death. Our Arthur occasionally likes to treat us as children." (Welles was nicknamed Arthur.)

Ruth held out her cigarette case to Pat, and the latter took a cigarette, though she very seldom smoked. Ruth said:

"What do you really think about the ghastly business, Pat?"

"Just what everyone else is thinking. I'd like to believe that Pompfret pulled that Canova monstrosity down himself. I don't want to believe that someone in this place planned to murder him."

"It needn't have been someone in this place."

"Oh yes, it must," said Pat. "I know what you're going to say—somebody from outside could have walked in perfectly easily and hidden themselves. That's true, but whoever did this knew the building and the routine of the building. They knew the night watchman did the stoking when he came on duty, they knew where the fuse box was, they knew that Pompfret hated that Canova bust." She paused for a moment and then went on: "You said a little while ago that Pompfret was just somebody you passed on the stairs. Do you remember the way he always came downstairs?"

"Yes. I thought of it as soon as I heard what happened. He always went up or down in the centre of the stairs, quite deliberately. It was the same if you passed him in the corridors. He walked in the centre and saw to it that other people made way for him. It was a sort of pose."

"Deliberately is the right word," said Pat slowly. "It was partly that affectation of deliberation that made him seem so pompous. He'd walk to the head of the staircase and pause at the top, right in the centre, and then walk down looking important, so that people always made way for him. It had become a habit. That's another thing that 'they' knew—the person who killed him. If they could only think out a way of shifting Manderby as Pompfret went downstairs, then Pompfret would have been hit by Manderby."

"But wouldn't Pompfret have spotted that the bust had been moved forward? After all, barring an explosion, it couldn't have been done all in a second or so."

"Wasn't he very short-sighted?"

"Good lord, yes, so he was. I've seen him going right up to a picture to stare at it. Perhaps that's the answer, Pat. Someone counted on him being so short-sighted that it was a safe bet he'd never notice if Manderby had been jacked forward."

"The pilot light in the hall was out," said Pat slowly. "He'd have had the light on in the corridor that led to his room. When he got to the main landing he'd have realised that the pilot light in the hall wasn't on, so he probably left the corridor light burning and walked on to the top of the stairway. Don't you think he'd have stood there for a moment, and probably thought 'What the hell have they turned the light out for?' while he fumbled for matches, or a lighter. Did he smoke, by the way?"

"I've no idea. I've never seen him smoking," said Ruth, and then hurried on: "But Pat, the corridor lights are good ones. The light would have shone right across that main landing. If there had been anybody standing by the Canova, wouldn't Pompfret have seen them?"

"I don't know. They might have been in the shadow. But perhaps there wasn't anybody there, not on the landing."

Ruth Kenton stared: "You mean... Oh, goodness, you've got me utterly muddled. You've said you don't believe Pompfret did it himself."

"I'm certain he didn't. He was too stereotyped in mind, in spite of the corduroy jackets and gaudy ties. Don't you ever remember learning that formula 'to obtain a greater ratio of resistance to effort' etc., etc., etcetera..."

"Good lord!" Ruth gave a gasp, and then sat with her chin on her hands, pondering deeply. At last she said: "It's no use pretending I don't see what you mean. Once it's occurred to you, it's so obvious. But... need you tell them?"

"Not if they don't ask the operative question. But they're bound to think of it. I don't believe in the idea that policemen are fools. The C.I.D. aren't fools, far from it, and this man Rivers is bound to see it. It's inevitable."

"Why? Oh, lord, yes. I suppose he is. And there's the Minister. Do you remember…?"

"Yes," said Pat. "I do. But Rivers will see it first."

Ruth stubbed out her cigarette. "Let's get back to our damned projects," she said. "I feel a bit sick."

"And I feel a good deal sicker," said Pat slowly.

CHAPTER XI

RIVERS AND LANCING HAD THEIR LUNCH SENT IN TO THE SMALL waiting-room they had adopted as an office. (It was a very small room and had once been a servery to the family dining-room.) Rivers read some reports as he ate, and Lancing studied the lists he had been compiling.

"Good old routine, always pays a dividend," said Rivers softly and Lancing cocked an eye at him.

"List of items found on deceased's person," went on Rivers. "All the usual, nothing unexpected. It appears that he was a non-smoker, which is relevant, and that he hadn't a good digestion, which may not be relevant. He wore glasses for reading: most men of his age do. They were in his pocket. He had no glasses on when he was killed. Not wishing to ask too many leading questions, I did not ask any of our witnesses whether the late Deputy Permanent Secretary was in the habit of wearing glasses when he walked about the building and so forth."

"Not even the Minister?" queried Lancing.

"Certainly not the Minister," said Rivers firmly. "You can ask me about that later on. No. I sent Mr. Pompfret's reading glasses to the firm of opticians who had had the honour of supplying them and asked for a report on the state of his eyes. Leaving out all the lovely terminology, Pompfret was what blokes like you and me would have called as blind as a bat. He was as short-sighted as say-so and he always wore glasses. He was so short-sighted that he probably needed to feel for his glasses when he woke up, because he couldn't see the case on his own bedside table."

"Didn't he have bi-focals?" asked Lancing.

"No. He refused to have them. He tried them once and fell down-stairs. Some people find it difficult to adapt themselves to bi-focals."

"All right—but he seems to have been a silly sort of chap," said Lancing reflectively. "He used two pairs of glasses, one for reading, one for getting around, and without the latter he was desperately short-sighted. The point is—what happened when he changed from one pair to the other?"

"That's it," said Rivers. "Most men put the ones they're not using in their pockets. My guess is that Pompfret kept his distance glasses on his desk when he was working in his office here. He wouldn't have been likely to forget to put them on before he got up or moved around because he was too myopic to be comfortable without them. And since he wasn't wearing glasses when his body was found, it's to be assumed that someone had taken his glasses away. If he'd broken them or lost them during the day, we would have been told about it."

Lancing nodded. "That's one of the clearest pointers we've had," he said. "No man who is as short-sighted as that would walk about without his glasses unless he'd lost them, or they were smashed. Your idea that he habitually put his glasses on his desk seems quite a likely one to me: he probably changed from reading to distance glasses when he had visitors, and found it more convenient to lay the alternative pair on his desk rather than put the case in his pocket."

"Could be," pondered Rivers, "in which case we can assume that he had not got a visitor in his office immediately before he walked on to the landing. Now what can we assume from the evidence we've got so far? First, that he wasn't going straight home when he went on to the landing, because he hadn't got his hat and coat on. Next, that when he looked for his distance glasses he couldn't find them. I don't think he rushed out of his office because of some sudden emergency, such as a call for help from the landing, because he'd put his reading glasses in their case and put them in his pocket. That indicates, as the tidy desk indicates, that he'd finished work for the night and was preparing to go home."

Lancing spoke again here: "Accepting the hypotheses we've made so far, how would this idea work: some time during the course of the evening, somebody went to Pomfret's office to speak to him. It wasn't anybody important, or anybody Pompfret wanted to talk to, so he didn't bother to change his glasses. He just said something like 'All right. Put it down. I'm busy and can't discuss it now,' and the visitor put something down on the desk and picked up the distance glasses without Pompfret noticing."

"Well, as a theory it doesn't collide with any of the facts we've got," said Rivers. "It has probability, in that it suggests that the visitor was someone known to Pompfret and somebody on whom he didn't have to waste time. The next most likely move, to my mind, is that Pompfret went to the cloakroom to get his hat and coat and also to make sure he hadn't left his glasses in his brief-case—if you can't find a thing in the place where it ought to be, you're driven to look for it in the place where it ought not to be. When he opened the door of his room he heard a call, or a groan, and went along to the landing to see what it was. The pilot light was out, and he stood for a moment, feeling addled, because he couldn't see a thing."

"And look here, sir," put in Lancing. "We've argued that the murder was carefully timed: it'd got to be done while Titmarsh was stoking, so the operator wanted to be sure that Pompfret would come on to the landing during that time. That suggests a definite appointment to get him where he was wanted at the time he was wanted."

"Quite a point," agreed Rivers, "so delete 'possible groan or call' as suggested, and replace by official chit: 'The Minister can see Mr. Pompfret in his study at 10.30 this evening.'"

Lancing whistled. "That's a bit near the ham bone, sir."

"All right. For 'official chit' read 'chit purporting to be official, marked confidential: please burn.' As an idea it fits the known facts. Further item of information for you: Pompfret hadn't lowered enough whisky to make him drunk. Just a comfortable tot—enough to give him confidence in himself."

Rivers finished the last mouthful of Vienna steak he had been consuming in the intervals of the discussion, and said: "Well, we've produced some ideas and now we'd better get on with the job and see if we can get any corroboration of them. I'll tackle the office staff about Pompfret's habits with his glasses. Also find out if I'm right in believing I've spotted how the booby-trap was worked."

"Oh hell!" exclaimed Lancing indignantly, and then added hurriedly: "Sorry, sir, but I'm still groping in a maze of motor jacks, steel wedges and mallets, and levers padded at the end to ensure no marks on fabric of building. Don't tell me. I swear I'll tumble to it in the end."

"If you don't, you deserve to be demoted," said Rivers unkindly. "When we first tackled the job last night we hadn't the data which suggested the means, inasmuch as we didn't know the records or attainments of the very odd collection of individuals in this building. You have been working like a beaver at personnel records, and you've known me for quite a while. So I'll leave you to co-ordinate private information with official fact, adding the use of your eyesight, which is quite as good as my own. Here's luck, and good-bye for now."

II

Rivers went up to Pompfret's office and removed every single object from the writing-table, concealing everything in such a way that anybody entering the room would not see the things he had removed. Then he sent for Miss Ellis, Pompfret's personal typist, who had replaced old Rosie Burke when the latter retired from the Civil Service some twelve months previously. Miss Ellis was a sensible-looking girl, neat, trim and business-like, but by no means one of the lovelies. She came in with pad and pencil saying "Yes, sir?" in a most official voice.

"I don't want to dictate," said Rivers. "I want you to sit down in your usual place and tell me exactly what objects were habitually on this writing-table when Mr. Pompfret dictated to you."

"Very good, sir," replied the unemotional Miss Ellis, and set about her task with the precision of an auctioneer's clerk reading through an inventory. Miss Ellis obviously possessed a visual memory. She described blotter, pen-tray, ink-pot, pens and pencils, in-tray, out-tray, telephone, mucilage, clips, pins, elastic bands and their containers with great accuracy. She finally said: "And a scarlet spectacle case. It was always just in front of the blotter and a little to the right, here. Mr. Pompfret was short-sighted and he changed his spectacles if he wanted to see across the room. It's a big room, isn't it?"

"It is, a very big room," agreed Rivers. Then he leant forward and dropped his voice. "Was Mr. Pompfret deaf?" he inquired.

"Not in the least," she replied.

"He didn't use a deaf-aid?" persisted Rivers.

"No. I'm quite sure he didn't. At least…" Her conscientious mind struggled for accuracy. "Not unless he had an invisible one," she said, and then, for the first time, forgot her precision and spoke as a rather agitated young woman does speak: "Why, he couldn't have; it's silly. My grandmother has a deaf-aid, and granddad too, and they get so mad with all those wires and gadgets." She flushed as she broke off and resumed primly: "I'm sorry, sir. I'm certain Mr. Pompfret wasn't deaf. Quite the reverse. He was almost too keen of hearing and complained if there was ever a noise outside in the corridor."

"Thanks very much. You've been most helpful," said Rivers.

Miss Ellis went out without attempting to ask any of the usual questions—she was evidently a very well-disciplined young woman—and Rivers chuckled to himself a little. His question about deafness had only been put to distract Miss Ellis's attention from the real focus of his inquiry. Rivers did not want her to connect Pompfret's glasses with the matter in hand, and he was pretty sure that his query about a deaf-aid would exclude any thought of his real target.

Leaving Pompfret's room, after another glance at the Abstract over the mantelpiece, Rivers went up to the Architects' Branch and knocked on the door where the junior practitioners were housed. Two girls were sitting at their drawing-boards, and two serious pairs of eyes looked up at him.

"I'm sorry to interrupt your work," he said. "Miss Oxton, isn't it, and Miss Kenton? My name is Rivers. I asked the Minister to recommend me a guide to the intricacies of this building: in the absence of the Surveyor, he commended me to you. Would one of you take the job on?"

"Yes, of course. I'll take you anywhere you like," said Patricia Oxton. "I think I know the building as well as anybody does."

Her voice was calm and matter of fact, and she put her tools together carefully and methodically as Ruth said:

"Yes. You really know it better than I do, Pat, because you went round with the Surveyor. Would you like me to finish colouring up that drawing you're working on, so that you're not held up?"

"No. It's all right. I can do it afterwards," replied Patricia evenly.
She turned to Rivers: "Where would you like to start, and is there
anything particular you want to see?" Her voice was quiet and steady,
but Rivers was aware of tension underlying the studied quietness
of both girls: it was as though they were waiting for something to
happen.

"I want to get an idea of possible exits and entrances, apart from
the recognised ones," he replied. "I know there are fire escapes: there
are also, doubtless, manholes to give access to the roofs, as well as
hatches for delivery of goods in the cellars. Could we start with a
glance at the roof?"

"Of course. There's a fixed ladder in our Plans room. Shall I go
on ahead?"

She led him out of the room and along the passage where the
Minister had once turned in the wrong direction, and Rivers asked:

"Is it a flat roof?"

"No, not for the greater part. There's a flat leaded section in the
centre, around the low glass dome, but apart from that the roofs
slope down to the parapet. It's only a slight slope, but it simplified
draining and guttering. This is the Plans room—we keep some of
our drawings on screens here, for easy reference. The ladder's against
the wall there. I'll go up first, I know the trap-door."

"Does the trap-door give direct on to the roof?"

"No: it takes you to the lofts below the sloping leads: they're
very low, you'll need to be careful of your head. There's another
trap-door which takes you out on to the roof."

She went up the ladder, opened the trap-door and went through it
with complete assurance, and Rivers heard her unbolting the further
trap-door. When he went up, he found himself in a low loft which
stretched away into the darkness on either side, a seemingly interminable distance. The floor consisted of beams spaced at intervals

on which you could walk, bent nearly double: above were the spars and battens of the sloping roof. There was sufficient height to stand erect under the further trap-door, because the roof rose to meet one of the chimney breasts.

"This is interesting," said Rivers. "Can you get right round the building by way of the lofts?"

"You can—but it'd be a pretty grim scramble and a very dirty one."

"But I suppose the electricians had to work up here when they wired the top floor?"

"Yes. You can see the conduit pipes, and the cisterns are up here. It's quite possible to get round, but not very pleasant."

"I suppose architects always arranged so that workmen could get access to the upper surface of the ceilings, to get at pendant fixtures and so forth?"

"I don't know about always. It was done here. In vaulted Gothic buildings you can generally get access to the space above the vaulting and below the pent roof. We call it the extrados—the upper surface of the vaulting. You get rather a good view outside here."

Rivers got up through the second trap-door and stood beside Pat, gazing across to the Green Park and St. James's Park, with a glimpse of the Thames beyond the towers of Westminster.

"That's a grand view," he said.

They were standing on a level strip where the roof met the parapet which concealed the sloping slates from ground level. Rivers said: "Are there other trap-doors, and if so, can you get round from one to the other?"

"Yes, to both questions," she said. "There's always likely to be repair work on a roof, particularly pointing the chimneys and seeing to the lead flashing on the chimney breasts. You often get a roof leaking where the slates join the chimneys. I think Decimus Burton was a very sensible architect. He remembered that gutters have to be cleared and chimneys inspected and slates replaced, and he made it possible for builders to get up here without using long ladders or putting up scaffolding every time they wanted to inspect the roofs."

"I think that's quite a point," said Rivers. "Do you admire Medici House?"

"As a building, not as a Ministry," she said. "I think they'd have done better to use the house to display pictures and craftsmanship—the furniture and glass and silver and china of the late eighteenth and early nineteenth century—and they could have had chamber music in the music room and full-dress receptions in the ballroom and a specialised library, and made it seem worth while. It's a pity the country's so poor. All the pleasanter ideas are guillotined by the Treasury."

"Well, there's your Small Towns Gallery Project," put in Rivers, and she laughed.

"Who told you about that?"

"Oh, I'm learning quite a lot," he replied. "I've been concentrating on the Loans Collection. Isn't that one of the pleasanter ideas?"

"It was," she said soberly. "The idea was all right, but it was strangled at birth. Do you want to walk round the roof or not? It's cold up here."

"Sorry," said Rivers. "No, I needn't go right round now: I've got the idea. Could you tell me where the other trap-doors lead to?"

"Yes. I can show you that from inside. They're all locked from inside, anyway, so we couldn't go down by a different route."

III

From the roofs they eventually worked their way down to the vaulted cellars. Patricia Oxton was a very good guide, and Rivers learnt quite a lot about building and construction work. The vaulted cellars fascinated him. Using a torch, because the electric wiring did not go all the way, he saw the old wine racks and even some tremendous barrels and tuns which had once held the pipes and hogsheads of wine essential to Regency nobility.

"That explains Manderby's countenance," Rivers said to Pat, and she gave a cry of expostulation.

"Must you? I'd managed to forget Manderby."

"Sorry, but I can't afford to forget him," he replied. "How did they get those barrels down here?"

"There's a hatch and there was a ramp. Look, there's the hatch. All comfortably cob-webbed over."

"Yes, but the hatches they used for the coal aren't cob-webbed over," said Rivers. "What it amounts to is this: anybody who knew this building had a choice of half a dozen exits, apart from the doors. They could have played hide and seek indefinitely in the lofts, with a choice of ways down to the four different corners of the building, and they could have got out of these hatches without bothering about doors. Or they could have stayed up in the lofts until morning and then joined the throng when everyone turned up. One person who has specialised knowledge of this building could defeat an army of searchers. As you've probably realised for yourself, specialised knowledge is the answer—in more senses than one."

"Any intelligent person could find their way about this building, provided they had the time to study it," said Pat. "It isn't like one of those ancient buildings that have been added to again and again in the course of centuries. This is a rational building, designed by one man who was an expert planner as well as a good architect."

"Yes. I see your point, but it would take me a long time to get a clear idea of the planning, especially in the old service staircases and the smaller corridors upstairs," replied Rivers. "How much did Mr. Pompfret know about the building?"

"I've not the least idea," retorted Pat. "I knew nothing about him. You see, we're very departmental here and architects aren't thought highly of by permanent Civil Servants. We're only temporary and attached and liable to be axed any moment. Have you seen all you want to see in these cellars?"

"No, but I can come back now you've shown me my way about," said Rivers. "I'm most grateful to you: you've been an admirable guide and I shall tell the Minister so. If ever you're axed, let me know and I'll get you a job in our establishment."

"Thanks very much, but I'm thinking of going to Australia if the worst happens. I'm told they welcome architects there—but don't tell the Minister so. Don't you think we're very fortunate in our Minister?"

"I do, indeed. Does he show an interest in your department?"

They had got back to the steps by the central heating furnace, and as she went up Pat said: "He takes an interest in everything. He even came into our department and looked at our plans and talked most sympathetically about them. That's an unheard of thing for a Minister to do. Mr. Pompfret wouldn't have dreamt of coming up to our garrets. If he'd wanted any first-hand information, our chief would have gone down to him. You see a Deputy Permanent Secretary belongs to the hierarchy."

Rivers paused on the top step, "Look here, Miss Oxton: you're a very intelligent person. I wish you'd answer one plain question. Was Mr. Pompfret generally disliked here?"

"I can't answer it, because I haven't the knowledge to do so. I can only give you an opinion. I don't think he was generally disliked, because of his nickname. 'Pompey' indicates that he was laughed at a bit, but not disliked. It was the typists who called him Pompey.

Most of them had no idea that he was quite a distinguished person in his own way. He'd been an able scholar—but that didn't matter to the typists. All they noticed was his pompous manner and stylised wording in dictating letters. He was very precious in a pedantic sort of way, I believe. But to us, as Ruth Kenton said, he was just someone we occasionally saw on the stairs. Not someone we spoke to, or who would speak to us."

"Thanks very much for a very sensible answer. I agree with you that a nickname generally denotes toleration And thanks again for all you've taught me about the building."

CHAPTER XII

I

"COME IN, DANVERS, AND SIT DOWN." THE MINISTER'S QUIET voice sounded very much as usual, save that it lacked its usual undertone of humour, but Michael Danvers guessed at once what was coming.

"You went to see Mrs. Edwin Pompfret last night after having told the Chief Inspector you did not know her address," went on Humphry David. "In view of what happened here last night, and of the police investigation which is now going on, I think I must ask for an explanation of your behaviour, Danvers."

"Yes, sir," said Danvers. "I suppose I was a fool. I don't know. The more I think it over the more difficult I find it to know whether what I did was right or wrong from the point of view of friendship. I'm not suggesting it was correct from the official point of view and certainly it was not dictated by self-interest. I'd been to the Highland Ball, and got home some time after three to find a phone message waiting for me with the news of Pompfret's death. It said he'd fallen downstairs here and they wanted to know about his next of kin. I came along here at once, under the impression that Pompfret's death was accidental. Chief Inspector Rivers let me see pretty quickly that he didn't regard it as accidental death, and that it might be due to murder."

Danvers broke off for a moment, as though to put his thoughts into order. "I don't know quite how to put it, sir, but it was a shock, in the way the totally unexpected is a shock. I know Pompfret's wife. She's a friend of mine—a friend and no more. I hope you'll believe that, because I don't think Rivers does."

"I will accept your word," said the Minister quietly.

"Thank you, sir. I knew that she had been living apart from her husband for some years, earning her own living, and that she's had a tough time. Incidentally, I had only learned recently that she was Pompfret's wife. Well, when I saw the trend of Rivers' mind, of course the first person I thought of was Virgilia Hill. I don't know what your reaction would have been, but I was horrified. The whole thing suddenly became a nightmare. I knew what Rivers was bound to think—the obvious thing. When he asked me if Pompfret were a bachelor, I tried to put him off. But it wasn't any good." Again Danvers paused. Then he said: "Look here, sir. I told Rivers I was a man as well as a Civil Servant. I hope you don't think I'm lacking in respect when I say that at the present moment I'm thinking of you as a man and not as a Minister, though I do respect you sincerely as a Minister."

"Believe me, I am listening to you as a human being, without any reference to other authority," said Humphry David, "but you must grant me the added experience which age implies. You are telling me that you were in a quandary: one of the most terrible quandaries a man can face, between personal loyalty and civic responsibility. Don't think I'm minimising your personal problem."

"Perhaps I fell down over it, sir. I don't know. I think I'd do the same thing again. Could I have said to Rivers: 'Yes, I know more or less where she lives, or at any rate I can take you there, and then you can jump the facts on her and deal with it in your own way'? The departmental slogan—'passed to you, please.' I don't know if you could have done it. I only know I couldn't. I had to find out for myself, and then—think. I hadn't time to think while I was with

Rivers." He gave a wry smile. "If I'd thought at all, I should have realised he'd do exactly what he did do—have me followed. Not that it mattered, because I did what I wanted to do. I found out if she knew anything about Pompfret's death. She didn't. I'm quite sure of that."

"Look here, Danvers," said Humphry David. "I can only tell you just what is in my mind—my personal response to your statement. You have said that there was nothing but friendship between you and Mrs. Pompfret, or Miss Hill, if you prefer to call her that. I have accepted your statement. But it seems obvious to me that your mind was activated by fear: the fear that she might have been concerned in her husband's death. Why did that fear possess your mind? Wasn't it because you knew she was associated with another man, and that that man was a friend of your own? In short, your fear was partly for him, not only for her?"

Michael Danvers sat very still for a moment or so before replying. Then he said: "Yes, sir. That's true to some extent. But it's also true that when you hear about the murder of someone you know, your judgment goes haywire a bit. The fact of a murder is so grim, so irrevocable, that something inside you panics and you postulate improbable things as a reaction to an improbable situation. If I'd sat down and thought things out, I should have realised that I was panicking, and there was no ground at all for the fear which leapt at me."

"I'll grant your main premise—that the shock of hearing about a murder can undermine your judgment, as any other shock can do," said Humphry David slowly, "but in this case you had a basis for your fear. I needn't enlarge on that because it is obvious. But there's one question that I am bound to ask, and which I think you should answer, however much it seems to go against the grain. A friend of your own is associated with Mrs. Pompfret. Is that friend employed in this building in any capacity whatever?"

"Good heavens, no!" There was relief in Michael Danvers' voice, and it was the vigour of that relief which made the Minister believe him at once.

"He's never been inside the place. He regards us as a red-tape machine," went on Danvers. "He and I were P.O.W.s together in Stalagluft Y. We haven't a great deal in common, perhaps, but we were mates in one of the biggest tunnel schemes ever attempted. We were copped on the last lap—but an experience like that gives you a feeling that endures, somehow. It was because he went about with Virgilia Hill that I met her."

"Yes. I see. I'm glad you told me that, Danvers. You asked me earlier on to believe you. I hope you'll believe me when I say that I'm not likely to forget that when you young chaps were digging tunnels I was sitting in a different sort of dug-out—in Whitehall, writing memoranda."

"That's all right, sir. I wasn't asking for preferential treatment on account of the tunnel, you know. It just happened to come out in the course of conversation. In any case, I think I'd rather have had my tunnel than yours, meaning no disrespect."

"Yes, I know," said David. "Well, I've got to go on, so here's the next question. You say your fellow tunneller is not a Civil Servant and that he has never been inside this building. What is his occupation?"

"He calls himself a jack of all trades and master of none. He's interested in the theatre and designs what he calls 'décor.' He writes a bit, topical verse, low brow and bitter. He paints murals, prefer-ably in pubs, and plays a flute, sometimes in an orchestra, more often in a pub. In short, he's the absolute opposite of the types in this establishment." Again Danvers broke off: then he said slowly: "The war, and being a prisoner, did something to the chaps who had imaginations. It didn't affect me, because I haven't got any imagination. That's why I'm here. I had the knack of passing exams and this is where that knack led me, but I don't think I'm the salt of the earth because I've landed a safe job and found it within my capacity."

"I'm not prepared to argue that point," said the Minister dryly, "but I've got to go on with this problem. It's either a case of me asking you questions, or of the C.I.D., and with every respect to Rivers, whom I find a very likeable person as well as an outstandingly able officer, it may be less painful if you and I try to get certain points cleared up."

"Very good, sir," said Danvers. "I will answer your questions as far as I can. If you reach a point where I can't answer, I can only say, as I said to Rivers, that I'm prepared to take the consequences."

"Can you tell me if Miss Hill is a painter?"

"I don't know. She may be. The only occupation she has mentioned to me is that of a writer."

"The situation is this. When Rivers went to see Miss Hill, there was a painting on an easel in her studio." Here the Minister gave a brief resumé of the Chief Inspector's statement. "It seems to me that Rivers is probably right in his assumptions," concluded David, and Danvers put in:

"He may be. I don't know. But one thing sticks out a mile. The police argue that here is a woman separated from her husband: she sees a lot of another man and that man frequently visits her at her studio. The husband is murdered. Therefore the answer is plain. It may be that Miss Hill claimed she had painted the picture to avoid saying who had painted it. Again, I don't know. She is being interrogated by the police about a crime she is absolutely ignorant of—and innocent of. If she tries to prevent the man she cares about being mixed up in the squalor of it all, she's a right to try." Danvers' hand went to his pocket. "May I smoke, sir?"

"Yes—of course. I don't smoke myself, so I didn't think of it."

"Thanks very much. Look here, sir. My fellow-tunneller—call him John—he didn't kill Pompfret. He wasn't anywhere near here. I know where he was. I'm not telling his name, nor where he was, but he wasn't here. And there's this to be considered. A lot of hot air is being talked in this Ministry about the method employed to shift that Canova thing, but everybody is agreed on one point. If Pompfret was murdered, the man who did it was a man who knew this building and the conditions that obtain here. John doesn't know it. He's never been inside the place. Neither did he know Pompfret, not even by sight."

"That being so, wouldn't it simplify things a very great deal if you gave his name?" asked the Minister. "I can give you my own assurance that, if the facts are as you state, his name will never be mentioned in connection with the case."

"I can't, sir. I've promised not to. It might be more simple, as you say. A lot of chaps would have found life quite a lot simpler, in conditions which both you and I have heard about, if they'd just produced a little more information than the minimum. They pre-ferred to keep their traps shut, as I do now, and the consequences of their refusal were definitely more uncomfortable than anything which is likely to be handed out to me. It's just not a thing you can argue about."

"Very well. We will leave it at that," said the Minister. "Now you have told me that you are satisfied that neither Miss Hill nor your friend John had anything to do with this affair: so far as you are concerned, they are out of it. You also are out of it. I gather that the police have proved your alibi. So I see no reason why I should not ask you to discuss the matter impartially. You were in Pompfret's department, his senior assistant. You know more about him than I do, probably more about him than anyone in this building. He has been murdered. Have you any idea at all which suggests a motive for such a crime?"

"No, sir. I have been thinking of that point all day. Pompfret was the last person I should have expected to be murdered. He was an able Civil Servant, with all that that implies in the way of achievement at school and university. I'm quite sure he was a man of integrity, so far as his job went. He had adopted a veneer of the picturesque, which, in my judgment, failed to impress. To put it brutally, he was heading in the direction of being a pompous bore. And the last man to get murdered, in my opinion, is the bore. People avoid them, but they don't murder them. I'm not being flippant over this, sir. I'm only trying to answer your question."

"But you have got to remember that Pompfret *was* murdered," said the Minister, "and probably murdered by someone in this building. The only suggestion that I can make is that he had become aware of some fraud or corrupt practice which he was making it his business to investigate."

"But what fraud *could* be engineered in an establishment like this, sir? The finance department is foolproof—and anyway Pompfret admitted that finance was a bug-bear to him: he would never have spotted anything in that line that the Finance people wouldn't have seen first." With frowning face, Danvers looked up at the Minister's "funnies." Then he said: "May I tell you a suggestion that somebody made to-day, sir? A lot of people are saying that Mr. Pompfret wasn't murdered: that he thought out a way of shifting Manderby himself. I argued that he wouldn't destroy government property, and somebody put in: 'But the thing was insured and it's valuable. If Mr. Pompfret smashed it up, he'd have got rid of a thing he hated and cashed in on the insurance money to buy a Henry Moore or something which he thought was worth while.' It did seem to me that that line of thought might be near the mark."

"You said that you believed Mr. Pompfret was a man of integrity, but you're prepared to believe he would swindle an Insurance company?" asked David.

Again Danvers looked round at the pictures, and then said slowly: "When people get modern art on the brain, I think they lose a sense of proportion and become extreme, like these things." He broke off, and flushed, as he added: "Sorry, sir. I realise that's an unjustifiable thing to say, but this modern stuff revolts me. But if Pompfret *was* murdered, I haven't the very faintest idea who killed him or why they killed him. I don't know of anyone who held any particular animus against him, and if he had uncovered any racket he never mentioned it to me."

"Very well, Danvers. That appears to be as far as we can go, but I'd like to add this. You have claimed the freedom to adhere to your own private loyalties. I'm not judging you on that issue. The circumstances you have told me constitute a bond which only those who have experienced them can apprehend. In your tunnel there was one imperative rule—not to let the other chap down. I grasp that all right, but I also know that individuals who claim absolute freedom for their own judgment always impinge on someone else's freedom. I ask you to think that one over."

It was when he got back to his own office that Michael Danvers said to himself: "Good God! He thinks I did it... 'Those who claim absolute freedom impinge on someone else's freedom...' If that alibi comes unstuck, I'm as likely a favourite as the next."

II

It was late that evening that Julian Rivers and Henry Fearon met to discuss progress in Rivers' room. There was only one picture on the walls: a reproduction of a portrait of Margaret Beaufort when

young, once exhibited in the National Portrait Gallery. Henry Fearon
looked at it gratefully.

"That's a very beautiful thing, Julian. Why *must* they...?"

"Oh, for God's sake, don't start being controversial, Henry. I got
her for the simple reason that I thought she was not controversial.
Now I'm told they've X-rayed her and found the painting isn't an
authentic contemporary portrait, confound them. But by the time
I'm through with this job we're on, I shall want to buy an Abstract.
Ben Nicholson for preference. Don't ask me why. I can't tell you. But
the things seep into one's subconscious and kill everything else stone
dead. Do you think it's possible that these contemporary paintings
are potent enough to arouse murderous passions?"

"No. I don't. I hate them as much as anybody does, but I would
neither commit murder nor lift a finger nor spend a sixpence for any
of them. But I'll buy that picture of yours if you're tired of her. And
now to get down to it. As soon as I heard of Pompfret's murder, I
knew there wasn't an earthly of getting anything useful from Files.
The letters the Minister spotted have gone, and the practitioner who
shifted the Canova on to Pompfret wasn't likely to have obliged by
leaving his fingerprints around. I've worked through lashings of
the stuff, with some of the clerks checking on serial numbers and
references. I haven't found anything that isn't in order, but I've got
one item for you: Pompfret put in quite a lot of work on them. His
prints are uppermost on some of the stuff: they're superimposed
on the Minister's in some cases. It looks as though he'd spotted
something—but why in hell didn't he report and have it properly
investigated?"

"I've been thinking about him quite a lot, but I want to tell you
the findings of my trio of eccentrics—the blokes who have been
working through the Loans Collection canvases," said Rivers. "They
dismissed most of it at a glance as authentic if not distinguished. The

amount those three men know between them is pretty impressive: they not only know the names of the painters who have missed being 'significant,' if you'll accept the word, they know the studios they worked in, the cliques they formed, the art schools where they studied and the exact prices their work will command. They also know the smaller dealers who market the smaller fry. And amongst this collection of the not-so-successful but obvious practitioners, my trio have spotted two canvases which ought not to be there. They are copies—and pretty expert copies—of early paintings by Matisse, but each one has some deviation, some variation, from the original."

"Are they signed?"

"Yes. They're both signed with the name of a man called Arlettier. Arlettier is dead. He died six months ago in Paris, but according to my trio, he did not paint these canvases. The record of the sales is all in order: they were bought by Joyce-Lawrence's instructions from a Paris dealer, but not delivered to the M.O.F.A. until after Joyce-Lawrence's death. They are listed as examples of the Fauviste school in the Ministry catalogues."

"Well, it's quite a story," said Henry meditatively. "Did your trio tell you where the original Matisse paintings are—the ones from which the M.O.F.A. canvases were copied?"

"They are both owned by private collectors, one of whom lives in France, one in Switzerland; so you may have your fun yet, getting around to check up. But I want to look at the facts from the point of view of deceased. Everybody, from the Minister to the typists, agree on one point—that Pompfret was conceited. I think it's a point worth bearing in mind, because conceit can have a deleterious effect on the character. Pompfret fancied himself as an art critic. He thought he knew. Doesn't it occur to you that it would have been a bitter pill to him to have to admit that he'd been had? That he'd got two canvases in his collection that he ought to have spotted as being incongruous if he possessed the flare and knowledge he claimed to have possessed?"

"Yes. I agree to that: so what?"

"I'm wondering if he tumbled to it, by information received, perhaps, that he'd been landed with two very odd fakes. His conceit prevented him from having the matter investigated officially. Perhaps he refused to admit to himself that the canvases were bogus. Anyway, he decided to do some private snooping, and not being very smart at it he gave away what he was doing, and somebody decided to liquidate him before he had time to take action."

"Might be," said Henry Fearon. "We've got to admit to start with that this case was coloured for us from the word go by the Minister smelling a rat over the files. It was that which determined the line we've worked on. If there hadn't seemed to be a ghost of a motive, would you have considered more sympathetically the idea that Pompfret had succeeded in moving Manderby himself?"

"I don't see how he could have done it," said Rivers, "though I gather some of the lads here have put some smart ideas forward. The notion of using a small hydraulic jack is very cunning. But I also argued that Pompfret wouldn't have destroyed government property. However, in the light of what we've learned, I'm not wasting any time on arguing as to how Pompfret could have done it, because I'm certain he didn't do it. The thing's tied up with some sort of racket over these pictures."

"Incidentally, where have the two pictures been all this time? How was it that the visiting experts whom Pompfret entertained didn't spot the things?"

"They didn't see them. The idea of this Loans Collection business is to lend the pictures to small towns and even villages which have no official art galleries of their own. The big cities which have their own municipal collections are outside the scheme, so the pseudo-Matisse canvases had been dazzling the eyes of worthies in small towns in the north and the midlands. It happened that they'd just been returned from loan, after having been sent around for months, and no expert eye had examined them. Of course we don't know how many other 'pseudos' may turn up eventually. You must remember that the Right Honourable Higginson axed all the resident experts, and no one in the place was really qualified to judge the things. None of those employed in the Loans branch can claim to be an expert."

"Well, it's quite a story," said Henry Fearon. "I'm disposed to agree with you that Pompfret wouldn't have wanted a public inquiry if he could have avoided it, though if he had the wits of a hen he ought to have realised that someone was working a racket under cover of a government department."

"And as for the exact nature of the racket, your guess is as good as mine," said Rivers.

"I heard rather an odd story to-day," said Henry. "It's not relevant, but it amused me quite a bit. I went into the Modern Art Centre this evening to look at their picture books, drink coffee, and listen in if any of the young intelligents got chatty about the M.O.F.A."

"What on earth do they take you for?" asked Rivers.

"Me? Oh, I'm an Essayist. It's a perfectly good description, because I always try hard," replied Henry equably. "There was a private huroosh on: they'd had an exhibition of ceramics and plastics, and while the stuff was on show a discussion group had had the use of the gallery. The next morning one of the exhibits was found smashed on the floor, and nobody knew anything about it."

Rivers grinned. "All I can say is that I'd have enjoyed the 'discussion' group."

"Quite. But some pert young thing pointed out that all exhibits are insured at the value put on them by the exhibitor."

"The old fire insurance racket applied to contemporary ceramics," said Rivers meditatively. "A most unworthy innuendo. Do you wish to point a moral to this squalid story?"

"As you know quite well, the moral is being chewed over at the M.O.F.A.," said Henry. "Ergo: did Pompfret collaborate in the shifting of Manderby—with the highest motives? Intention being to cash in on the estimated value of the Canova and buy a contemporary Abstract?"

"What base motives they do attribute to blameless Civil Servants," said Rivers. "Did that one emerge from Loans or Architects? The one thing that seems plain to me is that if the C.I.D. isn't careful, their own jargon will become infected by that of the M.O.F.A. The terms contemporary Abstracts, ceramics, plastics and mobiles have never sullied our reports before."

"Contemporary—what a word, what a senseless concept to pay homage to," said Henry morosely.

"As you say," murmured Rivers.

> "'What's time? Leave now for dogs and apes,
> Man has forever.'"

"*Not* contemporary poetry," said Henry.

CHAPTER XIII

I

WHILE RIVERS AND FEARON WERE APPLYING THEIR INTEL-
ligences "on the highest level" (as the most recent recruit
from Hendon Police College phrased it), and Lancing was working
overtime on the officially filed records of certain selected persons
who worked in the M.O.F.A., the rank and file of the C.I.D. were
checking the alibis and observing the living conditions of some of
those same selected persons. There were George Smith and Alec
West, housemen on the two to ten o'clock shift; there were Dick
Chandler and Bill Carter, packers for the Loans Collection; there
were Bob Titmarsh, night watchman and Albert Edward Baines,
day porter. On the executive side there were high-ups who had
to be approached with care, like James Dellison, Esq. (Deputy
Assistant Secretary, Loans Collection), Roger Welles (Director of
the Architectural Branch), and some of the juniors on the professional staff: John Dunne (junior Architectural assistant), Paul Weston
(assistant curator Loans Collection) and Ewart Blackwell (assistant
to Paul Weston).

Detective Shand, who was in charge of the inquiries into this
miscellaneous selection, had a busy day of it. He ranged from Leyton
and Walthamstow to Tooting and Morden and Camberwell, with
Wimbledon, Golders Green, Marylebone and Bloomsbury sand-
wiched in between. Having studied and arranged his districts, Shand

had applied for a police car—and got it, but his detective conscience would not permit him to drive up to individual doorways (humble or otherwise), in the handsome outfit provided. Shand alighted in each case some distance from his objective and thus put in quite a lot of pedestrian exercise.

The immediate purpose of Shand's inquiries was to determine the whereabouts of the persons on his list between ten o'clock and ten forty-five the previous evening. In some cases he made straightforward inquiries: in others he used the diplomatic approach (generally a hoary chestnut) calculated to obtain an answer without giving the real reason for his question. Witnesses to traffic accidents, persons suspected of loitering with intent, attempted burglary, bag snatching, car stealing, parking without lights—all these hypothetical occurrences, which were part of the daily routine to every police division, figured in the diplomatic approaches of Detective Shand.

Shand's first inquiry, however, was a straight one: it concerned George Smith, the houseman on the second shift, who had enjoyed a cup of tea with Bob Titmarsh only three-quarters of an hour before Bob had found Pompfret's body. Of course, George's wife knew all about the murder: George had been routed out of bed by the police and gone back to Medici House soon after midnight. According to his own statement, George had left the Ministry at five minutes past ten and gone straight home to Camberwell, where he had arrived "shortly before eleven o'clock." It was the hour of George's arrival at home that Shand sought to check. George said that he had walked to Piccadilly Circus and had there boarded a No. 12 bus, which put him down at the corner of his own road. The time taken by his journey was not unreasonable, in view of traffic conditions: the roads were fairly clear at that hour, and there were no traffic blocks. Nevertheless, if George had used a motor-bike, or got a lift in a car or taken a taxi, he could still have arrived home about eleven o'clock even though he had not left Medici House until after half-past ten. No one had seen him leave the Ministry, and the police had not found anyone who had seen him walking along Piccadilly.

Mrs. George Smith was a woman of forty-five with no nonsense about her. She knew exactly what Shand was after and she answered his questions without any sign of apprehension. Her husband had arrived home at his usual time—round about eleven o'clock, maybe a bit earlier. He always came straight home, George did: no, he didn't go into a pub before closing time, he came home and had his glass of Guinness over the kitchen fire. He hadn't got a motor-bike and he couldn't ride one, either, though their boy had one—twenty-one the boy was and making good money in a garage—Sun's garage in Pimlico. The boy had come in at nine o'clock and gone up to bed before his father got home. He'd been dancing the night before and he was sleepy. No, they hadn't got a clock in the kitchen, but she knew what the time was all right. She'd heard the ten o'clock news 'on the Light' and listened to the next programme and a bit of the dance music which followed, and then she'd switched off and put the breakfast things on a tray same as she always did, sat by the fire a bit and then George had come home and they'd talked about the boys out in Korea—George's old regiment was out there. "It was just the same as it is every night, and so was George," she concluded.

Shand left the house in some respects no wiser than he entered it, but his good sense, both as a man and a detective, inclined him to think there was nothing wrong about the George Smiths. The sturdy forthrightness of Mrs. Smith had the quality of a woman who had never been frightened or bullied and who wasn't going to be upset by detectives or anyone else. "After all, you've got your job to do," she had concluded reasonably, "and you've got to look at it all round."

Alec West, who lived in Tooting, was a straightforward job. Alec had left the Ministry at ten o'clock to the tick and reached home by ten thirty-five, the neighbours next door substantiating this fact, as they'd spent the evening "viewing" the West's new (hire purchase) television set, and had stayed on for a chat with Alec.

Thankfully crossing Alec West from his list, Shand went on to Morden to investigate Albert Edward Baines, day porter. Baines had been playing in a darts match at the local and hadn't left until closing time. Chandler and Carter, the packers, who inconveniently lived in Walthamstow and Leyton respectively, had only their wives as witnesses to the fact that they had been in their own homes during the entire evening in question. Shand, as an experienced investigator in a small way, wrote in his report that he accepted Mrs. Chandler's evidence, for she seemed a decent self-respecting body. Mrs. Carter, who was a slut (and nobody recognised a slut more quickly than Shand) was also shrill and disposed to be abusive, and from his glance at the domestic chaos coupled to shoddy smartness in the Carters' home, Shand entered a large question mark in his report. He sensed, rather than proved, rent in arrears, bills unpaid, too much of the wage packet going on Pools, Dogs, Drink, Perms and Finery. (The capitals were Shand's, also the order of the indulgences.)

Bob Titmarsh, the night porter who had found Pompfret's body, lived in Islington. Shand's business on this visit was to report on domestic conditions, and to get such opinions as he could glean from tradespeople (often a useful source of information) on the Titmarsh household. Bob, of course, was in bed, and Shand did not want to disturb him, but the detective had been primed with a question supplied by Rivers. When Bob's wife came to the door, Shand immediately gave his name and business, apologised for troubling Mrs. Titmarsh, and then came straight to the point.

"Did Titmarsh wear dungarees or a boiler-suit when he was working in the cellars at the Ministry?"

"Well, he's got some, not that he always bothers to put them on," said his wife. "I often have no end of bother to make him bring them home to be washed. I send them to the laundry once in a way, they're a heavy, dirty job to do at home. I know he's got a clean pair—or near clean—at the Ministry now. I only gave them to him a few days ago. He puts them on if the furnace has to be re-started, and you'd not believe how filthy he gets." She had answered quite naturally, but as she finished speaking, fear suddenly came into her eyes. "What d'you want to know that for—and why come asking me? Why didn't you ask him?"

"Now you don't get worrying, ma'am. In a case like this there's a lot of odd things we have to check up on. If anything's missing, or moved out of its place, it might give us a lead. If anybody borrowed those dungarees of your husband's it might be very important."

Shand knew at a glance that Bob Titmarsh was lucky in his wife, and a good husband to boot. They lived in a prefab, and it was in tip-top order, clean and neat and comely, with a tiny lawn and a flower border below the front window. Shand went on conscientiously to some nearby tradespeople, asked if they could tell him Bob's address—"once knew him in the army"—and he eventually heard just the sort of report he expected to hear—a sound chap, one of the best, got a good government job. Nice wife, too. Not like some of these dames who was always trying to get more than her share.

Mr. Dellison lived in Wimbledon—a very select neighbourhood. The front door was opened by a nice trim maid: she was an Austrian girl, but she spoke very good English. Mrs. Dellison was out, but the maid answered Shand's questions without hesitation. Her master had been out yesterday evening: he had dined out and had not got home until nearly midnight, so he could not have seen the car Shand was inquiring about, not if it was in this road between ten and eleven. Mr. Dellison had dined in the West End: he had taken a case with his dinner-jacket, Elsa knew that, because she had pressed and cleaned it for him and packed it in the case.

From Wimbledon Shand drove to Bloomsbury, where Mr. Welles lived in chambers just off Gower Street. Shand had expected this to be a difficult interview: Welles was not married, and the proprietors of gentlemen's chambers were not generally partial to answering any questions about their clients. Primed with a story about a stolen car and faked number plates which were identical with Mr. Welles's, Shand was prepared to induce a cod-eyed ex-butler to expand, but when the front door was opened, the C.I.D. man saw a familiar countenance, as ex-Police Constable Trimming of E. Division, clad in a very natty houseman's coat, stood at attention. Shand said "Thank God, Fred," and meant it.

Trimming said: "This is a real pleasure, this is. If you'd care to step downstairs to our quarters, me and my missis'd be properly pleased."

Seated in a comfortable Windsor chair in front of a good fire, Shand knew he could talk without reserve, for Trimming was known as a faithful and responsible ex-policeman.

"Well, you've got a fair sized job on, Mr. Shand," said Trimming. "I'm told there's over a thousand employed in M.O.F.A."

"Ah—got around, has it?" asked Shand.

"It has that. I always keep in touch with the point duty men— like to talk a bit of the old shop, you know. Reckon I heard about it before Mr. Welles did. Matter of checking up, eh?"

"That's it," said Shand. "Routine stuff, but it's got to be done, and we're treating 'em all alike, from the porters to the Minister."

"Ar—you're telling me," said Trimming. "Murder by a Minister. That'd be a headline, that would. Now about Mr. Welles. He was out all last evening. He was lecturing if you want details: I saw the card on his mantelpiece: Junior Architects' Association. Vanbrugh House. W.I. Mr. Roger Welles on the Modulor of Le Corbusier."

Trimming grinned. "I took another dekko at the card when I did his room this morning. Him being at M.O.F.A. and having heard what I had heard about a fatal accident there, well, I thought I'd like to get it correct. Eight o'clock the lecture was, and discussion to follow. C-o-r-b-u-s-i-e-r, that was the subject. Not that I've ever heard of the place."

"Hearing about the place doesn't matter," said Shand. "Did you hear Mr. Welles come in?—that's what I want to know."

"Hear him? Me and my missis sleeps down here in the basement, Mr. Shand, and we don't hear the front door, not unless the bell's rung. I can tell you he wasn't in his room at 10.15. The boss couldn't get separate telephone lines for all these chambers, some of them are on an extension of the house phone until such time as the P.M.G. obliges with new lines. There's a switchboard down here for chambers 3, 4 and 5, Mr. Welles being number 5. A call came through for him at 10.15, I rang up to his room to put it through, but there was no answer. So I reckon he wasn't in then."

"Well, that's my answer, thanks very much," said Shand. "Not up to me to go any further in this case."

"Just so," agreed Trimming. The ex-policeman paused a moment and then curiosity urged him on. "But why ever should Mr. Welles have done a thing like that? He's what I'd call a highly respectable party. Never no goings on, pays on the dot, and works harder than any man I know. We gets to know a bit about the tenants, my missis and me. She provides breakfast for all, but does some other meals by arrangement. Mr. Welles, he's often at home of an evening and likes a tray sent up. Working at his drawing-board he is, or doing calculations. A very respectable party, he is, with his heart in his work if you ask me."

"Didn't I tell you it was a routine check-up, Fred? I'm not the only one on the job. While they're about it they're making a job of it."

"Ar. Chief Inspector Rivers on the case, isn't he? Great sense of detail, he has, so I'm told."

"You're telling me," sighed Shand. "Well, I must be moving. Glad to have seen you, Fred, and many thanks—you've saved me a lot of trouble."

II

From intellectual and poetic Bloomsbury, Shand proceeded to conservative and prosaic Marylebone. Mr. Weston lived in Derwent Street, an unexpectedly quiet road of unexpectedly small houses. Shand could tell from the window curtains (or lack of them) and from the front doors, which of these houses were still tenanted by the old-fashioned lodging-house keeper and which of them had been turned into flats or "service chambers"—that modern variant on furnished lodgings. To Shand's satisfaction, Mr. Weston's domicile was of the old-fashioned variety. An elderly or middle-aged landlady was a much easier proposition than the smart manageress or suspicious owner of one of the blocks of newfangled "self-contained" service chambers. The moment Shand saw the comfortable looking middle-aged body who opened the door he felt on good terms with her, and his patter came easily and naturally: he apologised for troubling her, but the police were seeking witnesses to a traffic accident just off the High Street yesterday evening—perhaps she'd heard about it on the radio?

"No. I'm afraid I didn't. My wireless hasn't been working—but step inside. Butler's the name—Mrs. Butler," said the stout dame. "Not that it's any good asking me, I was indoors all the evening. One of my young gentlemen was poorly: it's these cold winds, they're so treacherous."

"They are indeed, ma'am," agreed Shand, removing his hat politely in the comfortable fug of the hall. "Now it's a funny thing, but a witness thought he recognised a lodger of yours—name of Weston—near the scene of the accident: walking past the corner of Queen Anne Street about ten o'clock."

"But you've been told wrong," said Mrs. Butler. "Mr. Weston wasn't out at all yesterday evening. He came home early with a shocking bad cold and went straight to bed."

"But are you sure he didn't go out again afterwards?" asked Shand. "Maybe felt better, or thought he'd go and have a drink or such like?"

"That he didn't. I took his supper up myself, and later on I gave his chest a rub, him having a shocking cough," said Mrs. Butler indignantly, "and I remember it was well after ten before I left him, tucked up in bed with two hot-water bottles. Very poorly he was. I just went downstairs again to put the cat out and fasten the back door, and it was half-past ten as I went up to bed myself. I noticed the grandfather striking the half-hour as I went up—a very good timekeeper that is—and I hadn't left Mr. Weston more than ten minutes or so. And the other two lodgers, Mr. Evans and Mr. Price, they were away last night, having gone to a dance in Oxford, it being Miss Price's twenty-first birthday dance—Mr. Price's sister, that is. So I'm afraid you've come to the wrong house. Though maybe there's one thing I could tell you might help. Mr. Jones, at number 19, he's on shift working at the Power Station, and he gets home every evening just about ten and puts his car away in the mews there—it might be worth asking him."

Shand thanked her politely, glanced at the grandfather clock and observed it was correct to the minute and took his leave.

John Dunne, junior assistant architect, of Hatfield Close, Golders Green, was next on Shand's list. Why Mr. Dunne and Mr. Weston should interest the Chief Inspector it was not Shand's business to inquire—his not to reason why. Mr. Dunne lived at home with his family: the door of a very pleasant (architect-built) house was opened by a very lively looking schoolboy of about twelve years old. Shand asked for Mr. John Dunne, and the boy confounded him by retorting promptly:

"He's not in. You know he's not in, don't you? Is it about the murder?"

"What murder?" asked Shand in horrified terms.

"The murder at the Ministry. It *is* a murder, isn't it? John rang up and said he couldn't get off this afternoon because someone had been killed and they were all being third degreed," said the boy, adding as though in pity: "I know you're a cop, because I was at the window upstairs and I saw your car turn at the corner. You can always tell a police car, they're so posh. You can come inside if you like, if you don't mind me being in quarantine for measles. Everyone else is out and I'm bored stiff."

"You ought to be working at your school books," said Shand severely, and the boy replied:

"I'm fed up with school books. Did you come to find out where John was last night? He's my half-brother, by the way. John was in all the evening. He was working out plans for a country cottage we're going to build on the self-help principle. You can see his plans if you like, they're on his drawing board."

"You're taking too much on to yourself altogether, my lad, and being too clever by half," said Shand, who had no opinion of pre-cocity in the young. "I should like to know what time your mother will be in, if you please."

"I don't know, and neither does she," retorted the boy. "She's gone shopping and she's asked her bloke to fit her in for a hair-do some time and that may mean any time. So if you want to know anything on the tick you must take it from me."

"What time do you go to bed?" asked Shand, and the boy grinned.

"Eight o'clock—but my room's next to John's, and I bob in and out. And you can't get past that, can you?"

"I'm not trying to get past anything," said Shand, "and if you take my advice you'll go and wash your face and decide not to be so clever another time, and kindly tell your mother that the Rating Officer will call and see her about the new Assessment in due course. Good-day."

"And if his half-brother's anything like him, I wouldn't put anything beyond him," thought Shand, as he plodded in search of the car which was parked round the corner.

Shand's last call was in Kensington, where Mr. Ewart Blackwell, assistant to Mr. Paul Weston, lived in ascetic seclusion in an attic flat. There was no answer to Shand's ring: no answer at either of the flats below. He met an aged crone in the entrance hall as he went down: she was flicking a mop over the tiles in a dispirited way and when Shand addressed her she seemed not to hear him. He touched her arm and she produced a shrill yelp. When Shand spoke again she shook her head.

"I'm 'ard of 'earing and the Deaf Aid they gave me on the National 'Ealth 'as died on me, drat it." She was almost stone deaf, and Shand gave it best.

Returning in the car, it seemed to Shand he'd put in a fairly full day to very little purpose, and then he remembered Mrs. George Smith's sensible remark: "Has to look at it all round, don't you?"

He'd certainly done a round, and his items of evidence, if carefully set out, would make quite a substantial report. Shand liked to think he earned his pay and allowances—and he certainly did.

CHAPTER XIV

I

B Y SIX O'CLOCK ON THE EVENING FOLLOWING POMPFRET'S death, the entire staff of the Ministry of Fine Arts (with the exception of the two evening housemen and the cleaners) had vacated the building. A general directive had been issued to all departments that they were to leave the Ministry before six o'clock, no matter what work was in arrears, nor what ambitious Civil Servants had intended to work overtime on projects labelled priority.

George Smith and Alec West were on duty as usual. Each was charged to carry out his customary routine and to repeat in detail exactly what he had done on the previous evening. George and Alec were each accompanied by a C.I.D. man, whose duty it was to note down the movements and the timing of the two housemen and the cleaners they supervised, so that by the time the cleaning was finished it could be worked out exactly which rooms, corridors and staircases had been unoccupied at any given moment. It was perhaps not surprising that the Mrs. Mops of M.O.F.A. were in a state of jitters. Some of them expected to be accused of murder (or said they did). A larger proportion expected to be murdered themselves, being convinced that a homicidal maniac might pop out from behind desk or filing cabinet. It took Smith and West all their time to get the charwomen to work at all, and there were frequent screeches and wails from the nervous, especially when they met patrolling

C.I.D. men in the corridors and on the stairs. On one thing they were all agreed—the sinister quality of Canova's heroic sized Earl Manderby. "'Orrible thing it was. I always said there was something mac-a-ber about that there," said one cinema-going charlady. "If you asks me, it was old Nick in person came back and possessed that bust and made it afall down of itself just when Mr. Pompfret was passing by." (Great was the joy of Lancing and his pals to learn that this particular Cassandra was named Mrs. Gray: the "animated bust" became part of police records.)

Rivers and Lancing, after an interval spent in studying reports (including Shand's) returned to Medici House at eight o'clock. The cleaners had left by this time, and the diligent C.I.D. men were busy on the unattractive job of examining sweepings and of inspecting the contents of wastepaper baskets. George and Alec went to eat the suppers that neither of them fancied, still accompanied by their familiars—the two C.I.D. men—who made a much better supper than the housemen.

"Look here, mates," said George to the pair who had accompanied him and Alec, "no offence meant: we know you've got your job to do same's us, and we haven't taken a dislike to your faces or got a thing about your voices, but if we could sit at separate tables it'd be more comfortable for all parties."

"That's O.K., cock," replied the C.I.D. "We've met the same reaction before. You sit with your backs to us and give your digestions a chance."

It was just after eight o'clock that Rivers and Lancing went through the kitchens on their way to the cellars. The central heating furnace was cold now. It hadn't been re-stoked during the day, but its fire had taken an unconscionable time a-dying—as though insisting on being awkward to the last. Its ashes would be sifted when they had obliged by cooling. Rivers thought that the remains of the metal case holding Pompfret's glasses might be found in the furnace, and possibly some other properties as well. The Chief Inspector believed that the glasses in their case had been removed from Pompfret's desk by the murderer: Rivers had argued thus: "I don't think the murderer would have risked taking the glasses out of the building lest they were found on him if things went wrong. He didn't leave them about in some obvious place for us to find, as though they'd been dropped, so my guess is that he put them in the furnace. Decimus Burton so designed this building that it's possible to get into the cellars by two different entrances, one by the kitchens on the east side of the house, one by the servery on the west side."

Lancing nodded. "Yes, I see your point. The murderer might well have argued that once the night watchman had come up from his stoking job in the cellars and had found the corpse, the cellars would be the safest part of the building for a fugitive to take cover in, because the night watchman would be so busy over ringing the police and all that, that he wouldn't be likely to return to the cellars for the time being."

"That's the idea," said Rivers. "In addition to that point, the cellars can be regarded as an exit. It'd be possible to get out of one of the hatches into the sunk area which goes all round the house and beat it by way of the garden wall. What's worrying you, by the way?"

"You said earlier on that I'd deserve demoting if I couldn't work out for myself how Manderby was shifted," said Lancing. "Well, I've tumbled to that one, thanks to your personal pointers, if I may put it that way, but I deserve demoting on another count, I'm damned if I don't. I went down to the cellars with Titmarsh almost immediately after I got here, and I stood like a moron and watched him raking the fire in that antediluvian furnace so that it blazed up through the mountain of coal he'd shovelled on it. I tell you I watched him, and never thought of looking to see what was burning, or lifting the damned lid to see what was inside."

Rivers began to laugh. "It is pretty good, viewed in retrospect, but I've done plenty of things which were just as damned silly in my time. After all, we're not story book detectives, and we're not endowed with the miraculous foresight of such. What *was* the connection between Pompfret pulling Manderby down on top of him and that furnace? We didn't even realise the weight the thing was when we first looked at it. Well, this is where we improve our acquaintance with what Titmarsh calls the 'ollow cellars. Tate's been down there for the last two hours. He relieved James at six. I think Tate may be glad to see us. Our chaps don't like Decimus Burton's cellars."

"Takes 'em like that occasionally," said Lancing, "and the funny thing is you can never tell when it'll be. Our chaps are pretty tough, but even they have their fancies. I've often thought it'd be interesting to get a psychiatrist on to the fact that some places can make even a C.I.D. constable come out in a sweat."

"I think it's claustrophobia," said Rivers, "and in this case I must admit the fumes of that stove as it cools are pretty unpleasant—as you'll soon find out for yourself. I suppose when the draught goes you get the fumes seeping out from the clinkers."

They had been talking in the kitchens, while Rivers took a quick look round in scullery cupboards and glanced behind roller towels and under sinks and in the different squalid cubby-holes which always seemed to be a feature of early Victorian kitchens. He found nothing which interested him, shrugged his shoulders and said, "Oh, well, let's try the vaults."

He opened the door which led to the first steep stone staircase and sniffed disgustedly. The air was heavy with the smell of the not-quite-dead fires, a composite of sulphur and soot and smoke which offended the nose and made the eyes smart. There was a fairly good light over the steps, but lower down, after the first turn, the cellars were gloomy, as though the bulb were failing. Rivers ran down the steps with the neat crab-wise gait which was a hang-over from his sailor's days, and at the bottom of the flight he paused and called:

"Tate, are you there? Tate…"

There was no answer, and Rivers exclaimed: "Lord… don't say we've killed him. Is this abomination leaking carbon monoxide or something?" He pulled out his torch, for the light seemed very dim, and Lancing went and fastened back the door at the top of the stairs to let some fresh air in.

"We'd better open one of the coal hatches," said Rivers. "I can't believe this fug's lethal, but it may have been enough to turn him dizzy."

Lancing scrambled over the mounds of coal and shot back the bolts which held the hatch in place and let it down. It fell with a slam and Lancing called through: "Thompson—are you there? Lancing here."

"Here, sir," came a voice from outside.

"Stand by here. We've lost Tate and think the fumes down here have laid him out. If I want you, I'll whistle."

Lancing scrambled back down the coal pile and followed Rivers farther into the cellars: they went round the evil-smelling furnace and on through the vaults, past the great barrels, flashing their torches around and beneath them. It was an eerie business: the vaults were not open, like a crypt, but were a series of compartments with arched openings which led from one chamber to the next. There was no lighting beyond the furnace space, and there were occasional unexpected steps.

"There's a well, or pit of some kind in the centre here," warned Rivers, "possibly an ice pit—elementary cold storage. It's flagged over, but the ground's rough, so watch your step. Hallo… there he is."

Tate lay prone on the flagged floor, as Pompfret had lain at the foot of the grand staircase the previous night. Rivers bent over him, and a moment later said:

"He's not dead. Simply knocked out. Probably came a cropper over one of those baulks and pitched on his face. Can you find your way back? Don't think it's easy—it isn't. It's a fair catacombs."

"I'll cope," said Lancing.

"Bring a couple of chaps back: we can't carry him and light the way simultaneously and if we trip up and drop him we may finish him," said Rivers.

Lancing hurried off, and a few seconds later came the sound of his police whistle. Rivers bent over the injured man, ran practised hands down his limbs and over the back of his head without finding any injury. Then, very skilfully, he turned Tate over on his back. He was breathing stertorously and his face was contused with bruises, a cut stretching from eyebrow to scalp still bleeding. Rivers fished out a clean handkerchief, folded it into a pad and laid it over the wound. So far as he could see, with the light from his torch, the injuries were just those which might be suffered by a man who tripped and fell flat on an uneven stone-flagged floor, rather than those of a man who had been laid out by a blow from a weighted stick. Flashing his torchlight around, Rivers found Tate's torch a yard or two away, where it might have rolled if he had dropped it as he fell: his wrist-watch, which had a guard over its face, was still going.

Rivers stood up and sniffed the air: admittedly the furnace spread its abominable smell throughout the vaults, but were the fumes enough to have rendered a man dizzy? It was difficult to say, because the fact of having opened the door and hatches had allowed the colder air from outside to seep into the vaults.

A moment later came the sound of footsteps and voices and Lancing came back with two stalwarts who lifted the unconscious man and carried him through the complex of vaults and upstairs to the kitchens to await the ambulance which was already on its way.

II

"So far as I could tell, he tripped and went flat on his face," said Rivers, when he and Lancing had returned to the vaults, "but even if the explanation is as simple as that, it doesn't explain what Tate was doing so far away from his beat, so to speak. I posted a man down here to ensure that no one interfered with the hatches or came down here unobserved. They had orders to keep clear of the lighted cellars but to stay where they could observe any visitors. I did not post a man by the entrance up above because I didn't want to discourage anybody who wanted to come down here for their own purposes."

"Who was on duty when you came down here with Miss Oxton?"

"James. He knew I was coming, and he kept well out of the way behind one of those barrels. I saw him—or part of him. The part I saw was very much like a barrel and was unobserved by Miss Oxton. Now Tate was supposed to have remained somewhere between the furnace and the barrels, not to have been in the further catacombs."

"On the other hand, Tate might have felt muzzy thro' breathing the aftermath of that hell of a furnace," said Lancing, "and decided to patrol a bit in search of some fresher air."

"He might have, but I don't think he did, because all our chaps took a dislike to these vaults," said Rivers. "My own belief is that Tate would have kept as near to the steps as duty permitted unless he heard something in the inner vaults which he felt he ought to investigate."

"But could anybody have got down here without being observed?"

"I hoped not, but it looks as though I was wrong. I know there are only two stairways, but there may be another manhole which

Miss Oxton didn't know about. But it's also possible that Tate was enticed to his tumble by some queer trick of acoustics in the pipes of this crazy heating system. If sound travels up the pipes from the cellars, it'd travel down them to the cellars as well. However, it's no use chewing it over any more. We've got to make a job of it and decide if the things are here or if they're not here."

III

"The things" were there. Crammed behind a barrel, in the darkest of obscure corners, Lancing found a boiler-suit—a pair of filthy dungarees. In one of the pockets was a scarlet-covered spectacle case.

It was nearly midnight when the two C.I.D. men found what they sought. Lancing carried the dirty bundle up to the kitchens and spread it out on a table under a naked electric bulb. Then they sent for Bob Titmarsh. He came straight into the kitchen and Rivers pointed to the boiler-suit.

"Do they belong to you?" he asked.

Bob came and examined them: found a patch on the seat and nodded. "Yes. They're mine—but they were clean last time I wore them."

"When did you wear them last?"

"One day last week, when the old b— went sour on me. Wednesday, it was. But I didn't get them in a muck like that. From the look of 'em somebody might have crawled right through the bloody furnace."

"Where did you keep them?"

"On a peg in that cupboard there—behind the door."

Rivers flicked the dungarees back and exposed the scarlet spectacle case.

"Do you know anything about that? It was in the pocket of your dungarees."

Titmarsh stood with a frowning face, the lines on his forehead furrowed deep, his jaw clenched. At last he said: "I don't know anything about it except that it's not mine and I've never touched it. If it was in my pocket, somebody else put it there." He turned to Rivers, his eyes angry. "Whose is it? Mr. Pompfret's?"

"Why do you think it might be?" asked Rivers.

"Because I'm not a fool. I don't think quickly, like you chaps do, but that doesn't mean I don't think at all. I've seen Mr. Pompfret about the place one or two nights when he's worked late. He wore glasses—regular gig-lamps. But he hadn't got glasses on when I found his body last night. I should know. I had a good look at him. Christ… So you're trying to put this on to me, are you. I reckoned you'd have a bash at it. Always blame the working bloke and let the high-ups off easy."

"Steady, Titmarsh," said Rivers quietly. "That's not true and you know it. You say you think; why didn't you tell me straight away that Mr. Pompfret always wore glasses?"

"Why didn't the Minister tell you? He saw him, same's I did, and he knew a damned sight better than I did Pompfret always wore glasses. Anyhow, if you'd been knocked down a marble staircase by a bloody great statue, would your glasses have still been on your nose by the time you got to the bottom?"

"No, but the remains of them would have been either on the stairs or mixed up with the bits and pieces at the bottom of the stairs," replied Rivers. "Since you knew that Pompfret always wore glasses, didn't it occur to you to look for the remains of them? You had plenty of time before our men turned up."

"Well, it didn't occur to me," said Titmarsh. "Not at the time it didn't. I'm not so used to that sort of picnic as you and your mates.

But when I thought it out, after I'd had a sleep, I did think of his glasses and I knew there hadn't been any glasses, nor bits of glasses, on them stairs. I turned the other lights on, and I should've seen the glass shining. I didn't see any glasses and I never touched this here case. Never. So what about it?"

"Go and get on with your job—patrolling or going the rounds or whatever you call it," said Rivers, "and if you happen to think of anything else, you might tell me, before I've thought of asking."

Titmarsh went off, and Rivers stood looking at the boiler-suit. Lancing had already tested the spectacle case for fingerprints and found none on the outside save some blurred prints of Pompfret's. "This can go along to the back-room boys," said Rivers, nodding to the suit. "Now the more I think of it, the more likely it seems to me that our practitioner left the building by the coal hatch we found unfastened. Alec West says he *thinks* he bolted it after the coal had been delivered, but I think it's very doubtful. However, the only traces of prints on the bolts are Alec's, so I think this is where we do some additional searching—or researching—outside the premises."

CHAPTER XV

I

MICHAEL DANVERS LEFT MEDICI HOUSE WITH THE CROWD shortly after half-past five. He had never before in his life tried to outwit the police, and he was by no means sure if he could do it now. It seemed to him that there was bound to be an element of luck in evading a "shadower"—good luck for him meant bad luck for the police and vice versa. He strolled down to Piccadilly, which was thronged, and boarded an east-bound bus while it was moving fairly fast. He was a very active fellow, and in jumping on the moving vehicle he took a chance—greatly to the indignation of the conductor. However—nobody had boarded the bus behind him: hastily paying his fare, he alighted again when the traffic lights turned against the bus at the corner of Bond Street. He turned into Bond Street, where the north-bound traffic was moving at its usual rush-hour crawl and crossed the road, twisting and turning with considerable skill—and at considerable risk—among the moving vehicles, and turned east down Burlington Gardens. He knew that no police car—or any other sort of car—could have followed him during this manœuvre, and if anyone was following him on foot, he was prepared to give them a run for their money. Burlington Gardens was less crowded than the main streets and Danvers took to his heels and ran, swerving like a rugger player to avoid other pedestrians. At the corner of Sackville Street he turned south towards Piccadilly again, deliberately loitering a little and studying his watch to make sure that his timing was right. Then he strolled into Piccadilly, turned left, and went into the Piccadilly Hotel. He glanced round, as though looking for somebody he expected, and then strolled over to the Regent Street entrance. He looked calm enough, an obviously well bred, well-dressed, pleasant looking young man, but his heart was pounding a little. He had thought out every move very carefully, but he was still uncertain whether he had got away with it, or if an unknown C.I.D. man was somewhere behind him.

The next move depended on the London traffic: no one knew better than Michael Danvers that it was exceedingly difficult to bring a car to a given point in Regent Street at a prearranged time during the rush hour. But his luck was in: just at the moment he glanced out of the glass doors he saw Billy Waring's car creep in to the kerb and almost before Billy had come to a dead stop Michael had crossed the pavement and boarded the car and it moved on, insinuated itself into the stream of north-bound traffic and got across the next traffic lights in the nick of time.

"Jolly decent of you, Bill," said Michael, "that was very skilfully done."

"Well, I suppose you know what you're doing," said Waring. "The stories that are going round London about events at your show are just nobody's business. Certainly not mine. I take leave to hope you haven't really attracted the attention of the C.I.D."

"I think I've attracted their attention all right," responded Michael, "but they've got rather a lot of us to keep an eye on. The whole thing's a jolly mess up. However, as zero hour was around ten-thirty last night and you happen to know where I was at that hour, you needn't charge your conscience with aiding and abetting a fugitive. And if you'll let me slide out somewhere in the vicinity of Marble Arch, all I can say is I'll do as much for you another time—and thanks a lot."

"No need. Delighted to oblige. Don't go getting involved in anything too murky."

Waring asked no questions, and hardly spoke again until they were approaching Marble Arch.

"Here's Mr. Bumpus, his book shop—that do you?"

"Grand, thanks."

Michael Danvers changed buses three times between Marble Arch and the Brompton Road: a number 2 took him to Grosvenor House, a 74 to Hyde Park Corner and a 30 put him down at the corner of Redmayne Gardens. By this time Michael knew that nobody was following him, for the street was empty: there were neither pedestrians nor cars to be seen as he walked round the quiet square and eventually descended to the basement entrance of a big double-fronted house. It was dusk now, and there was no light in the passage when the door was opened, but it was Virgilia Hill's husky voice which greeted him.

"Hallo. It's the room at the end where you can see the light. Go straight in."

Danvers did as he was bid, but when he turned and saw Miss Hill come into the room he stared helplessly, utterly confused. The woman who faced him had black hair, smoothly brushed back from her face and held by a plait which was poised on her head like a coronet. She was dressed in a severely tailored black skirt and trim white blouse: she wore glasses and her eyebrows were plucked to fine curves of blackness.

"It's all right. It's me," said the husky voice. "I was a bit tired of myself; I've been tired of myself for some time, so I thought I'd have a change. My name is Constance, which is a bit inappropriate, I admit, and I am the assistant Superintendent of the Redmayne

Residential Club. My cousin, Olivia, is the Superintendent and she's taken me on: six months' training with full board and a salary at the end if I suit."

"But how on earth…?" gasped Michael.

"I walked out and went to the hairdresser's—Betty Tucker, just off Haverstock Hill. She did my hair and dolled up my face and let me out by her back entrance. Then I came on here, by devious routes, and Olivia did the rest including dressing me. Sit down, and try not to gape."

"But why?" asked Michael, and she responded with sudden energy:

"Because I'm through. Through with all of it. When I saw that damned C.I.D. man summing me up this morning, I suddenly knew I was sick of it all. Sick of being a dud everything. He gave me the driving power to do what I'd been thinking of doing for a long time—to walk out on myself and start again. Of course, I oughtn't to have let you come here, but you might have been a nuisance if I hadn't. Were you followed here?"

"I don't think so. In fact I'm pretty certain I wasn't, but Virgilia—"

"Constance. It really is my name—my second name. You'd better get used to it."

"Do you really think you can get away with it?" asked Michael. "The police—"

"You've got police on the brain, Mike. It's not the police I'm eluding. They've got nothing on me. It's my wretched self. When I saw that Rivers man making up his slow mind that he'd got another variant on the Thompson-Bywaters case I could have laughed at him like a hyena if I hadn't been so angry. You see, Tony's gone. Gone for keeps. It's all over and done with. 'For to stay love is to rue it and the harder you pursue it, the faster it's away'—to the tune of a Day Lewis hornpipe. 'Too true,' as Edwin would have said."

"I'm sorry," said Michael, and his voice expressed more than the brief words.

"It's all right. It had to come. It always does," she replied. "You see… the Tony you knew, in your famous tunnel, isn't the Tony I knew. He used up his last reserve of constancy on you and the tunnel, and there wasn't any left for me."

"Where has he gone?"

"Back to France somewhere, among the wild Fauves and all the crazies he knew in the old days. He's gone, vanished, *disparu*." She met his eyes, and through the disguising horn-rims he saw the unhappiness in her own eyes.

"But you don't need to think Tony killed Edwin to get me," she urged. "He didn't kill Edwin. He was in Paris when Edwin was killed."

"All right. I'll accept that," said Michael slowly, "but did he know anything about it—about the reason for it? I don't want to plague you. You've got enough to live through without me pestering you, but you see—we've got to find out. Otherwise this thing will hang over us for the rest of our lives. Over you and me, over the Minister and the night watchman, over the packers and the porter: it's a nightmare. It may be fun to do what I did this evening, just for once—to use your wits to get away from the police. But it wouldn't be fun to make a habit of it."

"I'm sorry, Michael. You shouldn't have come out to tell me about it last night."

"I had to know," he said slowly. "Perhaps I was a fool; I just drew attention to you, but the only thing I could think of was to come and find out—"

"About Tony," she said bitterly. "Always Tony."

"All right. About Tony. I've always wanted to help him."

"You can't help a person like Tony. Nobody can. I should know."

"Again—all right. But now I'm asking you to help me. You know I won't repeat anything you say, but can't you understand I've got to know?"

"Yes, but I don't *know* anything, Michael. I can only guess, as you're guessing. I've heard Tony talking about Edwin and I do know from what Tony said that Edwin was made a fool of by some of these phony French dealers."

"How so?"

"Well, when the Ministry was started, Joyce-Lawrence began to look for pictures. He didn't use the famous dealers. He hadn't got the money. He negotiated with some of the less reliable gentry who buy up promising work for a song. Joyce-Lawrence could afford to do it, because he did know painting when he saw it. Then he died, and that Higginson man became Minister. He was an economy measure. You know all that."

"Yes. I know. And he was a very competent administrator. So what?"

"That left Edwin in the post of adviser. It was Edwin who negotiated with crafty French dealers, and Edwin didn't know a thing. He only thought he did. Well, I think he was had, and somehow it gradually percolated to his mind that he'd been had."

"You mean he'd been landed with worthless pictures?"

"Yes. It wouldn't have mattered if he'd been a sensible person. He could just have suppressed the rubbish. Kept it in the cellars. But being Edwin, his conceit got the upper hand. Somebody had fooled him: well, he was going to find out who and make them sorry for it. He was vindictive, you know. He would have taken a lot of trouble to ruin anybody, not because they were dishonest, but because they'd fooled him."

Michael Danvers sat with his chin in his hands, thinking furiously. "You're assuming there was a swindle," he said slowly. "Rivers is on

to that. He's had all the people in Loans shifted to the basement
and he's been haunting Architects and Acquisitions and Files. But
if it was a swindle over pictures, it's the dealers who would have
worked it, and everybody is certain that the person who murdered
Pompfret—if he *was* murdered—must have been employed in the
building."

"The dealer might have had an agent in the Ministry—one of
the packers, most probably. I'm trying to remember what Tony said,
something about two-way traffic—that it was possible to fool an
inexpert buyer in two ways—to palm off a dud as a valuable painting
or a valuable painting as a dud."

"Good lord!" exclaimed Michael. "I hadn't thought of that one."
He sat and thought again. Then he said: "Do you think Tony knows
anything, or was he just guessing?"

"He wasn't even guessing. He was just holding forth one evening,
after he'd read some scorching critique of one of the Ministry Loans
shows. He said that any dishonest dealer could fool an inexpert buyer
on this modern stuff—and Tony didn't count even Joyce-Lawrence
as a real expert. But we don't know that it's anything to do with a
dealer's ramp. It may be something quite different. Some wretched
porter or clerk who snaffled something. Edwin was so damned
self-righteous." She saw Michael's face harden and added: "Sorry,
Mike. I know you don't like me to say things against him. You can't
realise how remote I feel from him. For three years he bored me
so hideously I nearly went mad. It was my fault. I ought never to
have married him. I know I was loathsome to him, always quarrel-
ling, always mocking him, and he was thankful when I packed up
and left him to his own meticulous, finicky ways. But once I'd left
him, I didn't hate him any longer. I just didn't care. He could have
divorced me if he'd wanted to, but he didn't want to. Neither of us
wanted to get married again. We'd had enough of that." She broke

off, and then added wearily: "I don't know why I'm boring you with all this. I know you don't care a damn about me. It was Tony who mattered to you. But you've been so damned good to both of us, kind and generous—"

"Oh, forget that," said Michael quickly. "The only thing that matters is that somehow we've got involved in this grim business: you and Tony and me. We're all suspect, as accessories if not as principals. That's why we've got to clear it up. What was the silly business you tried to put over Rivers with that painting of Tony's?"

"Oh, that. Of all the fool things... Tony left that canvas because it was too big to take away and he hadn't finished it anyway. It was clever, you know. I thought if I splashed some colour over the bare patches I could sell it. I was just about broke. Besides that, if the C.I.D. came along, as I knew they might, I didn't want them to get asking who had painted the tulips."

"Why not?"

"Because I didn't want Tony dragged into the mess-up over Edwin's death. It's nothing to do with him. He'd never even seen Edwin. Tony had taken all his things away from the studio except his paint box and easel and canvas. I said I'd send them along later. Well, I thought I'd do a painting act. It didn't come off. That's all."

Michael Danvers looked at her steadily. "Is Tony mixed up in this ramp at M.O.F.A.?" he asked quietly.

"No. He isn't. He knows nothing about the place. You've no right to suggest things like that, Michael. If you're going to try to get Tony mixed up in this, you'll be asking for trouble, and you'll get it."

"Oh, don't be so childish," said Michael. "You know perfectly well that the one thing I'm interested in is making certain that Tony isn't mixed up in it."

He realised the moment he had spoken that he had made a mistake in answering her sharply. Virgilia Hill had a flaring, uncontrolled temper and Michael Danvers knew it. Moreover, she was inevitably oppressed by an almost intolerable sense of strain and unhappiness. Whatever her faults and foolishness, she was deeply devoted to Tony.

"Look here, I'm sorry," he said. "I'd no business to snap back. I do realise you've had enough upset to knock any woman flat. Honestly, I'm terribly sorry about everything."

But Virgilia wouldn't listen to him: it was as though something had snapped, and sullen rage overwhelmed her. She turned on Michael furiously.

"What did you start interfering for? If it hadn't been for you the damned police would never have found me, never have heard of Tony. You only came to the studio to lead them there, to turn suspicion on to Tony to save yourself. You've been sitting here pumping me for information so that you can pass it on—"

"That's enough," said Michael quickly. "You don't know what you're saying. The strain of the whole business has got you down and you're just imagining things."

Suddenly she threw herself sideways in her chair, put her head down on her arms and began crying, in dreadful choking sobs. Michael Danvers got up and left her. There were some things he was helpless to cope with, and he knew it.

II

When he went out into the passage he saw a tall woman standing there, as though waiting for him. She gave a nod and indicated a door on the right and Michael followed her. She closed the door behind them and he said:

"Could you go to her? She's in a wretched state, crying her heart out."

"So much the better," she rejoined quietly. "It had to come. Let her cry herself to sleep. You're Michael Danvers, aren't you? I'm Olivia Wainwright. I've been trying to get Constance to leave that wretched studio for months. She's a maddening person but I'm fond of her, and I couldn't bear to see her living the way she was living. But I didn't count on all this hideous complication of Edwin Pompfret being killed."

"She hadn't anything to do with that," said Michael quickly.

"I know she hadn't. She's not wicked, not in any sense: just a fool who believes in all this modern clap-trap about freedom of association between men and women. Neither do I believe that Tony did it. The only thing he cared about was to get free of an association which had become hateful to him."

"Yes. I see that," said Michael, "but in running away as Virgilia has done, hasn't she done the very thing to make the police believe she's involved in Pompfret's death? The very fact that she's disappeared will make them track her down. It's crazy."

"So it may be, but I'm not," she rejoined coolly. "What you say is perfectly true, and it's almost impossible for anybody to walk out and disappear so that the police never find them. The police know she's here. I've told them, and I've made myself responsible for looking after her. I told them it was impossible for her to go on living in that studio by herself."

"Good lord!" exclaimed Michael helplessly, and she went on coolly:

"I've got my living to earn, and I don't intend to get mixed up in any criminal proceedings if I can help it. Neither did I want a red-haired Virgilia Hill here for any of our residents to recognise, so the 'new look' suited me all right. Here she is, and here she'll stay—at least until such time as Scotland Yard makes up its mind who did the dirty work. I'm a great believer in Scotland Yard. I don't think they often slip up."

"Don't they?" said Michael.

"Well—not often. And now—I don't want to be uppish, or over-bearing, or anything like that, but I think it'd be better if you didn't come here again until all this mess-up is over."

"Very well," said Michael, and added rather bitterly: "and if I do, you'll ring Scotland Yard?"

"I wouldn't put it beyond me," she said. "Good night."

CHAPTER XVI

I

AT ELEVEN O'CLOCK THAT SAME EVENING, RIVERS AND LANCING
sat down to a sandwich meal at the Ministry, accompanied by
good coffee and plenty of it. One of the C.I.D. sergeants (who had
been instructed in the art by the Chief Inspector) had made the
coffee: it was strong and hot and clear, and in Rivers' opinion did
more to keep sleepiness at bay than any other beverage. Despite the
fact that they had worked the greater part of the previous night, both
Rivers and Lancing wanted to put in another night's work while they
had Medici House to themselves, and were not "tripping over typists
or stalling off Assistant Secretaries" as Lancing put it.

While Rivers drank his coffee, he read the reports which were being
sent on to him as they came in from Headquarters. "I wonder how
many people realise the trouble we take," he grumbled, as he tossed
sheet after sheet across to Lancing. "Everything from a cradle to a
coffin, as the old firm used to say. Date of birth, home town, profession
of parents, school, university, subjects of study, army, navy and air force
records, passport photograph, present acquaintances, hobbies, income,
probable expenditure… it's marvellous how we're all tabulated. Here's
Michael Danvers—everything he was so careful not to tell us."

Lancing took the file and looked through it eagerly. "Stalagluft
Y… Cripes, he was one of those tunnellers—longest job on record…
Anthony Devinton worked with him—"

"Yes, and Tony Devinton's photograph supplied by the ever watchful Press—they gave him a special par when he got home—has been recognised by all Miss Virgilia Hill's disapproving neighbours around the studio. Michael Danvers doesn't lack brains when it's a matter of passing exams which would plough you and me to the tune of gamma minus, but he hasn't the wits to realise that we know our own job if we don't know his. Then there's young John Dunne: a very promising architect. He's done special designs for the Build Your Own Homes brigade, with particular attention to labour-saving devices in the hoisting of roofing materials for the amateur builder. He seems to be one of those inventive chaps, interested in gadgets. Paul Weston still goes in for gliding as a hobby—you'd have thought he'd have had enough of that on D-Day. He also belongs to a flying club in Sussex and has a pilot's licence. Blackwell, also in Loans branch, does a bit of painting on his own account and has exhibited in the Civil Servants' Art Exhibition. Roger Welles once won the Diamond Sculls and still keeps his own boat at Teddington, and Mr. Dellison landed a First and a Boxing Blue the same year, which isn't bad going. I'll leave you to sort out which items interest me and which don't."

Lancing grinned. "Thanks for kind offer. About this Tony Devinton. Said to be a skilled artist. Forged all the documents for escapers while in Stalagluft Y, also decorated the huts with murals. Query, did Tony Devinton also paint the canvas you saw in Miss Hill's studio?"

"I should think so. But before you produce any beautiful theories, remember that Tony Devinton has never been employed in this building and so far as we can judge has never even been in the place. He's got an unusual face—not the sort of face you forget. I've showed his photograph to a fair selection of people here, including the doormen, porters, messengers and others who're about the entrance hall and corridors a good deal, and they all swear they've never seen him here. And as you and I have reason to appreciate, this building isn't an easy one to get to know. And one further reminder, in case you need it: Michael Danvers was at the Highland Ball, probably dancing a sixteensome, when Pompfret was killed."

"I hadn't forgotten that. Incidentally, what did the tickets for that ball cost?"

"More than you and I would care to pay, but Danvers has a comfortable private income in addition to his wage packet—and that, I may tell you, is not to be despised, especially for a bachelor."

"He's a nuisance, isn't he," said Lancing. "That was a very snappy get-away he did in Piccadilly."

"Very snappy, but as he was one of the most accomplished escapers of the whole band of brothers, I don't feel disposed to blame our lads for being bested by him. And so to work: as Pepys did not say. I'm asking you to concentrate for a few minutes." Rivers sat silent for a second or so, then he said:

"We have made an assumption about the mechanics of this murder, and the movements of the murderer before and after. We are justified in assuming that he used his knowledge of the building to enable him to get around it, from top to bottom—or from extrados to foundation, if you prefer to be architectural. We have no proof of the murderer's identity: no proof, that is, that the D.P.P. would accept. My own belief is that the proof may exist if we can find it." He paused, intent on doodling with a government pencil on a government pad, and then he went on: "It's safe to assume that the murderer got very dirty during his peregrinations in this house. He took a chance and borrowed Titmarsh's boiler-suit, which was an intelligent thing to do. The boiler-suit protected him from most of the soot, but my guess is that he was careful what he wore underneath it: something like a seaman's jersey with a roll collar and dark slacks. It's pretty certain he wore gloves—he wouldn't have forgotten those. Perhaps also a balaclava helmet to keep his head clean. He wouldn't have wanted to go home filthy. And probably Plimsols or gym shoes of some kind, which would enable him to walk silently and get a good grip on the floor. Now I've been guessing all this, and the basis of my guess work is what I myself should have worn in similar circumstances. I've supposed an outfit which could have been got rid of easily, but I've omitted one item which I think he must have used. We've been over this place pretty carefully, haven't we? What haven't we found—what didn't we find last night which we might have expected to find?"

Lancing sat and thought, his chin on his fists. It took him quite a long time. Then he said: "Yes. I think I get you. But there was that damned furnace."

"Yes, there's that," agreed Rivers, "but somehow I don't think so. However, by this time the electricians have got their drums of flex in the cellars and up top. We shall have enough light to see by this time. So now you know what you're in for—a detailed examination of the whole area of this house, first the cellars, then the lofts, with particular attention to footprints, if any."

Lancing grinned. "What about following the example of the bloke who's giving us all this exercise and borrowing some overalls?"

"They've sent us some from the mechanics department—but we shall be like sweeps before we're done."

"A Turkish bath to celebrate on my next free day," said Lancing.

II

For two solid hours Rivers and Lancing searched the cellars, carrying portable lamps with them. It was a fantastic party. The two officers went ahead, armed with bulbs and flex which trailed in their wake. They searched old boxes, bung-holes, crevices in the masonry. They studied the flagged floors and arched vaults: they discovered unsuspected manholes giving access to ground level, both in house and garden. In the dust that lay heavy on the floors of the further cellars they found plenty of traces showing that other people had been there before them—but it was impossible to say when these traces had been made. The surveyor's party, and also the inquiring architects, had been down in the vaults within the last few months, and the dust was shuffled and disturbed. Footprints there were in plenty, and these were photographed, but as Rivers said, they didn't prove a thing. Following up behind the Chief Inspector and his companion, came C.I.D. men, reminiscent of the "seven maids with seven mops": they swept the dust into piles for future examination. The result was that dust hung in the air like a fog: the fine dust of pulverised mortar, the dust which always develops on the surface of flagstones, dust from the old furnace, coal dust which had spread when Titmarsh did his strong man act on the coal heaps: in addition to all this was London soot—the deposit which hangs in the London air and which settles on every foggy day. It was about the filthiest search Rivers had ever experienced, and he and Lancing and their attendant minions coughed and wheezed and grumbled—and carried on. It was nearly two o'clock in the morning before they came up from the vaults, having found nothing which was of the least interest to them. Their only satisfaction was a negative one—they knew there was nothing to find.

The two officers went outside into what had once been Earl Manderby's garden: now a waste of coarse grass around the air-raid shelters. They stayed in the cold night air while they smoked a cigarette each and Lancing demonstrated how easy it was to climb the containing wall and drop down into the quiet Mayfair street outside.

"This building is a murderer's delight," said Rivers morosely. "Any number of opportunities for playing hide-and-seek: exits at every corner of the building, official or unofficial, and about a thousand employees to put the blame on to."

"Leave out the poor typists," said Lancing. "Not one of the poor girls can be blamed for shifting Canova's outsize. They wouldn't have known how to begin."

"Maybe not, but there are a few intelligent young women here who could have told their boy friends just how to set about it. Well, we've had a surfeit of cellars: now we weigh in on the lofts. They're as filthy as say-so and give about as much head room as some of our choicer mines, so I can promise you a happy time."

When they got inside again, a messenger was waiting for Rivers with a report about Tate—the constable who had been found unconscious in the cellars. Tate had "come to," but was suffering from concussion and the doctors were unwilling to have him questioned in any detail. He said that he had tripped over something, after going to locate a noise—a hammering noise, like someone trying to "break out."

"My own opinion is that the noise he heard was provided by someone hitting one of the radiator pipes on the ground floor," said Rivers. "Any old lag could tell you—if he chose—how to communicate with his fellow convicts in gaol by tapping a code on the pipes—the sound travels along them in an uncanny way. The idea behind this demonstration was probably to give the impression that somebody was playing games in the cellars, but the executant couldn't have counted on a C.I.D. man being fool enough to knock himself flat out by tripping over a baulk left on the flagstones."

"And counsel for the defence will tie Tate up into knots and make him admit he was tripped up or attacked in the darkness, while accused was busy about the nation's business in his private office," said Lancing. "Everybody who saw the ambulance arrive will have been busy reporting another murder in Medici House. Incidentally, do you think it's possible for a big tough like Tate to have stunned himself by taking a header on to a stone floor?"

"Not in normal circumstances," said Rivers, "but the air down there was fouler than I would have believed possible: also it's probable that Tate wasn't using his torch to light the floor and look out for snags: he threw the beam ahead to light the farther cellars. If he rushed at the job like a bull, his own velocity would have helped to crack his silly skull when he met the pavement. Well, this is where we do our bending double act, and for the love of Mike don't go splitting *your* skull on a beam because your zeal outruns your gumption."

Under the leads and slates and rafters and battens, over the beams and joists they crawled through the lofts of Medici House. The cellars had been unpleasant, choking and chill and confusing, but the lofts were a great deal more unpleasant. Rivers and Lancing were both tall fellows and neither of them enjoyed crouching: in addition to physical discomfort and over-close contact with a film of soot which had lain in the lofts ever since the blitz, was the complication of the variety of places to search. Lancing said afterwards that a whole forest must have been felled to provide the timbers in the roof of Medici House. Every beam and joist and rafter concealed crevices which were potential hiding places.

There were four manholes which gave access to the lofts from the attics: each had been opened more or less recently, when the roofs had been inspected because war-time damage seemed irreparable and rain persistently leaked through some fresh fault in a roof which had suffered the rain of shrapnel from London's barrage. If—as Rivers believed—the lofts had been visited by Edwin Pompfret's murderer, the latter had been provided with good camouflage by the builders who had patched up the cracked slates and damaged lead of that great roof. There was nothing to prove which manhole had been used to gain access to the lofts: the Plans room in the Architects' branch, the store room of Establishments, the cleaners' scullery and the one remaining museum piece of a Victorian bathroom—all these four apartments had fixed ladders which led to the four manholes provided by Decimus Burton or his obliging builders. So along the four long lofts the C.I.D. men crawled and stumbled, swearing and sneezing, hunting in every crevice, collecting every bit of rag, mis-laid tool, length of flex or piping, and fag-end of illicit cigarette left behind by the artisans who had worked in the loft.

One of the more interesting jobs was handed over to two young C.I.D. men whom Rivers described as "Frogmen." It was their privi-lege to raise the cover of the surprisingly large water cistern which was established on the joists in one corner of the loft. The cover was of wood, held in place by its own weight, but the timber was old and had been attacked by mice, rats, beetles and other enemies. When it had been pushed to one side by the muscular Frogmen, a waterproof electric fitment was lowered into the cistern, so that it was well illuminated. When the cistern had last been emptied and cleaned was a matter of history, but, despite its cover, the deposit at the bottom of it was, in the vernacular, "just nobody's business." The Frogmen reported that anything might be hidden there, because once they disturbed the deposit at the bottom the water immediately became clouded with a surprising density of suspended matter. Rivers came to inspect the phenomenon while one of the Frogmen murmured: "Don't say anybody drinks it… not really drinks it."

"Don't fuss," said Rivers. "It's only carbon deposit—pure soot. You're breathing it every day of your life. It's no use stirring it up, you poor fool. You'll have to empty the cistern. Go and find the main stop-cock, turn it off, and then turn on all the taps in the building. The furnace is cold by this time, but see there aren't any electric boilers on in the canteen. When the tank's empty, you can toss up for who is to have the unique privilege of getting inside and finding out what's really there."

The rest of the time spent in the lofts was enlivened by the surprising amount of gurgling that went on when Rivers' orders had been carried out, and every tap and drain in Medici House (there were a surprising number of them) helped to empty the "father and mother of cisterns" which had been introduced into the loft some hundred years ago, when eminent Victorians were beginning to regard baths with favour. By what means the tank was got into the loft remained an unfathomed mystery, since there was no aperture large enough to admit it.

While the tank was being emptied, Rivers had the pleasure of showing Lancing the most sensational item in the loft: this was a small, carefully covered aperture which, when opened, gave a view of the main staircase and the empty plinth where the Canova bust had stood. It was this small trap-door which gave access to the hook and chain from which had once been suspended the great candelabrum whose picture Patricia Oxton had shown to the Minister. Lancing looked down, fascinated.

"Anybody could have shot Pompfret from here," he observed.

"Quite easily. But he wasn't shot," said Rivers dryly. "Look here: a change of occupation is as good as a rest. I'll bet you a couple of quid you can't get from this spot to the entrance hall in five minutes—by any route you like to take."

"Done," said Lancing, "provided no one gets in my way. Can I order them off?"

"You can."

A moment later Lancing was scrambling over the joists like an animated crab, making for the nearest manhole: ignoring the ladder, he let himself down by his hands and jumped. Then he ran, swiftly and silently, in his rubber-soled shoes, out of the Plans room, along the passage, down the twisting service stairs, and so to the ground floor and the entrance hall, whence he yodelled derisively at Rivers, two minutes in hand, two pounds in pocket. It was some minutes later that he rejoined Rivers, who was perched on the ladder in the Plans room, gazing with satisfaction at the trail of sooty footsteps which Lancing had left over the scrubbed boards of the floor.

"Crikey!" said Lancing. "That shows, doesn't it? Every picture tells a story."

"Yes," said Rivers slowly. "Soot. That's what we didn't find, and we might have expected to find. Whoever goes up to those lofts will leave, a sooty trail when they come down. The man we're wanting went up there all right: he wouldn't have wasted time cleaning up his footprints—he hadn't got the time to waste. So he'd have worn something over his shoes and discarded the something before he finally came down the ladder."

"He might have pulled socks over his shoes," said Lancing.

"He might have, but I don't think he did," said Rivers. "Socks tear on nails and splinters—and they can trip you up if they catch. I think he wore goloshes and shoved them under the timbering before he came down. At least, I hope he did. And if he did, it'll be all Lombard Street to a china orange that he left a fingerprint on them at some stage. Here's your two quid—and cheap at the price. Now come on and find those goloshes. They're there somewhere— I'm certain of it."

CHAPTER XVII

I

WHEN MICHAEL DANVERS LEFT OLIVIA WAINWRIGHT, HE walked on slowly, hardly noticing where he was going, his mind in a turmoil of confusion and uncertainty. Common sense bade him go home and leave things alone: he knew that he had drawn attention to himself too much already, and in so doing had focused attention on Virgilia Hill also, but the thing which troubled him so much at the moment was that he had suddenly lost confidence in his own judgment of Virgilia. When he had talked to her last night, he had been confident that she had spoken the truth when she told him that she knew nothing about Pompfret's death, and that Tony knew nothing about it, either.

He thought back to Virgilia's puzzled sleepy face when she had opened the studio door last night and demanded angrily what on earth he was dreaming about to come and wake her up at such an hour. She *had* been puzzled, she *had* been sleepy; her hair tousled, her eyes heavy, her face still flushed with sleep, at first she had refused to listen to a word about Edwin Pompfret. "He's dead," Michael had blurted out, and she had retorted angrily, "Who cares, and why come and wake me up to tell me so…?"

It hadn't occurred to him then that she could be putting on an act, but now Michael's mind was veering to and fro, like a weather cock when the wind is changing. He realised suddenly why it was that his confidence in her was thus shaken: it was her changed appearance. She now looked so utterly different: she had become a stranger, somebody he didn't know. Would any woman have taken such pains to alter her appearance unless she intended to run away, to escape... from the police? As for Olivia Wainwright, what proof was there that what she said was true? She had said: "The police know, because I've told them"—and she would have felt quite certain that Michael would take no steps to ascertain if that statement were true.

Walking slowly along Brompton Road, Michael wondered again if he had evaded the C.I.D. man whom he was certain had tailed him as he came out of Medici House. He had no means of knowing, and suddenly realised that he didn't greatly care: but he did care about Tony Devinton, and his mind was troubled by the recollection of some cryptic phrases of Tony's which Virgilia Hill had quoted: "... two-way traffic... you can fool an inexpert buyer in two ways." Michael Danvers had not got the artistic sensitivity to respond to the symbolism of modern painting, but he had an exceedingly acute mind so far as other problems were concerned. It was as though something clicked in his brain—or gears engaged smoothly and began to turn, and their movement made him realise the potentiality of phrases which had certainly been Tony's. And being Tony's they had a precise meaning, for all the casualness of the phrasing. Michael Danvers looked about him with a sudden interest in his surroundings: he was near South Kensington station, and he remembered that Ewart Blackwell lived somewhere near here, in one of those roads between Cromwell Road and Harrington Gardens. Blackwell—like Michael, he was keen on dancing reels, that was how they had got to know one another—but Blackwell was in Loans branch and consequently in touch with Acquisitions. Michael crossed the road and began to pursue a devious way, now north, now west. He'd been to Blackwell's flat once. He could find it again if he tried.

II

Blackwell was working hard. He was an ambitious young man and believed that promotion comes to the studious, so he was sitting humped up by the fire, concentrating on *The Philosophy of Modern Art* by Herbert Read and dismissing from his consciousness the fact that he had acquired the new Agatha Christie from *The Times* library at the same time as the Herbert Read. Blackwell's "unk" (a term he had recently picked up which denoted his subconscious) had already decided that one hour's concentration on *The Philosophy of Modern Art* would earn him two hours' relaxation on Mrs. McGinty, but he was aware that he looked pleasantly studious when the front-door bell rang: carefully placing a marker in the one book, he left it with its title showing impressively uppermost on his sheaves of notes: the other book he moved to a side table before he went to the door.

When he saw Michael Danvers he gave a slight gasp. "Lord... I thought it'd be Scotland Yard. They've been breathing down my neck all day. Come along in. Any news?"

He led the way into his pleasant sitting-room and pulled a second chair up to the fire, adding: "Do you think they're getting anywhere, these Yard men?—and would you like some beer?"

"Thanks very much," said Michael, lowering himself into the chair. "The answer to A is I don't know: to B, in the affirmative, thanks a lot. Sorry if I disturbed you when you were reading."

"Don't worry about that. I think I was glad to be disturbed. I'm not really up to contemporary standards. My powers of appreciation lag around at the end of the fifteenth century, but an occasional quote sounds well when we get some of these high hats along. Here's hoping..."

He handed Michael a glass of beer and added: "Do you really believe Pompfret was murdered? Because I do not."

"I don't think it matters what we believe," said Michael, "it's what Rivers believes that matters, and there's no doubt whatever about what he believes. Anyway, it's hardly worth arguing about, because Pompfret couldn't have shifted the thing."

"I don't agree. The thing *was* shifted, so why not Pompfret? He'd got more brains in some ways than most people gave him credit for. If he'd wanted to shift the Canova, he was as capable of working out ways and means as anybody else. And he'd got a thing about his marble namesake, you know."

"I don't care if he'd got twenty things," said Michael. "Alternatives aren't on in this act. Rivers knows that Pompfret was murdered. I'm pretty certain he knows how it was done, and it's my belief that a few other people in the Ministry know, too. The Architects gang know something. Welles has been going round with a face like something out of a Last Judgment mural, and those two girls are studiously avoiding speaking to anybody."

"Well, how was it done?" asked Blackwell.

"The lord knows, I don't. It's why it was done that interests me, and the why must be somewhere in your line of country."

"Mine? What was Pompfret to me, or me to Pompfret?" demanded Blackwell indignantly.

"I don't mean you personally. I mean the answer's connected with Loans or Acquisitions. Those V.I.P.s who've been sitting in committee on all your stuff are doing it because somebody's spotted something, either the Minister, or Rivers, or one of your crowd in Loans. There must have been some dirty work going on somewhere, and Pompfret must have realised it."

"I hope you don't kid yourself you're being original," retorted Blackwell. "We've been chewing it over all day, and the answer's a lemon. There isn't a thing in Loans that's worth pinching."

"Look here, Blackwell. How much do you really know about

all these canvases you bung around? No, don't interrupt. It's no use saying you know them all by heart and they're all there. How much do you know about the artistic value of them—what they'd mean to the artists and critics who have spent their lives studying this modern stuff?"

Blackwell sat with shoulders hunched and meditated for a while. "You're challenging me, personally," he said at last. "Well, the best answer I can make is to show you two reproductions, common or garden colour prints. They'll make my point for me better than any amount of blethering about values."

He got up and rummaged among his books and came back with two which he laid on the table, open, showing two colour prints. "You probably know them both even though you haven't seen the originals," he said. "The first is 'The Holy Family,' by Michael Angelo. The second is a contemporary Still Life—'A Colander with Beans.' Now the first can be recognised as a great painting by any ordinary intelligent person; no matter if they've never looked at a picture in their lives before, they'll still recognise the inherent greatness of that one. The second is regarded as a great painting by the contemporary experts and critics: that is to say, it's important enough to be reproduced in colour in authoritative treatises on contemporary painting. And how many ordinary intelligent people would recognise it as an important painting if it was shown to them for the first time without comment or commendation?"

"Certainly not me," said Michael. "It doesn't convey anything to me at all except a deliberately naïve rendering of commonplace objects."

"There you are," said Blackwell, "and you can at least recognise what those objects are. With abstracts it's even more difficult to judge. What I'm saying is that the ordinary chap, blokes like you and me, simply can't assess the things on our own judgments alone.

It's only the specialists who can assess them. And whether the critics of to-day will have their judgments endorsed by the critics of to-morrow is anybody's guess."

"All right. I agree with all you've said so far," said Michael. "Now in Loans Collection you've got a lot of stuff which looks to me on a par with that Still Life. It may be immortal art or it may be a leg-pull so far as the uninformed are concerned. You say that only the specialists know. Leaving the specialists out of it—and I gather you don't claim to be one—how do you know whether the stuff you've got is damned good or damned bad?"

"Oh, we know from extraneous evidence," said Blackwell. "The things are signed—not like the Minister's 'funnies'—that was Joyce-Lawrence's idea of humour. We know the sort of esteem the painters are held in, the prices they command, the galleries they exhibit at. And we've nothing in Loans that isn't very middle class indeed—"

"But how do you *know*?" insisted Michael. "You're going by what you call extraneous evidence. Can you, or Weston, or Miss Barton, or any of you, swear that you haven't got a single picture that's a pure leg-pull or a single picture that's an epoch-making contemporary? It seems to me that since Joyce-Lawrence's death, none of you knows the one from the other apart from its label and provenance."

"Look here, what are you getting at?" demanded Blackwell, and his voice told that he was becoming irritated.

Michael said hastily: "Sorry if I'm being a bore. I mean this. You showed me two colour prints. I'll quote you two statements you've just made. One is, 'Joyce-Lawrence was a humorist.' Two is, 'We know from extraneous evidence.' Now if your extraneous evidence was faked, would you still know if a humorist had been indulging his own brand of humour?"

"I still don't follow you."

"Well, to get down to brass tacks, say if Joyce-Lawrence followed his own ideas by acquiring one or two valuable pictures and made up the rest of the collection with canvases which cost virtually nothing?"

"So what?"

"Well, there's the possibility of a fraud. Some smart copyist copies the valuable work, leaves the copy with you and sells the original at a high price. Would any of you in Loans collection really know a copy from an original, when the original is deliberately child-like in treatment?"

Blackwell sat and puffed at a pipe which he had just filled. "I don't know," he said slowly. "I suppose you've got the idea from Rivers."

"I haven't," retorted Michael indignantly. "Apart from a few personal raspberries Rivers said nothing to me at all."

"Well, if it's your own idea, it may be a bit too close to the target," said Blackwell, "because I happen to know that Rivers asked Weston if he could tell a copy from an original. But it won't wash. We know the value—or lack of value—of all these pictures we've got. They're not worth copying because the originals have never commanded a market price. I'll show you our catalogue if you like. I doubt if a name in it would mean a thing to you, and even you must know the names that command big prices. You must have heard Pompey raving about the élite."

"Well, why have the C.I.D. turned the big three on to Loans?"

"I've not the least idea, unless it's because Pompfret haunted us like a shadow. Look here; you've made quite an interesting point about copying these moderns. It does seem to me that such a thing is possible in the case of some of these infantile still-lifes and some of the abstracts, but I still can't see the point of doing it, and even if it were done I don't see the connection between copying not-so-good paintings and murdering Pompfret."

"He might have spotted the fraud, traffic, or what have you."

"My good ass, we've blown that one sky-high. Pompey was less capable of judging pictures than any of us. And if you're suggesting that one of his visiting experts tried to put him wise, that won't wash either. He was so conceited that no criticism could penetrate his hide. Once he'd made up his mind, it was made up permanently. A picture was good because he'd said it was good and further comment was redundant."

"Look here," said Michael, "you're making a mistake if you try to dismiss Pompfret as a hundred per cent fool. He wasn't anything of the kind. I worked for him and I know. He may have been a fool over pictures, but he wasn't a fool about human beings. He was pretty shrewd over people and he could get the gist out of a letter or report as fast as any man I know."

"Well—you should know." Blackwell sat and stared at Michael and then said: "I gather you've got an idea. D'you want to share it or not?"

"I've got too many ideas," said Michael unhappily. "I hoped you'd be able to scotch some of them for me."

"You don't believe anything I've told you," said Blackwell. "You've got this bee in your bonnet about the chance of some valuable object in Loans—and the hell of it is you're infecting me with your own dotty ideas. Look here: let's leave Loans out of it and transfer our attention to the Minister's 'funnies.' I've never had a chance to really look at them, but I believe they're much better than the Loans things."

"Perhaps you've spotted it," said Michael excitedly. "Joyce-Lawrence might have plunged for one first-rate picture in his own study…"

"Yes, I'll grant you that, but it'd have been spotted. Joyce-Lawrence had a lot of people in there, people who really knew."

"But Higginson didn't!" shouted Michael. "Higginson hated art experts."

"Cripes!" said Blackwell. "Now you've got something. Alf would never have spotted it if the whole lot of funnies had changed colour in the night. Anything might have happened. And our present Minister not only can't make head or tail of them, he admits it quite frankly. But the argument breaks down. Pompfret couldn't have spotted it either. A copy would have been just the same to Pompey. He was myopic as a man can be, anyway."

"Yes, but since Humphry David's been Minister, he's allowed Pompfret to bring visiting experts in to the ministerial study. There was that melancholic little Austrian—Weissonnier. He might have upset the apple cart and set Pompfret detecting and deducing things. Did Weissonnier come into Loans?"

"I believe he sniffed around. I didn't see him, but Miss Barton did. He didn't utter the whole time he was there." Blackwell sat forward, staring into the fire: then he said: "You've put forward an idea. It's an interesting idea. But how was it worked? You've postulated a copy. It's not impossible, but who was the copyist and when was it done? Higginson certainly wouldn't have known a copy from the original, or vice versa, but he'd have known if one of the pictures had been taken away. How was the copy done, and when?"

"Well, you know much more about painting than I do. You do paint yourself, don't you?"

"I wondered if that was coming," said Blackwell, and Michael put in quickly:

"Don't take me wrong. All I'm asking you is if my own ideas are all at sea. We can take it for granted that no official copyist has worked in the Minister's study. We should have heard about it—or at any rate, I should have, because Pompfret would have talked about it. Therefore, if a copy has been made, it's been done on the q.t. What I want to know is this: if the original were photographed and measurements taken, could a copyist, who knew the original well, have produced something near enough to a replica for an inexpert observer not to have noticed the difference, once the copy was framed and hung?"

"Might be," said Blackwell. "There are one or two of them which look as though a child could have done them. But I don't like your trend very much. And incidentally I haven't got an alibi for last night. I was here, by myself. And how can I prove it?"

"You haven't got to," said Michael quickly. "The only person who could have done a copy in the way I'm postulating is someone who has been in the Minister's study quite a lot to study the original. Not blokes like you and me, who have hardly ever been in there."

"I see. You're meaning a high-up: someone important enough to have been called into consultation with the Minister fairly frequently, and who would have been admitted to the study even if the Minister hadn't arrived."

"That's about it," agreed Michael. "I know this is only guess work, but everybody's agreed that if Pompfret was murdered, the murderer must be someone in the Ministry: someone who knew Pompfret's habits and the routine of the place. Well, I suggest two more qualifications: someone who was likely to have been called into consultation with the Minister fairly often and someone who was a fairly skilful painter. Finally, someone who needed money, because the only object of the fraud we're postulating would be to make money by marketing the original canvas."

Blackwell turned round and stared at Danvers with raised eyebrows: "Do you realise that you're making out a case against one particular person? There is only one person in the Ministry who fulfils all your qualifications—and frankly, when it comes to imputing murder to any particular person, I don't like it. Accusation is a two-edged tool."

"But I wasn't accusing any particular person. I was stating a general case," said Michael.

"You might have thought you wcrc, thc wish bcing father to the thought," said Blackwell. "It just happens that the individual who fits your case is a man who had a hell of a row with you not so long ago."

It was Michael's turn to stare. Blackwell went on: "Did you, or did you not, have a row with Welles over those papers of his which got lost—in your office or his. He said you'd held up his letters, you said the file had never reached you. The row got through via the typists and messengers."

"Welles…" said Michael.

"Yes. Welles. Some architects can paint, and he's one of them. He fulfils all your qualifications, including being an extravagant bloke. He's one of those bibliophiles who are crazy over first editions. He also knows a bit about contemporary painting."

Michael Danvers sat silent for a moment or two: he realised—as he had not realised before—that discussing a murder case is a nervy business when it gets down to chapter and verse.

"Look here," he said slowly. "I was *not* thinking of Welles. The thought of him never occurred to me."

"So you say. But the cap fits," retorted Blackwell. "Welles is a very decent chap, and I happen to know it. Whoever murdered Pompfret, he didn't. You might as well say I did. If I'd wanted the opportunity to study the Minister's pictures, doubtless I could have made it. Don't you see you're just making trouble by being too clever?"

"Sorry," said Michael quickly. "I hadn't realised the way the argument was going. I'd been worrying about something quite different."

"I can well believe it," said Blackwell. "Trying to get out of your own troubles by loading them on to someone else."

Michael stood up quickly. "All right. I'll clear out," he said. "I'm honestly sorry you think I was trying to frame anybody. I wasn't."

"Oh, all right. This damned business has got on everybody's nerves, including mine. The C.I.D.'s doing a cat and mouse act with all of us—you and me, Weston and Welles, Dellison and Dunne. They're following the lot of us. And it's all too easy to say so and so fits the facts. For God's sake let's leave it alone."

"All right. Sorry and all that," said Michael quickly.

III

After Danvers had gone, Blackwell sat and brooded miserably. He couldn't read any longer, and both the volumes he had got from the library seemed equally unsuitable to his present mood—both modern art and murder were topics he could not at the moment enjoy. Again and again he chewed over Michael Danvers' arguments, and again and again the word "copy" sent a shiver down his back. At last he got up, went into his bedroom and rummaged in his wardrobe. At the back of his clothes was a stretched canvas and he carried it into the sitting-room. Blackwell enjoyed the business of painting, the putting on of colours, but he had no creative ability. The canvas he held was painted with some skill: it was a very flat still life, the colour, form, and method being a frank imitation of a study in the Loans collection. Blackwell looked at it with something akin to panic. Then he took out his pocket-knife and slashed the canvas to bits and threw them on the fire. The wooden frame he wrenched in pieces and burnt also. But even then he couldn't settle down again in his silent room. He jumped up, saying to himself, "I'll go and see Weston. He'll soon blow Danvers' dotty ideas sky high. I can't go to bed and think about it all night. Weston will just hoot at the whole thing, and see all the weak points in the argument."

And with that he got into his top-coat and went out into the chilly evening.

CHAPTER XVIII

I

THE SEARCH IN THE LOFTS OF MEDICI HOUSE WENT ON PAIN-fully and wearily throughout the small hours until the searchers had quartered the lofts. The huge cistern had drained dry and its sooty sludge had yielded up sundry items, including small fragments of shrapnel, bits of slate and stone, a good many nails and the skeletons of various birds and a mouse. It was when the search party who had turned eastwards along the lofts met the searchers who had turned west that Lancing said "Do we do it all over again?"

They were weary and filthy and dispirited, and Rivers was just on the point of ordering them to go home when he suddenly gave an exclamation.

"I must be weak in the head. Sorry, chaps. I think I've got an idea."

He had suddenly remembered seeing Patricia Oxton standing on the ladder which led to the higher trap-door—the one that gave access to the roof itself. She had pushed up the trap-door, which was a hinged one, and it had gone back flat on to the leads, where it had stayed until she had pulled it back into place when she and Rivers re-entered the loft.

"Why didn't I think of that first instead of last?" said Rivers. "Softening of the brain. That's my trouble."

He went up the ladder to the first trap-door, opened it to the chilly night air and got out on to the leads, followed by Lancing.

"It'd be a perfect place to hide anything," said Rivers. "When you open the trap-door it goes back flat on the leads and anything underneath it would be hidden. You don't raise the trap-door again until you're going inside, and anything beneath it would still be concealed. Moreover, you're immediately above the manhole into the attics."

"Let's hope he was a sensible bloke," murmured Lancing.

There were four trap-doors giving access to the roofs—north, south, east and west: beneath each was another manhole leading to the attics, and any of the four might have been used if Rivers' theory was correct. He went up the ladders in turn, having groped his way over the joists along each side of the interminable lofts: north, south and east he drew a blank. It was under the trap-door at the west corner he found what he had hoped to find—a pair of goloshes, or rubber overshoes.

"They're here," said Rivers, "and for once it hasn't rained. Get me that box—treat 'em tenderly, treat 'em with care."

II

The goloshes were swathed in soft wrappings, enclosed in the box and despatched to Scotland Yard. Rivers refused to allow any examination before the rubbers were handed over to the experts in the fingerprint department.

"It's a chance, and only a chance," he said. "He'd have worn gloves all right while he was on the job, but those goloshes aren't new ones. He probably pulled them on dozens of times since he first had them, and even though he wiped them there's still a chance his fingerprints left traces, because you grip a golosh pretty hard when you pull it on."

Lancing agreed. "If there's not a single dab the experts can swear to, it'll be just too bad. What's the next item on the agenda?"

"A wash," said Rivers. "If there isn't any hot water in the cisterns we'll boil up kettles. Talk about stokers!"

They scrambled down again into the Plans room and Rivers dismissed the other searchers with a blessing. Then he and Lancing looked at one another They were clad in adequate boiler-suits which had once been blue. Close contact with the lofts of Medici House had blackened them comprehensively: their faces were smudged with black and there were sooty rims round their eyes. Taken all in all, they looked as typical a pair of sweeps as could be wished.

Shaking themselves to dislodge any loose soot, and wiping their feet on a mat thoughtfully collected for them by a constable, they stripped off their overalls and made their way downstairs. Rivers chose to go by the grand staircase, and he stopped in front of the plinth whence Earl Manderby had once stared out with globular marble eyes.

"We'll reproduce the lighting effects of last night," he said. "The lights would have been on in Pompfret's corridor, but the hall and staircase were dark."

He called to the man on duty down below and the hall lights went out, leaving the landing lighted only with the glow which came from the corridor. It shone across the landing and the top stair, leaving nothing but gloom below.

"We've guessed our way along in grand style," said Rivers, "and I think we've got a fairly comprehensive idea of what happened. Here's my final suggestion. The murderer wanted Pompfret in a particular place at a particular time. The time was arrived at by making an appointment—possibly with the Minister, possibly in Loans department. To get Pompfret into the identical spot which was necessary, I suggest that his own scarlet spectacle case was put on the middle of the top stair. He was desperately short-sighted but I think he'd have recognised it—and it's the one thing he would certainly have stopped to pick up."

Lancing gave an appreciative chuckle. "Speaking with due respect, sir, that is what I call a most intelligent suggestion."

Rivers snorted. "The chap who did this was intelligent all right," he observed. "He lacked one item of information—that Pompfret had a weak heart. Pompfret was a big chap. He looked tough. The murderer thought there was a perfectly good chance it'd be assumed that Pompfret shifted Manderby himself, especially in the absence of any indication of how Manderby was shifted."

"Yes," agreed Lancing, "but there was another thing as well. The murderer didn't know that the Minister had been browsing in files."

He broke off suddenly, as they heard the hall door open down below, and Rivers called for the lights to be switched on. Then they saw Humphry David standing down below, staring up at them with astonished eyes.

"Have you been sweeping chimneys?" he inquired.

"Sweeping, but not chimneys," said Rivers. "We'll go and get clean before we come to report, sir."

III

"I've told you how I think it was done, sir, but I'm not going to tell you who I think did it because I admit my theory has no evidence to prove it. You can argue out for yourself the qualifications needed, but even when you've got those tabulated, there are several persons who have no alibi to clear them: that's why I'm waiting for a report from the fingerprint people before I make a move."

The Minister nodded. He was heavy-eyed and weary, having just left the House after a stormy sitting which had prolonged itself until early morning.

"How it was done," he mused. "I suppose I ought to have tumbled to that—I had all the data. Why it was done: because someone accepted a bribe to perpetrate a fraud: and because the nature of modern art makes it difficult for any save the specialist to see through the fraud. And I suppose that Pompfret couldn't reconcile it with his *amour-propre* to report to me that he had been as blind as the rest of us. This is what comes of putting administrators in charge of works of art. I never imagined that murder would result from Civil Servants setting themselves up as connoisseurs of the fine arts, but I did envisage the possibility that they'd make laughing stocks of themselves."

"I've told you that I've guessed my way along, sir," said Rivers. "It had to be guesswork, because there was no concrete evidence to examine. Apart from possible fingerprints on an old pair of goloshes we've still got nothing positive, but I'm prepared to risk another guess. The fraud was possible because nobody in this place was qualified to judge between a picture by a world-famous modern artist and a copy of that picture. The probability is that one of Mr. Pompfret's visitors—Weissonnier for example—informed Mr. Pompfret that a picture in his beloved Loans collection was a phony picture. Mr. Pompfret inquired into the matter on his own account, studying the correspondence in files to assist him in his inquiries. My guess is that Mr. Pompfret spotted the culprit—"

"But why didn't he report it to me?" cried the Minister.

"Because he didn't want to admit that he himself had been made a fool of," said Rivers. "The culprit—who wasn't lacking in brains—may have said: 'Yes. I stole the thing. But I stole it because I valued it for itself. I, at least, knew what it was. You didn't. You saw it, but you didn't realise what it was. At least give me a chance. I will bring back the original picture, and you can have the credit of

discovering it.' It's possible that a man like Pompfret, swelled with
his own conceit, might have fallen for that one."

Humphry David sat with his head in his hands. "I suppose that in
all detection you've got to put yourself in the other chap's place and
puzzle out the motives which may have led him to such and such
a course of action," he said slowly, "and I agree that your diagnosis
may fit the facts—but there's an element of the grotesque in the
whole thing—"

"There's often an element of the grotesque in crime," said
Rivers. "This particular crime was, *au fond*, like the majority of other
crimes—a fraud perpetrated for profit. The method was unusual,
the environment was unusual, the person murdered was unusual,
but the original impulse was the lowest common denominator
which every detective meets every day—personal profit. I've admitted I've guessed my way along, but every guess I've made, whether
as to mechanics or individual reactions, had some material basis to
support it."

He broke off as a discreet knock sounded on the door.

"That will be my phone call, reporting from the Yard, sir."

"All right, Rivers. I'm not asking any questions. You can tell me
the rest when it's substantiated," said the Minister quietly.

IV

The first pallor of dawn was showing above the house-tops when
Rivers and Lancing got into the police car. They had got their one
item of indisputable evidence—fingerprints on the goloshes.

"Qualifications," murmured Lancing. "I looked through records
again. I spotted the essential—but it's shared by several persons in
the Ministry. A knowledge of architecture, and acquaintance with
building in course of construction—was that it?"

Rivers nodded. "Yes. Add that to a youth spent in Paris and an interest in gliding, plus a wireless that went out of order and the simplicity of stopping a pendulum clock."

"Gliding?" asked Lancing, but Rivers left him to think that one out for himself.

The London streets were empty of traffic at that hour—it was just after half-past five—and when the police car turned into Derwent Street there was nobody in evidence in the quiet roadway, but a man emerged from some basement steps and came up to Rivers as he got out of the car.

"Nothing to report, sir. It's been perfectly quiet all night. There's no back door to the house, and the ground floor windows at the front are barred. There was a visitor at ten o'clock last evening—name of Blackwell. The landlady was very unwilling to admit him, but he went in and stayed for a few minutes. Since then it's been as quiet as a graveyard. Very quiet respectable folk in this street."

"I'm delighted to hear it," said Rivers dryly. "Well, I'm sorry to disturb respectable folk at this hour, but I'm not feeling disposed to hang about."

He went up the steps of Mrs. Butler's house and rang the bell. It was an old-fashioned bell-pull, and he heard the bell jangling somewhere in the hall. It was at his third ring that the door opened and an indignant grey-haired man demanded the reason for being woken up at such an hour.

"I'm sorry to disturb you, sir," said Rivers. "We are police officers from Scotland Yard. I want to see Mr. Weston."

The other gaped at him in a horrified way and then stood aside.

"His room is the first floor front," he said. "Just above mine, to the right here. Will you find your own way up? Mrs. Butler sleeps at the top of the house, poor soul... Never had police in the house before..."

Rivers and Lancing went upstairs, quickly and quietly. There was no answer to their knock on the bedroom door and the door was locked. Rivers flashed his torch beam into the key hole, ascertained there was no key in it and got busy with his pick-lock outfit. It took him a very short time to open the door. He switched on the light and for a moment Lancing thought that the occupant of the room was asleep in bed—the bed clothes were humped up as they would have been over a body. Rivers pulled blankets and sheets away from the pillows which had simulated a human shape and said:

"Well, he's got away—probably by the roofs. He knows all about roofs."

"How did he guess we were on to him?" groaned Lancing.

"I expect Blackwell got talking. Confound them, they're all too talkative in that place. But I'll lay any money Weston's tried to get to France. He's got contacts there. And he'll try to fly. He belongs to that flying club in Sussex and he's got a motor-bike."

"If it's a club, it's hardly likely he'd get a plane away before daylight," said Lancing.

Rivers nodded. "Well—it's another guess. I'll put Brady on to phoning—aerodrome and gliding club."

"But aren't we going ourselves?" demanded Lancing.

"Of course we're going. We can identify him. The Sussex men can't. And the roads'll be clear at this hour."

v

The roads were clear all right. With a traffic cop on a motor-bike preceding the police car they bucketed through London at an incredible speed: over Chelsea Bridge and through Clapham and Streatham and Thornton Heath, past Croydon Airport and on to the Caterham by-pass, where the police driver grinned and showed what a police car can do. Rivers sat in the back and went to sleep, sensibly and characteristically. Lancing sat in front and saw the glory of a frosted March dawn over the north downs: through Godstone and Felbridge and Forest Row they speeded, where local policemen were on the *qui vive* to keep the road clear for the C.I.D.: through East Grinstead and Uckfield and a right-hand swing towards Lewes while the south downs rose clear and blue against a pale sky.

It was full daylight now. Rivers woke up as the car decelerated on a minor road and said:

"Hell! That's a plane! He's beaten us to it…"

It was Lancing in front who replied: "If it's Weston, he's had it. She's not climbing properly. He can't get height…"

As though instinctively, the driver pulled up with a screech of brakes. They heard the aero engine roar, splutter, cut out, and they saw the small aircraft dive, spin and crash; it hit the shoulder of Firle Beacon as the first rays of the sun lighted the long man of Wilmington.

CHAPTER XIX

I

"HOW WAS IT DONE?" REPEATED RIVERS. HE WAS SITTING in the Minister's study, avoiding looking at the pictures by a determined effort of will. "It was a problem which puzzled me considerably at first. How was that weight of marble moved so that it fell with such precision right down the middle of the stairs? I think I tumbled to it when I looked at that 'abstract' in Mr. Pompfret's office. There's a piece of string in the composition, running right down it. Somehow, inside my own mind, the string suggested rope, and because I once used to sail a boat and was once in the Royal Navy, the rope suggested tackle—blocks and pulleys. And that was that. Given the possibility of fixing a pulley above the weight, the shifting of that weight presented no difficulty."

"A pulley," echoed Humphry David. "You told me I had the data—"

"And you had the data, sir," said Rivers promptly. "It was given to you by Miss Oxton when she told you about the great candelabrum which hung above the main staircase. A candelabrum of that size is a considerable weight. It is hung on a chain, and the chain is attached to a ring or hook screwed into a beam in the ceiling. I didn't know about the candelabrum, but I spotted the hook because I looked for it. Later I learnt that, on account of the height of the building, access to the hook was provided by a small trap-door in the ceiling, to facilitate examination of the chain and its attachment. After that, the means of shifting the weight seemed clear enough."

The Minister shook his head. "A pulley. I should never have thought of it," he admitted.

"Every man to his own job, sir. A sailor uses pulleys: so does a builder. How often have you seen a builder's bucket of concrete being run up the side of a house by the simple expedient of a rope over a wheel—the essential mechanism of the pulley? Well, there was the fundamental idea. Given the possibility of access to the hook from the lofts, it seemed to me that a pulley could be hung without difficulty from the hook, and the rope or cable dropped to ground level. One end of the rope or cable could be affixed noosewise to Earl Manderby's neck, one end dropped to the ground floor where the haulier would stand. And because the hook was forward of Earl Manderby, when the cable was hauled on, Manderby would lift and come forward at an angle. If the cable were released suddenly Manderby would fall—plumb down the centre of the stairs. It's a perfectly simple piece of mechanics. Only a slight lift was necessary—just enough to shift the weight forward from its centre of gravity. Gravity did the rest."

"It was an extraordinarily ingenious idea," said the Minister, "even though it seems improper to say so."

"I don't see why it's improper to say so," responded Rivers. "The fact that a man uses his ingenuity for criminal ends doesn't mean that he's not ingenious. This was a cleverly thought out job and I'm not denying it. Now having assumed that a pulley was used to shift the weight 'to obtain a greater ratio of resistance to effort' as the text books say, the next point I considered was the rope or cable. A fine steel cable seemed probable, but there were two arguments against that. Steel might well have scratched or marked the marble, and there was no such scratch. It also occurred to me that a steel cable, or even a rope, would have shown up very obviously both on the marble itself and against the white walls. The murderer had to fix his pulley and drop his cable from the observation trap in the lofts. He then had to get downstairs leaving the cable hanging, and he would have wanted to use a cable that was as unnoticeable as possible. He had cut the fuse wire downstairs which meant that there was no light in the hall, but Pompfret was certain to turn on the passage light when he came out of his room, and though Pompfret was short-sighted he might have spotted a rope or fine steel cable against the white marble and the white walls. I considered this problem as though I were doing the murderer's job. What was the best sort of cable—something white, something non-abrasive. The answer seemed to me to be a section of nylon cable, such as was experimented with in glider towing. Nylon is very strong and can be obtained in dead white. It can also be burnt more easily than a rope of similar strength. Well, there you have my original guesses, my answer to 'How.'"

"I can only say that you showed an intelligence which puts me to shame," said Humphry David. "I have no sense of mechanics. I can never fathom how things work."

"It's our job," said Rivers simply. "We're always being confronted with 'hows.' Now, as I reconstructed events, the pulley was fixed up shortly after ten o'clock when the housemen had gone home and the night watchman was stoking. Sometime shortly after that the noose was put round Manderby's neck and the murderer stood in the darkened hall with the nylon cable end taut in his hand, in a position where he could see the top stair. As he stood there he would have heard the row Titmarsh was making in the cellars. It's an eerie thought—it must have seemed an interminable time before Pompfret came to the head of the stairs and paused there—to pick up his scarlet spectacle case, if my guess is right. Then the murderer hauled on his cable until he felt he'd got the weight moving—tilting right forward. Then he let go. The result was inevitable: it was a neatly reasoned bit of mechanics."

Humphry David shuddered. "And the murderer stood there, listening, to discover if Titmarsh was coming rushing upstairs," he said.

"I've no doubt he listened, but I'm quite sure he didn't do any standing still," said Rivers. "I'm certain he'd have leapt to Manderby's broken head, freed his noose and pulled the nylon cable right down so that it cleared the pulley, fell to the ground and could be coiled up so that it was portable. Then he had to collect the spectacle case. I think he made a mistake there. He'd probably meant to smash the spectacles and throw the bits down the stairs. Perhaps he panicked when he heard that Titmarsh had left off breaking up the coal. He certainly went back to the loft and removed his pulley next. He'd recovered his nerve by this time, because he must have put on his overshoes again before he went back to the lofts, to avoid leaving sooty footmarks. As I argue it out, he hid the goloshes under the trap-door, wrapped pulley and cable in the boiler-suit which he took off before leaving the loft, and proceeded to reconnoitre the situation downstairs. He had turned off the passage light which Pompfret left burning, and he would have been able to see when Titmarsh had replaced the fuse and the hall light came on again. When Titmarsh discovered the body, the murderer went down to the cellars, stuffed his cable into the furnace and hid the dungarees. Then he got out of one of the hatches and went home. The subsidiary staircases and passages in this house made it easy for one who knew it well to get down to the cellars without any difficulty. Incidentally, he took the pulley away with him. It was found by the Westminster Corporation Sanitary authorities, having been dumped with the refuse collected in the bins so carefully put out for collection by responsible ratepayers."

"So much for the 'how,'" said Rivers. "The answer to 'why' was suggested by yourself, sir, when you first called Henry Fearon into consultation. The answer was fraud, the fraud being concerned with some of these contemporary pictures which the average man is incompetent to assess. It was you, sir, who pointed out to us that nobody in this building had the qualifications of training, experience and knowledge of contemporary painting technique which could enable anyone to judge the paintings of to-day. We have uncovered the fraud—or rather Henry Fearon, collaborating with the responsible art dealers in Paris and with the officers of the Sûreté, has uncovered it. May I read you his letter to me—unexpurgated?"

The Minister chuckled: "I should be delighted. I like Henry Fearon."

Rivers read: "I've had the enlightening experience of listening to some opinions uttered by the hangers-on of the dregs of the Parisian art world. These gentry were pulled in by the Sûreté (whose officers are politely scandalised by the whole racket). Even responsible artistic opinion here was derisive over the setting up of an English Ministry of Fine Arts. When the Minister himself set his agents on the 'buying cheap' projects, a number of scallywags, shaking with mirth, said 'Anything in this for us?' The ragtag of the studios, co-operating with experienced thieves, thought out a bright scheme which was made possible when Higginson replaced Joyce-Lawrence. It was known that certain early pictures by Matisse, in the possession of wealthy bourgeois, were coveted by rapacious collectors in U.S.A. A painter of considerable skill and extreme poverty was commissioned to copy the Matisse pictures when they were on exhibition. The copies were then foisted on the unsuspecting owners, and the stolen originals were ready for export. The difficulty was to get them out of France. It was here that the Ministry of Fine Arts became an unconscious collaborator. Two genuine pictures by Matisse, signed 'Arlettier,' were duly delivered at the Ministry and became part of Loans Collection."

"Oh my God!" groaned Humphry David, and Rivers hastened to console him.

"You never saw them yourself, sir. They were re-exported before you took office."

"It wouldn't have made any difference if I had seen them," said Humphry David. "I don't understand Matisse. I can recognise a Dürer engraving or a Rembrandt etching, but to me a Fauviste is a Fauviste—a wild savage denizen of wild territory. It may be shameful but it's a fact."

"I don't see anything shameful in it," said Rivers. "What seems to me to be shameful is to pretend to understand the things when you don't. But let us get on. The Matisse pictures were delivered here. The Loans Collection staff saw them: the typists and the filing girls doubtless said, 'Coo! Look at that!' Miss Barton painstakingly and in detail described the new acquisitions for the catalogue. Mr. Blackwell stared at them. And Paul Weston, who did know what they were, accepted a bribe to replace the paintings by copies. The copies weren't identical: a few variations were made lest any informed person said 'That's simply a copy.' And nobody noticed the difference. In short, the fraud worked perfectly—until some busybody in an industrial town in the north wrote to the Minister and stated that these pictures were plagiarisms of Matisse."

"Who dealt with the letter?" asked the Minister.

"Mr. Pompfret. He gave an authoritative denial and a disquisition on Arlettier. This has emerged after a prolonged interrogation of typists who have retired into private life and the blessings of holy matrimony. The correspondence doubtless fizzled out, and your researches into Files indicate that the letters were suppressed or altered. Now here we have a gap in the record. Pompfret is dead. Weston is dead. We can only guess the intermediate stages. Pompfret smelt a rat. He got Weissonnier in to report—but the pictures in dispute were on loan. My own belief is that Pompfret caught Weston tampering with files—and Pompfret was shrewd enough to make a guess at what had happened, but was too conceited to report to the Minister. Pompfret was caught on the horns of a dilemma. He didn't want to admit his own fallibility. He tackled Weston himself, and Weston, facing disgrace, dismissal and a police investigation, organised an 'accident' for Pompfret, based on Pompfret's often reiterated loathing of the Canova."

III

"How. Why. Who," said Rivers. "Who was easy. What were the probable qualifications of the murderer? Certainly a knowledge of architecture. Nobody but a person acquainted with architecture would have known about the ease with which you could reach that hook which held the candelabrum. It's forty feet above ground level: so high up that you need good eyesight to spot it, and the inspection trap is concealed in the decoration of the ceiling. Neither do I think that anybody save an architect would have realised that the lofts were accessible. From ground level the house gives the appearance of having a flat roof, because the parapet hides the sloping slates. So a knowledge of architecture was indicated. Now there were several architects here, but in Loans Collection was a man whose record, in your admirably filed personnel details, included a partial training in architecture before he was called up during the war. Yet that man—Paul Weston—carefully omitted to mention that part of his training when interrogated."

David nodded. "I knew that myself. I remember Miss Barton said he was an architect when I admired his lettering over the Loans picture racks."

"Point one," said Rivers. "Point two. He had been in a glider squadron. That struck my ear at once. It was the gliders who experimented with nylon cables. He was familiar with Paris. He obviously knew more about pictures than the majority of people here. And he kept up his interest in flying—he was a member of a flying club—and flying costs money. All these observations were what I called 'pointers,' but I don't want to pretend I picked out Weston as anything more than a possible culprit. There was Welles—a sardonic, morose fellow, who seemed capable of vindictive dislike; he had all the qualifications so far as knowledge of the building was concerned: so did young Dunne. There was Blackwell, who is given to painting 'funnies' himself, and there was Virgilia Hill and her faithless *amant du cœur*—Devinton. I admit that I confidently expected to find Devinton involved in the copying ramp, but I have realised since that I underestimated the skill of a good copyist." Rivers turned and looked at the pictures at last. "It looks so easy, doesn't it?" he said. "Or again—doesn't it?"

"I just don't know," said Humphry David. "It's not my sort of painting. Look at the surface of that one—"

"Morainal detritus," said Rivers, "but I'm told it isn't easy at all."

IV

"Weston's alibi? Well, very far from foolproof. He did go to bed early: earlier than his landlady realised, because he stopped the grandfather clock and disorganised the wireless. Mrs. Butler went up to rub his chest, but the time she did it must have been half-past

nine, not just after ten. After his kindly landlady left him, tucked
up with two hot-water bottles, Weston slipped out of the house,
got his motor-bike and raced down to Medici House. He must have
gone up the fire escape to the roof, got in by one of the trap-doors
which he had left open, and continued with his prearranged scheme.
When he got back home he put the clock on again and nobody ever
noticed that it had been wrong. A grandfather clock is so easy to
stop, just by checking the pendulum, and if you stop it by different
stages, checking it ten minutes at a time, very few people have a
keen enough sense of time to notice it. They just think the evening
is going more slowly than usual. I didn't think a great deal of his
alibi, but I was interested in the fact that an alibi had been arranged
for. However, once we'd got the fingerprints on the goloshes I was in
no doubt that my points had been added up correctly. We got final
corroboration when the Parisian gentry denounced him, trying to
make out that he was responsible for the whole fraud. The reason
why Weston bolted was that Blackwell, after arguing the case over
with Danvers, gave Weston the impression that the whole fraud
was discovered."

v

"And you think Weston took it for granted that Pompfret's death
would be taken for an accident?"

"I'm sure of it. He argued that in the absence of any evidence to
the contrary, the obvious explanation would be accepted. Pompfret
hated the Canova: he'd talked about tilting it off its pedestal. Ergo, he
did it. Like many another criminal before him, Weston assumed that
policemen know nothing outside ordinary routine police work. The
very last thing that policemen were likely to take an interest in was
contemporary painting, and as for spotting the pulley idea—well,

perhaps he had bad luck there. He couldn't have expected a Scotland Yard man to think in terms of pulleys. Then, sir, if you won't take it amiss, there was yourself. You have the gift of understatement, of sounding simpler than you are. You *say* you know nothing about these things." Rivers indicated the pictures. "You've even said you're not interested in them. Well, it's just not true. You *are* interested in them. You're beginning to know about them. And you already know a great deal about human nature. It was you who predetermined that Weston's plan would fail, when you realised that certain letters in files didn't conform to probabilities."

"Thank you for your kind intention, Rivers. I value it. I think very highly of you and I should like you to think well of me. I know you're a very trustworthy chap so I'll let you in on a matter which isn't yet made public. I've resigned from office, after tendering my last Ministerial advice: that in the interests of national economy the Ministry of Fine Arts be abolished. You see, I want to ensure that never again shall Civil Servants, either singly or in committee, be entrusted with buying works of art for the people. I said it wouldn't work and I maintain I was right."

Rivers laughed outright. "Well—that's rather an overwhelming consequence, sir. It means that when Weston rigged his tackle he brought the whole show down, not merely the Canova."

"So perhaps we can say of Pompfret that he did not die in vain," said David. "And I don't mean that flippantly. I'd have perished myself with pleasure for the same result. And now for a final indiscretion. I've bought you an Abstract. I hope you'll accept it. I've seen you looking at the things... Was I right?"

"Yes, sir. Perfectly right. I've developed an interest in them. And the beauty of an Abstract is that it *is* abstract."

The Minister nodded. "Remote," he murmured. "The fine arts devoid of human fallibility."

"Eminently suitable for a policeman," murmured Rivers. But the expression on his face as he studied the picture which Humphry David gave him was neither remote nor abstracted. It was quite passionately interested.

THE END

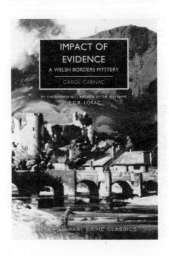

Near St. Brynneys in the Welsh border country, isolated by heavy snow and flooding from the thaw, a calamity has occurred. Old Dr. Robinson, a known "menace on the roads", has met his end in a collision with a jeep on a hazardous junction. But when the police arrive at the scene, a burning question hints at something murkier than mere accident: why was there a second body—a man not recognised by any locals—in the back of Robinson's car?

As the local inspectors dive into the muddy waters of this strange crime, Chief Inspector Julian Rivers and Inspector Lancing are summoned from Scotland Yard to the windswept wilds, where danger and deceit lie in wait.

Puzzling and atmospheric, this exceedingly rare mystery from one of the masters of crime fiction's Golden Age returns to print for the first time since its publication in 1954.

On a bright autumn morning, Superintendent Macdonald boards the plane bound for Vienna to visit his old friend Dr. Natzler. His detective's eye notes some unusual passengers including Elizabeth Le Vendre, new secretary to the diplomat Sir Walter Vanbrugh—but this is supposed to be a holiday. After arriving with the Natzlers and crossing paths with Elizabeth again, Macdonald settles into the trip as best he can, determined to relax for once.

But when Elizabeth is reported missing and a string of violence and murder encircles Vanbrugh and Natzler's social set, Macdonald's short-lived stint as a tourist comes to an end—and the race to stop a killer on the loose begins.

First published in 1956 and steeped in the turbulent history of post-war Vienna, this edition ushers E.C.R. Lorac's characteristically atmospheric classic mystery back into print for the first time in over 65 years.

ALSO AVAILABLE
IN THE BRITISH LIBRARY
CRIME CLASSICS SERIES

Big Ben Strikes Eleven	DAVID MAGARSHACK
Death of an Author	E. C. R. LORAC
The Black Spectacles	JOHN DICKSON CARR
Death of a Bookseller	BERNARD J. FARMER
The Wheel Spins	ETHEL LINA WHITE
Someone from the Past	MARGOT BENNETT
Who Killed Father Christmas?	ED. MARTIN EDWARDS
Twice Round the Clock	BILLIE HOUSTON
The White Priory Murders	CARTER DICKSON
The Port of London Murders	JOSEPHINE BELL
Murder in the Basement	ANTHONY BERKELEY
Fear Stalks the Village	ETHEL LINA WHITE
The Cornish Coast Murder	JOHN BUDE
Suddenly at His Residence	CHRISTIANNA BRAND
The Edinburgh Mystery	ED. MARTIN EDWARDS
Checkmate to Murder	E. C. R. LORAC
The Spoilt Kill	MARY KELLY
Smallbone Deceased	MICHAEL GILBERT
The Story of Classic Crime in 100 Books	MARTIN EDWARDS
The Pocket Detective: 100+ Puzzles	KATE JACKSON
The Pocket Detective 2: 100+ More Puzzles	KATE JACKSON

Many of our titles are also available
in eBook, large print and audio editions